the

QUEENE'S CURE

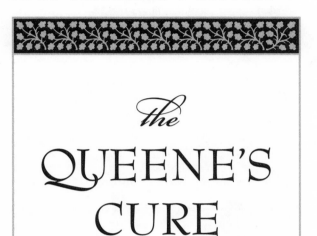

the

QUEENE'S CURE

KAREN HARPER

DELACORTE PRESS

Published by
Delacorte Press
a division of
Random House, Inc.
1540 Broadway
New York, New York 10036

Copyright © 2002 by Karen Harper

Map by James Sinclair
Book design by Laurie Jewell

Library of Congress Cataloging-in-Publication Data
Harper, Karen (Karen S.)
The queene's cure / Karen Harper.
p. cm. — (An Elizabeth I mystery)
ISBN 0-385-33478-8 (alk. paper)
1. Elizabeth I, Queen of England, 1533–1603—Fiction. 2. Great Britian—
History—Elizabeth, 1558–1605—Fiction. 3. Queens—Fiction. I. Title:
Queen's cure. II. Title

PS3558.A624792 Q44 2002
813'.54—dc21
2001047430

Printed in the United States of America
Published simultaneously in Canada

April 2002

10 9 8 7 6 5 4 3 2 1
BVG

FOR TRACY DEVINE,
EDITOR EXTRAORDINAIRE,
AND ELIZABETH'S AND MY
PARTNER IN CRIME.

THANKS, SUNNY, FOR THE
FABULOUS ELIZABETHAN GOWN,
WHICH HELPS ME UNDERSTAND
THE QUEEN EVEN MORE.

AND FOR DON,
AS ALWAYS, FOR PUTTING UP
WITH ELIZABETHAN MANIA
AND TUDOR TRIVIA.

ELIZABETH I — *the Young Queen*

1518 London Royal College of Physicians founded.

1533 Henry VIII marries Anne Boleyn, January 25. Elizabeth born September 7.

1536 Anne Boleyn executed. Elizabeth disinherited from crown. Henry weds Jane Seymour.

1537 Prince Edward born. Queen Jane dies of childbed fever.

1544 Act of succession and Henry VIII's will establish Mary and Elizabeth in line of succession.

1547 Henry VIII dies. Edward VI crowned.

1553 Lady Jane Grey forced to wed Guildford Dudley. King Edward dies. Mary Tudor overthrows Northumberland's attempt to put Protestant "Queen" Jane Grey and her husband, Guildford Dudley, Northumberland's son, on the throne. Robert Dudley sent to Tower for his part in rebellion. Queen Mary I crowned. Northumberland executed. Queen Mary weds Prince Philip of Spain by proxy; he arrives in England in 1554. Queen Mary begins to force England back to Catholicism.

1553 College of Physicians receives power to search shops and imprison apothecaries who sell faulty stuffs.

1554 Protestant Wyatt Rebellion fails, but Elizabeth implicated. Elizabeth sent to Tower for two months, accompanied by Kat Ashley.

1555 John Caius visits Italy and becomes president of College of Physicians. Elizabeth lives mostly in rural exile as queen sickens.

1558 Mary dies; Elizabeth succeeds to throne, November 17. Elizabeth appoints William Cecil Secretary of State. Robert Dudley made Master of the Queen's Horse.

1559 Elizabeth crowned in Westminster Abbey, January 15. Parliament urges the queen to marry; she resists, February 4. Mary Queen of Scots becomes Queen of France at accession of her young husband, Francis II, July.

1560 Death of Francis II of France makes his young Catholic widow Mary Queen of Scots a danger as Elizabeth's unwanted heir.

1561 Now widowed and not permitted to pass through English territory, Mary Queen of Scots returns to Scotland, August 19.

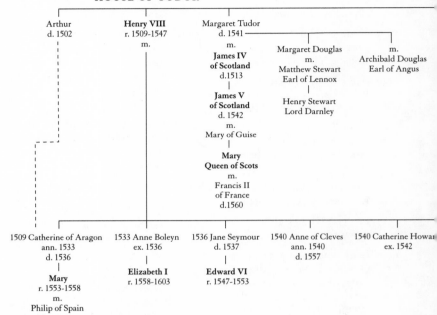

House of Lancaster   *House of York*
Henry VII   m.   Elizabeth of York
r.1485-1509

HOUSE OF TUDOR

Arthur
d. 1502

Henry VIII
r. 1509-1547
m.

Margaret Tudor
d. 1541
m.
**James IV
of Scotland**
d.1513

**James V
of Scotland**
d. 1542
m.
Mary of Guise

**Mary
Queen of Scots**
m.
Francis II
of France
d.1560

Margaret Douglas
m.
Matthew Stewart
Earl of Lennox

Henry Stewart
Lord Darnley

m.
Archibald Douglas
Earl of Angus

1509 Catherine of Aragon
ann. 1533
d. 1536

Mary
r. 1553-1558
m.
Philip of Spain

1533 Anne Boleyn
ex. 1536

Elizabeth I
r. 1558-1603

1536 Jane Seymour
d. 1537

Edward VI
r. 1547-1553

1540 Anne of Cleves
ann. 1540
d. 1557

1540 Catherine Howard
ex. 1542

THE DUDLEYS

John Dudley
Earl of Warwick
Duke of Northumberland
Lord Protector
ex. 1553
m.
Jane Guildford

John Dudley
Earl of Warwick
ex. 1554
m.
Anne Seymour

Ambrose Dudley
Earl of Warwick
d. 1590

Henry Dudley

Robert Dudley
Earl of Leicester
m.
Amy Robsart
d. 1560

Guildford Dudley
ex. 1554
m.
Jane Grey
Queen 1553
ex. 1554

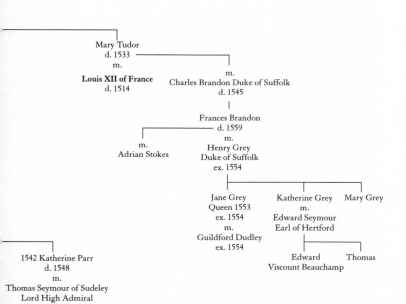

Mary Tudor
d. 1533
m.

Louis XII of France
d. 1514

m.
Charles Brandon Duke of Suffolk
d. 1545

Frances Brandon
d. 1559
m.

m.
Adrian Stokes

Henry Grey
Duke of Suffolk
ex. 1554

Jane Grey
Queen 1553
ex. 1554
m.
Guildford Dudley
ex. 1554

Katherine Grey
m.
Edward Seymour
Earl of Hertford

Mary Grey

Edward
Viscount Beauchamp

Thomas

1542 Katherine Parr
d. 1548
m.
Thomas Seymour of Sudeley
Lord High Admiral

Mary Seymour

TUDOR FAMILY,
FRIENDS, *and* FOES

Jane Dudley
m.
Henry Seymour

Mary Dudley
m.
Henry Sidney

Catherine Dudley
m.
Henry Hastings
Earl of Huntington

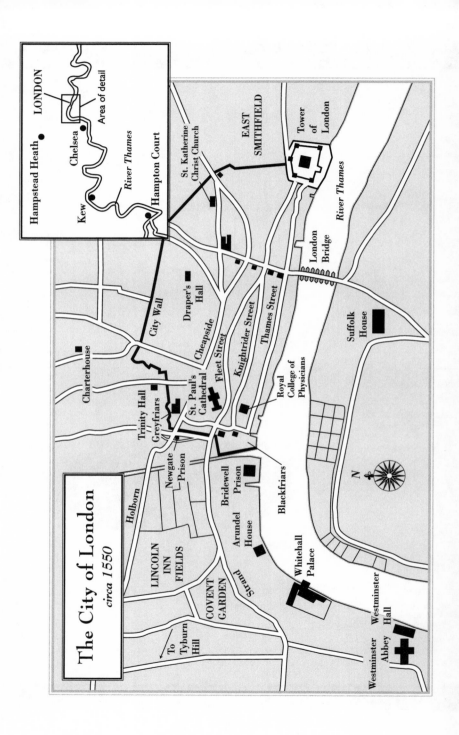

The City of London
circa 1550

Hampstead Heath   LONDON

Chelsea

Kew

River Thames

Hampton Court

Area of detail

To Tyburn Hill

Holborn

LINCOLN INN FIELDS

COVENT GARDEN

Strand

Arundel House

Whitehall Palace

Westminster Hall

Westminster Abbey

Charterhouse

Trinity Hall
Greyfriars

Newgate Prison

St. Paul's Cathedral

Bridewell Prison

Blackfriars

City Wall

Draper's Hall

Cheapside

Fleet Street

Knightrider Street

Thames Street

Royal College of Physicians

St. Katherine Christ Church

EAST SMITHFIELD

Tower of London

River Thames

London Bridge

Suffolk House

River Thames

N

the

QUEENE'S CURE

PROLOGUE

WHITEHALL PALACE, LONDON
SEPTEMBER 15, 1562

S HE MUSTN'T DIE. YOU *WILL NOT* LET HER DIE!" THE
queen commanded the foreign physician when he was
brought to the entrance of Kat Ashley's bedchamber.

Though Kat's fever had made her insensible for hours and
naught seemed to disturb her but her own delirious ravings,
Elizabeth Tudor stepped quickly out into the hall and closed the
door on the sickroom. With a yeoman guard standing sentinel,
she studied the short, German doctor.

After a quick, slipshod bow, the wiry, bearded man squinted
up at her in the dim corridor. Gripping a worn leather satchel to
his chest, he was shabbily garbed, especially compared to the im-
peccably attired palace doctors she had lately despaired could
ever cure Kat.

"*Gott in Himmel* alone," Dr. Burcote muttered in his thick German accent, "not even you, Majesty, can decree such things."

"Lady Ashley has been like a mother to me," she explained, wringing her hands. "I cannot lose her."

"Den ve best tend to her, *ja?*" he said impatiently with a sharp nod at the closed door.

For his impudence Elizabeth would have liked to box his ears, but they were covered by the flaps of a traditional physicians' skullcap with its loose ties. Instead she nodded, and the guard swept open the door for them.

As the stale smells of the room assailed Elizabeth again, she tugged on Dr. Burcote's long-sleeved gown. "Do all you can," she mouthed to him. "All!" A brusque nod was her only answer as he shoved the tapestried bed-hangings farther open. Elizabeth's four favorite ladies-in-waiting shifted to make room for him.

The slender, red-haired queen had turned twenty-nine a week before, and Kat had been with her for twenty-five of those years. Katherine Ashley had been her first girlhood governess just after that dreadful time her mother, Queen Anne Boleyn, had been charged, tried, and executed.

Now the queen's First Lady of the Bedchamber and Mistress of the Robes, Kat had been so sore ill that the chief royal physician, Dr. Huicke, could not break the fever, nor could the other palace doctors, Browne or Spencer. The learned men of the Royal College of Physicians, usually but a short summons away here in London, had journeyed to Cambridge for some sort of meeting, curse them. And since she'd banished from court her favorite household herbalist, Meg Milligrew, there was no one of that ilk she cared to trust either, not that mere apothecaries were permitted to prescribe physick.

So it had come to this, Elizabeth thought, gripping her hands before her stiff brocade bodice. All hung on an irascible foreigner, though she had to admit that the seat of superior medical learning was on the continent and not in her realm—yet.

As she held tightly to the carved bedpost and held her tongue, too, the doctor took command of the situation. He smelled Kat's sweat, drew and tasted a drop of her blood, and examined a flask of her urine, which even the common rabble knew was the watery overflow of the blood and so showed its purity.

"Sour blood—impure vater," he pronounced. "And she vas born under . . . ?"

"Scorpio the Crab," Elizabeth's lady-of-the-bedchamber and dear friend Mary Sidney put in before the queen could answer.

"Den signs are propitious for purging her bad blood," he muttered to himself as he felt Kat's wrist pulse while staring at a mechanical timepiece he'd fetched from his satchel. At least that showed he was a modern physician, Elizabeth assured herself. She'd seen English doctors time the pulse with old hourglasses, and some country quacks still counted the beats by the time it took to recite the Lord's Prayer.

"Be certain 'tis not the pox," Elizabeth hissed, unable to contain herself longer when he gave no more pronouncements. However much her people feared the plague, it was the pox that terrified her, for she had seen its power to kill many and disfigure most. Might as well be molding in one's grave, she thought with a shudder, than have one's skin pocked and pitted for life.

"It isn't, is it?" she prompted when the wretch said naught.

Silence from the brazen man. Kat moaned and thrashed about again, but at least she threw no more fits. The poor woman had thought they were back in rural exile with no new clothes to wear. She had screamed that Bloody Mary Tudor would kill the Princess Elizabeth just the way King Henry had killed two of his wives. Worse, she had shrieked that Elizabeth would lose her head, when indeed her delirium made it seem Kat already had.

"Not the small pox," Dr. Burcote spoke after an interminable, rude silence. "Bone-ache, digestive complications, and her heart's furnace has overheated. She is of a heavy, phlegmatic humor but has contracted hot, choleric disturbances, and they are at war with each other in her weak woman's frame."

Elizabeth fumed at those last words, for *her* woman's frame could brook no weakness. "And what will you do for her weak frame?" she demanded icily.

"As I said, Majesty, bleeding to restore humoral imbalance."

"Not with leeches," Elizabeth ordered. "Kat and I both detest leeches."

"*Gut,* if she holds still for a lancet and bowl," he muttered as much to himself as Elizabeth. "I do not hold vit tying patients down as your doctors sometimes do."

As he produced a lancet, tourniquet, and bowl, Elizabeth stepped forward and took Kat's hand on the opposite side of the bed. Memories of Kat holding her hand and bending over her bed, Kat comforting her through childhood night terrors, Kat teaching her sums and spelling, Kat . . .

"I said, Majesty, vill you stay?" Doctor Burcote asked, unwinding his cowhide tourniquet.

"Yes. Anything to help her. And you surely realize that recompense is no object."

"Rank and title of patients and der friends does not change how I vill diagnose or dose her. Feverfew in a tonic and nightshade leaves pressed to her temples to vard off headache after I bleed her. And herbs in an electuary for the next few days, powdered unicorn horn vit double doses of strong ginger. Ve must send to an apothecary for the ingredients."

Elizabeth dared to hope. Everyone knew that the more pungent the smell of the medicine, the more powerful the remedy. She had been going to insist on one of the new-fashioned panaceas of powdered unicorn horn or ground mummy. If the learned doctors of her realm, including the twenty select Fellows of the London Royal College of Physicians, thought their queen knew naught of physick they were much mistaken. She had several bones to pick with them about that, and soon.

While Dr. Burcote tied the tourniquet around Kat's brow, Elizabeth bent close to hear what she was muttering. "The royal physician, lovey—he's here?" the old woman asked, her eyes pinched closed.

"Yes, my Kat," the queen said, though that was not quite the truth. "Do not fret or fear. Dr. Burcote, highly recommended."

"Dr. Boorde, you say?" Kat murmured, stirring restlessly again. She tossed her head, pulling her silvered hair free from her bed cap and the tourniquet awry. The faint facial lines hidden by her plumpness seemed to etch themselves more deeply. "Poor Dr. Boorde," Kat cried, her eyes still closed. "He's always trying to salve your father's leg ulcer, but His Majesty still rants in pain and anger."

Elizabeth startled, then recovered herself as Dr. Burcote leaned over the other side of the bed to pull the tourniquet back into place. Dr. Boorde, King Henry VIII's favorite Doctor of Physick, had died shortly after her royal sire, over fifteen years ago.

As Dr. Burcote positioned his lancet and bowl, Elizabeth suddenly could not bear to watch. So many nights she had waked from horrid dreams of her real mother's head spurting blood . . .

"Mary, hold her hand one moment," Elizabeth said to the watchful woman who had come to stand behind her. Mary was Robert Dudley's sister and nearly as dear to her as he was—and without all the public and privy complications. "I will send for Dr. Burcote's unicorn horn and herbs and be back straightaway," Elizabeth promised and swept from the room.

Out in the fresher air of the hall, she wanted to collapse sobbing against the linen-fold paneling, but she summoned the guard with a flick of her wrist. "The doctor requires strong ginger, feverfew, and ground unicorn horn," she told him. "Have Lord Cecil send his new man for it—to the closest apothecary shop, that one in the Strand—but the man is not to say it is for the palace. He will pay well for it and bring me the reckoning. Go now."

Clifford, the crimson-clad, tall yeoman guard, who was part of her personal watch, bowed, backed up a few feet, then turned to hurry away. Momentarily alone, Elizabeth leaned one slender shoulder against the wall.

Ordering the cures from Meg Milligrew's shop was the least she could do, she told herself, for her lost Meg as well as for Kat. She hated having to banish people to whom she had once shown favor, whether it was her own deceitful cousins, Katherine Grey and Margaret Douglas, or a dear servant like Meg. Even Elizabeth's beloved Robin had been sent from court for a time and was yet best kept at arm's length. Standards must be set.

She smacked her hands so hard into her full satin skirts they bounced and swayed. 'S blood, why did being sovereign mean that when others were punished or lost, she felt that way too?

Elizabeth nearly jumped out of her skin as Kat screamed. Bolting back into the room, the queen ran to the bed. Three of her ladies were helping to subdue the struggling woman. Dr. Burcote had not yet begun to bleed her so that was not what was amiss.

"Treason! Assassin!" Kat cried, her eyes wide for the first time in days as she pointed at Dr. Burcote's lancet with one hand she'd yanked free. "This lunatic doctor means to kill the queen!"

Chapter

THE FIRST

*Other distinctions and difference I leave to the learned
Physicians of our London College, who are very well
able to search this matter, as a thing far above my
reach . . . none fitter than the learned Physicians of
the College of London.*

JOHN GERARD
The Herball

SEPTEMBER 25, 1562

QUEEN ELIZABETH WAS MOUNTED AND WAITING.
She shaded her eyes and waved up at the parapet of
Whitehall Palace where Kat Ashley was taking her
first constitutional walk in the ten days since Dr. Burcote had
cured her fever.

Kat smiled wanly and waved back. The old woman's recovery would have ordinarily been enough to make the royal spirits
soar, but Elizabeth Tudor was en route to visit the Royal College
of Physicians in the City. She was even less pleased with them
than she had been ten days ago when she had needed them and
they were gone. For since then, they had begged off a royal
visit—twice.

"A lovely day for an outing." Mary Sidney nearly sang the words as her brother, Robert Dudley, whom they both affectionately called Robin, helped her mount directly behind the queen. Ever the optimist, Mary was quite as pretty as she was pleasant, though that lighthearted humor ill suited the queen today.

Her Majesty heard a rumbling noise and glanced behind. Boonen, her coachman, was bringing up her round-topped, wooden and leather coach, pulled by the eight matched white mules. Though a ride in it over ruts or cobbles could shake the teeth out of one's head, Elizabeth's use of the three coaches she had ordered had set a new trend.

This one, her oldest, was upholstered inside with black velvet embossed with gold and outside was richly gilded. Like all of them, it was adorned with ostrich plumes. The effect of the equipage was exactly the awe she wanted, though folk had finally stopped calling it The Monster. She had not wanted to ride in it on the way today, but perhaps it would do for her return if the weather changed or the visit was as trying as she expected. She could, of course, have summoned the College fellows here, but she had wanted to beard the lions in their own den and see exactly what prey they had been hunting lately.

After all, that pride of lions was lorded over by two men who did not wish her well. Peter Pascal, their past president, gossip said, had never forgiven a personal tragedy for which he blamed the Tudors. When the Catholic Church was cast from England, her royal father had ordered Pascal's beloved mentor, Sir Thomas More, imprisoned and beheaded. Some said Great Henry could have saved More, but was angry with his former friend for censuring the king's conscience.

Elizabeth felt that Sir Thomas and others were legally judged guilty only for their refusal to take the Oath of Supremacy. This act granted Henry and his heirs—especially, at that time, the newborn Protestant Princess Elizabeth for whose mother the Catholic Church was dissolved—the right to head both the kingdom and the new Church of England.

But all that was before the torrent crashed over the mill dam: Anne Boleyn beheaded, Elizabeth declared bastard, and four other stepmothers paraded through her young life. Elizabeth could grasp bitterness over someone beloved being beheaded, but she was not to be blamed for what her father had done or for being Protestant either. She was willing to let men, even Papists like Pascal, follow their consciences as long as they didn't rock the royal ship of state.

But of even more immediate concern was the eminent physician John Caius, the current president of the college. Also an ardent Papist, he had never forgiven Elizabeth for dismissing him from his lucrative, prestigious post as court physician when she came to the throne four years ago. But it was precisely the fact that he had served their Catholic majesties, Queen Mary and the Spanish King Philip, so assiduously that made her mistrust the man.

Actually, she didn't approve of Pascal's and Caius's actions any more than they did hers. Though both were learned men, she felt they had their feet mired in the past. Surely new methods and remedies were needed to fight disease today, not old physick. Yes, those two heading the Royal College of Physicians needed a close watch as she urged them to lead England's struggle against common workaday disease and the tragedy of random, sweeping pestilence.

"Isn't it just a splendid day, Your Grace?" Mary's sweet voice repeated as if Elizabeth had not heard her the first time. Her hand on the pommel, the queen shifted slightly in her sidesaddle to see her friend better.

"The weather, my dear Mary, might as well have storm clouds after the learned doctors delayed this meeting twice," Elizabeth groused. "Delayed meeting with *me*."

"I understand, Your Majesty," Robin put in, looking up at her, "that they had an official convocation in Cambridge, then must needs go on to Oxford. And the second time they petitioned for a stay, their messenger said it was to be certain their premises were pristine for your perusal."

"As if they had something to tidy up or hide," she added ominously.

He flashed a smile as he took her reins from a groom, patted her white stallion's flank, and tried another tack. "It is true that they overvalue their power and always have, Your Grace."

"Indeed," she replied crisply, tugging the reins from his big, brown hands, "for I have known others to do such and pay the price." With a narrow look at him, she spurred her horse before he could mount his.

Others fell quickly into their appointed places in the royal retinue. Usually the queen traveled by river barge but she was a splendid horsewoman. She always felt more in control when mounted than encased in a coach. Yet armed guards with swords circumspectly sheathed rode ahead of and behind her.

Only two ladies-in-waiting accompanied her today, Mary Sidney and Anne Carey, the latter wed to her dear cousin Harry Carey, Baron Hunsdon. Two men rode her flanks, Robin, her Master of the Horse, who scrambled to catch up, and, because she always felt safer when he was at her side, a man of no rank but in her lofty regard, her longtime protector, Stephen Jenks. If any of the horses balked, a mere look or touch from Jenks would calm them. With the carriage rattling over cobbles behind their mounts, they clattered out of the King Street Gate into the busy flow of London foot, cart, and horse traffic.

The queen gave but a quick glance back at the white towers and glittering, bannered pinnacles of the palace that symbolized the Tudor monarchy. Kat still stood on the parapet of sprawling, rose-bricked Whitehall, the queen's official London seat. Its twenty-four acres stretched between two main east-west thoroughfares of her capital, the broad River Thames and this passageway cutting through Whitehall's grounds. The latter was called King's Street, or more simply The Street. Though the city was awash with people, it was good to be away from the overly ambitious, watchful two thousand hopefuls who always jostled each other for place and position around her. In bright sun and crisp breeze, she waved to the common folk.

"Give way! Uncap there, knaves! Give access to the queen's majesty!" her first two guards began to shout in repetition. When her people heard the cry or glimpsed the queen herself, they parted like the sea. Men hoisted boys on their shoulders to see better; maids waved scarves or hats; old women peered from second- or third-story windows. The faces of her people turned and tilted toward their queen like flowers to the sun. It was always that way, and her love flowed back to them.

"God save Yer Grace! Long live our good queen, Bess Tudor!" and a hundred other jumbled cries assailed her ears. Ordinarily, that was enough to buoy her up; today it only slightly sweetened her sour humor.

But the shops and taverns did have their doors ajar. She caught glimpses of the wares within. Sometimes she wondered what it would be like to stroll the streets and peek in with no one noticing, to be simply English and not the English queen. Once, when she had Meg Milligrew in her household, she had planned to do just that, for the girl resembled her and, on a whim, she had thought to change places with her for a brief hour. But that was tomfoolery and best put away like so much else. Nothing mattered but being a good queen and a strong one. And commoner to courtier, ignorant carter to learned physician, the folk of her realm had best realize she meant to rule and not just reign.

As the queen's party turned into the long, broad street called the Strand, Elizabeth averted her eyes from the apothecary shop that Sarah Wilton, alias Meg Milligrew, her former Strewing Herb Mistress of the Privy Chamber, managed. She worked it with her husband, Ben Wilton, once a bargeman who now lorded it over the shop, the lazy lout. Through Ned Topside, the queen's fool and principal player, and two other sources of town gossip, Bett and Gil Sharpe, Elizabeth knew Meg's fate. But Meg had misled her queen about being wed. Worse, she had dared to pass herself off as the queen without permission and had even forged her royal signature.

Her Majesty always looked straight ahead as she passed, even when she knew Meg stood in her door, because she could not bear to look into her eyes or admit she had sent the girl away too hastily. God forgive her, she'd far rather trust Meg than her own treason-tainted cousins, Katherine Grey and Margaret Douglas, who coveted her throne.

Katherine was currently confined to the Tower on the other side of town that also housed Margaret's dangerous Scottish husband, Matthew Stewart, Earl of Lennox. Margaret, who favored Mary, Queen of Scots, for the English throne, was herself under house arrest with her son, Lord Darnley, at Sir Richard Sackville's home at Sheen. Her Royal Majesty was not backing down from dealing with anyone who challenged or defied her.

"Don't see Meg—I mean Sarah—today, Your Majesty," Jenks called to her. "She's always hanging out the door or window when you go by. Seen her on boats in the Thames when the royal barge passes too. But look, there's Bett waving!"

"Leave off," Elizabeth said without letting her gaze waver. "I don't give a fig if you and Ned visit the shop, but do not try to cozen me into taking her back."

"But I din't mean—"

"Ride ahead and tell the eminent doctors that their queen is on her way and she has much to say."

≈   ≈   ≈

H ER STOMACH KNOTTED WITH CHURNING EMOTIONS, Sarah Wilton watched and waited. Cocking her head, she listened too. Ah, there was the distant clatter of a goodly number of horses' hooves. Huzzahs came closer, echoing in the narrow, crooked streets of the City, the heart of London within the old walls and gates. She tugged her hood closer about her face, then gripped her hands tightly under her russet cloak. The queen was coming.

As the entourage and its crowd spilled into the end of Knightrider Street, Sarah stepped back into the narrow mouth of an alley so she would not be seen by the palace folk or the robed and flat-capped physicians who were slowly filing outside their ornately facaded guildhall. Their large, four-storied, black-and-white framed building was a place the barber surgeons and apothecaries of London knew all too well, but she wondered exactly why the queen was visiting today.

Sarah, who still always thought of herself as Meg Milligrew no matter what her husband or the others called her, reckoned she knew most things about the queen, even those that had happened the last two years since she'd been sent away in disgrace from royal service. And one thing Meg Milligrew knew was that Elizabeth of England seldom made purely social visits, not that clever queen.

Pressing herself against the plaster wall, Meg peeked around the corner as the noisy rabble filled the street. She picked out the queen's one-time favorite, Lord Robin Dudley, and skimmed the queen's retainers for Her Grace's Secretary of State, the wily William Cecil. Fortunately, he wasn't here, because not much escaped his eyes. Then Meg saw, in the center of it all, Elizabeth.

Meg's skin prickled, and her mouth went dry. Her Grace looked fine as ever—maybe a bit thinner, if that was possible—but Meg could read vexation in the clenched set of the high, pale brow and purse of the narrow lips. Aye, Bess Tudor was here apurpose for more than reveling in public adoration or a pleasant chat with the chief doctors of her realm. Meg could see Elizabeth's dark eyes assessing the small cluster of cloaked and befurred master physicians before she intentionally turned away from their set smiles to wave again with a slender, gloved hand to the crowd. The people responded as if she'd caressed them, the dolts, for Meg, like Lord Robin, knew well that royal affection lavished one day could languish the next.

Under her dark blue riding cloak, the queen wore another new gown Meg hadn't seen, a dark green brocade edged with sable that set off the gleam of her red-gold hair peeking out from her feathered hat. Her Grace's detested summer freckles still looked faded. Mayhap she was yet using the tansy and buttermilk face wash Meg had suggested when Elizabeth was but a princess and lived in exile.

"But four short years ago," Meg whispered as a shiver raced up her spine. She clasped her hands and glared as those black-guards who were Fellows of the Royal College bowed to the queen and gestured for her to come inside. They were always trying to rule Meg's—and all apothecaries' lives—with their dictums and pronouncements. An apothecary could even go to prison for hinting a particular medicinal cure would work, for they wanted every farthing for their own purses for giving prescriptions.

Physicians' cooks, the carping, complaining jackanapes were fond of calling those of her profession, and they treated women the worst of all. And neither the Company of Barber-Surgeons nor the Guild of Grocers, Apothecaries, and Spicers were getting visits from the queen!

"But then, I'll never get to visit with her again." Meg spit out the words, suddenly more angry than sorry for herself as the queen dismounted and went inside. "Tender and terrible, the worst, cold, cruel, and unforgiving . . ."

"Eh, you talking 'bout our queen?" a blue-coated apprentice behind her demanded so loud she jumped. He had come down the alley but now rounded on her. "Who you be, darin' talk 'bout our queen?"

Lest the lout make a scene and wishing that she had the brilliant thespian Ned Topside here to bail her out with some fantastical tale, she lied. "I'm talking about my husband, and if I have to call him over here, you'll be sorry. He's one of the queen's guards."

"Go on, then!" the simpleton said, gaping. "God's truth? Eh, you," he went on, leaning closer to peer into her hood, "you know you look a wee bit like the queen, I mean coloring and all?"

Without answering, Meg ducked away into the press of people. Standing on her tiptoes to catch another glimpse of the woman she once would have died for—and now could kill for—Meg scurried between two other tight buildings, crosscutting into the same alley where she'd hidden her goods. She had a lot to do before Her Majesty came back out.

❧   ❧   ❧

ALL OF YOU HAVE A LOFTY HERITAGE TO LIVE UP TO IN this fine edifice and historic site," the queen remarked as she completed her escorted tour and was led into the large front chamber of the College. She had been shown every room with the exception of what they called their dark cellars. As the twenty Fellows filed to their seats at the long, dark oak table, she surmised this served as their council room. She decided to forgo the plates of suckets, comfits, and an elaborate marchpane castle—bribes, all of it, she thought—they had laid out for her. But she took the proffered goblet of wine because she expected this to be thirsty work.

Before anyone could answer her subtle challenge about their guildhall, a fuss fomented outside. People on the street peeked in the front windows set ajar and began to cheer again; the royal guards evidently shoved them away. During the moment's respite, Elizabeth surreptitiously studied the assembled physicians, especially Pascal and Caius on either side of her at the head of the table. The two men were physical opposites, she noted, however much they had seemed to covertly conspire with silent, unreadable glances during her tour of their sprawling building and gardens.

The forty-eight-year-old Peter Pascal was as severely dressed as if he were a cleric. Or as if he were still in mourning for, no doubt, his illustrious mentor, whom he managed to mention incessantly. Pascal was plump, to put it nicely, as rosy-cheeked as a milkmaid, and quite effeminate-looking despite his total baldness. The man obviously shaved what hair he had, for its outline was a faint shadow above his ears and on the nape of his neck. Beards and mustaches, trimmed or long, were the fashion of the day, which he seemed to be directly flaunting in favor of older, clean-cut styles. His blue eyes bulged slightly, the way her father's had, and that made her even more edgy around him.

Unlike his black-garbed friend, John Caius, aged fifty-two, was ornately attired to show his status with a scarlet and gray taffeta cassock buttoned to his chin and his wide sleeves trimmed with fur. The current president of the College was, in contrast to Pascal, rake-thin with sallow skin and a long, gaunt face, accented by a salt-and-pepper beard and long mustache. Wisps of gray hair peeked from beneath his traditional physician's circular cap. He moved deliberately and spoke portentously. His dark eyes darted, even when he addressed her, as if his mind were flitting elsewhere or he was afraid to look her in the eye.

"Indeed, your observations about our hall are precisely correct, Your Most Gracious Majesty, *Maxima Regina*," John Caius said, grandly addressing the entire assembly. "This building was donated to the College in perpetuity by the brilliant Medieval physician Thomas Linacre after his death. I sometimes feel his spirit still lurks *inter nos* within these walls."

"Erecting edifices and libraries is a worthy goal," the queen agreed. "But above all, we must work together to find new cures and elevate English medicinal practices to rival those on the continent. My people stagger under the burden of too dear a price for some of the newer remedies to which they should have access."

"Bread and circuses, *panem et circenses ad infinitum,* that's what they'd like, Your Majesty," Caius muttered with a shake of his head. "Give them one step and they will want a mile, to wit that raucous crowd out there."

"I do not fear my people, but say on," Elizabeth commanded.

"Life is naturally unhealthsome," Pascal put in with a sharp sniff. "No utopias exist, as Sir Thomas More's great book made eminently clear. Besides, it is not just the fees for our learned services that cause the prices to rise but the outrageous reckonings of the apothecaries."

"Who," Caius said, rolling his eyes in feigned disbelief, "are ever clamoring for more freedom, when what they need is a firmer hand."

"But you already hold the power to place apothecaries who sell faulty stuffs in any prison but the Tower," she protested. "And you can legally enter their shops and search for defective and corrupted wares, which you can then destroy. I should think that would not only be enough to keep the herbalists in line but, sadly, to keep you from doing your duty to spend time learning and perfecting cures. I will not have my Royal College of Physicians waste their days being constables or bailiffs and not healers!"

"But, Gracious Majesty," Caius argued with a nervous, ever-shifting smile, "we must keep control of not only the barber-surgeons and apothecaries but other quacksalvers, mountebanks, and runnagates which—"

"Do you mean to say," the queen cut in, "that the shops in town which import and supply your cures are in the same category as quacks?"

"Indeed not," Pascal took up the discussion, steepling his fingers before his broad face as if to hide his expression. "But, just as in the days of your father, Your Grace, each area of mankind's expertise must be left to the experts and not encroached on by those who know not whereof they speak."

She stared him down, unsure if he dared such a direct affront at her, to the apothecaries, or if he was throwing Thomas More's so-called martyrdom in her face again. As the other fellows up and down the long table gaped and leaned out to listen raptly, Caius jumped into the moment's silence.

"*Id est,* there are certain apothecaries who are hardly trained as we by years of study and time abroad, *et cetera.* Why, madam, some who cannot even read or speak Latin and Greek but only cling to simple herbs dare to question the medical truths of humors within the body."

"Truths, you say, and not theories?" she challenged. "Of a certain we all rely on the wisdom of great men of past ages, but did they not make errors too? We have learned the world is hardly flat."

"Ah, but we do continually reexamine the old ways, though one out-of-town doctor, we've heard," Pascal said, shaking his head, "has been spreading the heretical belief that disease is caused not by warring humors, governed by the planets, nor by bad air. He—and he is not alone," his voice rang out and he pressed fingers fat as sausages on the tabletop as if to prop himself up, "claims that the airborne seeds of disease fall upon open pores of the skin and infect the person. Such a one claims that a man must be most careful shaving or his open pores will allow in certain harmful vapors! So much for new-fledged ideas!"

There was general nodding, head-shaking, or smothered sniggering down the length of the table. Elizabeth's ire rose, and she did, too, partly to make everyone stand. Men scrambled to their feet, and she heard her two ladies' skirts rustle as they stood behind her.

"But like all my people," Elizabeth said, "I am plagued by worry that I or those I love, God forbid, may be one of the persons who needs your expertise and wisdom someday, gentlemen. *Ergo,*" she added, staring now directly at the Latin-spewing John Caius, "the next time I send for help, I would expect some of you to be in London healing and not wandering hither and yon to attend meetings or chasing down apothecaries like a wayward constable-of-the-watch or harassing someone who has a new theory which you choose to mock without testing its good first. Never say something cannot be done without trying it, learned and yet-learning doctors. *I* am a new theory, a queen ruling alone, and it can be done, indeed!"

"But, Majesty," Peter Pascal dared to rattle on, after that speech with which she had hoped to make her exit, "about your Lady Katherine Ashley's recent illness. We all know disease is a gift from God to gild a martyr's crown, so each must suffer some in his or her turn in this life."

"And I say"—here she switched to speaking Latin with an occasional phrase in Greek—"that I hate to be ill, and I think illness is a personal affront which a kingdom's doctors must and will spend their precious time to battle. We have yet the small pox and the great pox and the Black Death and numerous other maladies, and there must be something, some way we can discover what the Lord God has given us to fight such. The status quo is not acceptable, and I expect occasional and detailed explanations of how you will strive to improve upon your past performance. Good day to you, Fellows of the Royal College of Physicians."

She smacked her goblet down for effect and started for the door. Caius—even the portly Pascal—raced to keep up.

"Your Grace," Caius cried, "you have put our credo so perfectly, has she not, Doctor Pascal?"

"Ah—indeed. We care deeply for all ill persons in our charge and care."

"As I care for and keep a good eye on all, even physicians, in my kingdom," the queen concluded and strode down the escutcheon-hung hall toward the street door. She wanted the final word, the fine exit, and these doctors clung like their own bloodletting leeches.

"Then, Your Gracious Majesty," Caius went on as he reached the door with her, "there is one request that would help us to fulfill your every desire for our work."

"Which is?" she snapped.

"I—we humbly request that we might have bodies," Caius said, "corpses here for dissection to learn the things you would have us to do."

"Corpses?" she cried, her hand flying to her bodice when she tried never to show dismay in public. "Corpses to dissect? I'll not have bodies so abused. Whose?"

The man dared to shrug. "I know not, Your Gracious Majesty, as the human body is all the same. The poor found dead in the streets. Prisoners or executed felons. Country rabble. Whoever."

"I shall think on it," she declared, raising her voice to its ringing tone, "for quite a long while. You may shrug, Fellows of the

College, at the earthly remains of your fellow human beings so abused, but I do not. And now," she concluded again, irked she had to find yet another closing line, "I shall take my leave, and next time I want to see you in the palace or here or anywhere, I warrant you will not be so busy."

Her guard on the front door barely pulled it open before she got to it. On the stoop, watching the crowd, Robin saw her and swirled open her cloak he'd evidently been holding. He offered his arm to escort her out, but she kept going on her own. Furiously blushing and wanting no one to see so in the light, she made for her coach. It waited for her but one house away, behind the line of unmounted horses, as they had obviously expected her to ride back. Coachmen and grooms alike scrambled from their lolling stances and grabbed for reins and bridles. Boonen, the burly coachman, swept open the door for her and banged down the folding, metal steps.

Robin haphazardly settled her cloak about her shoulders, and Mary and Anne tried to help control her voluminous skirts for her climb up and in. But she was too quick even for them. Though her cloak spilled back into Robin's hands, she felt him give her a hoist up, one hand on her waist and one under her left elbow.

And then she nearly stepped on the horrid thing lying on the floor of the dim coach. Gaping at it, despite her long-tended command of herself, the queen screamed.

Chapter

THE SECOND

*Nutmeg and mace are profitable for cold husbands
that would fain have children, but not for lecherous
bores and bullies.*

WILLIAM TURNER
The Herball

E LIZABETH'S HEART BANGED IN HER CHEST LIKE A
drum. Her knees went weak as she gaped at the thing—
the body—in the dim depths of her coach. Wedged between the seats, it lay faceup but with knees slightly bent to fit
upon the narrow wooden floor.

Evidently fearing someone lurked inside the coach, Robin
unceremoniously pulled her back out, thrust her at her ladies,
and lunged within, both sword and dagger drawn.

"What the deuce?" he cried, followed by a string of stronger
oaths.

Though trying to seize control of her trembling limbs, the
queen whispered, "Is it a corpse?"

"I—no, a big doll—like an effigy, I think."

Her ladies tried to tug her away, but she shook them off and peered inside between Robin's legs. He stood straddling the woman with red hair, a small circlet crown, and queenly clothes. Shading her eyes with both hands to peer into the dimness, Elizabeth was jostled by the doctors pressing in before Jenks and the guards shoved them back.

"God as my witness," Robin told her, "I think the damn thing is wax—no it's plaster, the face and hands, at least. And with a face, wigged and painted—"

"To resemble me," Elizabeth finished for him.

Her mind raced. When a monarch died, it was tradition to parade a full-sized likeness on top of the closed coffin through the streets for the people to mourn. She'd never seen such but she knew earlier monarchs, including her sister, had had such effigies made.

But now, did some simpleton deem this a compliment or joke? Was this the idea of the royal physicians who not minutes ago were asking for corpses to dissect? Their whereabouts had all been accounted for when this appeared, but their lackeys could have managed it by sneaking through nearby small alleys between the bigger buildings. This clever corpse could even be a death threat. Whatever the motive, the whole charade sickened and frightened her.

"Shall I drag it out, Your Grace?" Robin asked, finally tearing his eyes away to look at her.

"No," she said, lifting one hand to him. "Drag me up."

Robin reached for her, and she climbed the carriage steps again. To avoid stepping on the effigy and to make room for her, Robin was forced to kneel on one leather-covered seat.

'S blood and bones, Elizabeth thought, the thing even had a pair of fine satin slippers peeking from the petticoat hems. The crown was obviously fake stones wired to the wig. But—a plague on it—she recognized the gown as one of hers!

"It's still too dark in here to see the features well," Robin de-

clared as Elizabeth bent over it, "but we hardly need to open the
street-side door for the crowd to gawk."

"Roll up the flap a whit, and I'll get out of this doorway.
Jenks, tell the guards to hold people back and close that door!"

"Aye, Your Grace," Jenks muttered and shouted commands
to the other guards and grooms.

As Robin drew up the heavy leather flap and Elizabeth sank
on the seat opposite him, what daylight still sifted into the narrow street more fully illumined the effigy. It was slightly smaller
than life-sized, she realized—or was she indeed that small if it
was made to her form? Fringed by the familiar hue of red-gold
hair, the face was also a close copy, with features just a bit off.

As she leaned closer she thought the skin looked so soft and
real—alive. But as the light slanted in she saw that the white and
pink skin, the complexion of the forehead, cheeks, and chin, even
the graceful hands . . .

The queen did not scream aloud again, but in her own soul.
She covered her gaping mouth with both hands as she saw the
scars and grasped the dreadful threat that they implied.

のう   のう   のう

DON'T LIKE YOU RUNNING 'ROUND TOWN MAKING DE-
liv'ries even if Nick's puking his insides out today," Ben
Wilton told Meg the moment she rushed back to the apothecary
shop.

Nick Cotter usually ran Meg's errands. Ben liked him well
enough, and Nick was one of her few male acquaintances he
never seemed jealous of. Ben did not rise from his favorite chair,
but continued to tip it against the wall in a dull, disturbing *thud,
thud.*

"Late deliveries mean people keep ailing—and no payment,"
she said.

Removing her cloak, she draped it over a stool. She knew not to leap directly into an argument but to choose her comments carefully. Living with the queen had taught her that, though Ben Wilton was a far cry from that brilliant debater.

"For all I know," he went on, arms crossed over his big chest, "you're deliv'ring by dilly-dallying with certain men, Madam Sarah Wilton, goodwife a mine."

She avoided that challenge, though he was the bed-swerver in this marriage. "Bett was watching things here," she protested quietly, still out of breath as she skirted the back of the long work counter. That way she didn't have to walk by him to get to the tasks she'd left unfinished when she heard the queen was going calling on the College of Physicians. The last thing she needed was Ben's hard hands on the fresh bruises she'd treated this morning with the crushed root of Solomon's Seal. She had enough to do to keep him from mauling her in his idea of amorous attentions, even when he was in a good mood.

"Bett's not here that I saw," he mocked, his words accompanied by that ominous drumbeat of his chair against the wall. "You see her here? She musta vanished like a puff a smoke."

"Maybe she ran out just to check on Nick. She's a real help to me, Ben, and that nose of hers telling her which herb's which is as good as an extra pair of eyes."

"It still galls me both a you run out."

Meg sighed as a memory leaped at her, one of those she treasured but that also tormented her. She and Ned Topside had been given a chance to get out of the palace together. Again she saw and heard the dashing, clever—albeit stuck-on-himself—Ned. This scene was of the two of them together on an errand, sent by the queen to London Bridge when they had royal coin to buy any hats they fancied. Ned had insisted they playact that they were husband and wife as they strolled the shops and streets looking for information about a murder—

"I'd a done deliv'ries if you'd asked 'stead of just leavin' the 'pothecary without a heigh ho," Ben groused, shattering her reverie. The fact that he hadn't been around to ask when she left evidently meant nothing to him. Getting up from his chair, he swaggered toward her behind the counter. He forgot to duck and bounced the bunches of poppy heads, braided garlic, and lupin hanging in their little nooses. Cursing, he shoved a fist at them, so they jerked and swung the more.

Standing but a half head taller than Meg, Ben Wilton had straight, chestnut-hued hair hacked ragged because he cut it himself with a dagger instead of a razor. Meg was pretty certain he didn't trust her close to him with any sort of blade in her hand. His thatched brows bridged a crooked nose and wide-set, pale eyes that sometimes seemed to look straight through one. Yet it was not Ben's features that folks remembered, but his bulky build—massive, rounded shoulders, bull neck, thick thighs, and powerful arms from years of rowing barges. Now, though he'd never admit it and she dare not say it, he'd been living on her labors and was going to fat.

Meg shifted slowly, slightly away, forgoing her half-finished job of weighing lavender heads, one of her favorite, fragrant tasks. Instead, she shuffled down the counter to roll pills that smoothed wrinkles. The ingredients were crushed madonna lily root in wax, so her customers could get the herb down easily. Mildred Cecil, wife of the queen's Secretary of State, had sent her maid for them, but never came herself.

"Not likely you'd have been pleased to run errands," Meg picked up the strand of their talk, unable to keep from defending herself. She too wondered where Bett had ducked out to, but didn't want to get her in trouble by making a point of it. "Not unless it's a delivery down by the river landings and water stairs where you'd find your old rowing cronies, and it wasn't there. I did see the queen pass by, though," she added, knowing that would placate him.

"Heard she was abroad," he said, rubbing his calloused hands together as if he were washing them. "Didn't happen to see your old comrades-in-arms sticking to her skirts, did you? That run-off-at-the-mouth rogue Topside or the queen's fetch-it man?"

"No, I didn't see them, and Jenks is one of her bodyguards, not some sort of lackey."

"And Topside?" he challenged, his voice even sharper.

"Ben, you know he's her chief player, though some call him her fool, and she keeps him busy."

"Just you be sure he's not busy being love's fool, or I'll crack his crown," he threatened, fists on the counter as he leaned toward her.

Meg went on rolling pills. Sometime, somehow, she had to earn enough money to pay Ben off and get him out of her shop and her life. Even if she never had another man, she'd be better off. But for now she kept measuring out little fingernail-sized bits of bruised lily root and rolling each in a drop of warmed, malleable wax from a pewter plate over a small flame, then setting them aside to harden. Sometimes she used honey, flour, or animal fat as binders, but she always thought wax worked better, as long as her customers didn't leave the pills in the sun or too near the hearth. She worked with great dexterity, feigning interest in each small, round pill, but she was aware that Ben was sidling closer.

Ben Wilton wanted a son, as if it wasn't enough that she ran the shop and played wife and sometimes nursemaid to him, when she still could not recall for the life of her why she ever would have wed him in the first place. She'd made that miserable mistake in what she thought of as her "other" life, before she was kicked in the head by a horse and Sarah Wilton ceased to exist for her. Not only could she not recall Ben but she had no early memories of her now-deceased parents and how they'd taught her the herbs, although her knowledge of the trade strangely had stuck with her.

But Meg thanked God that Ben—and mayhap the queen herself—had let her hire Bett and Nick to help keep shop. Bett Sharpe tidied up both their shop and privy chambers and gathered and sorted herbs. Bett's husband, Nick Cotter, delivered goods if they were not picked up here. Bett was the mother of the queen's young artist, Gil Sharpe, who, like Bett, had begun life as a thief, but now drew portraits and pictures for the queen. Ned had said Her Grace might even send the boy to study art abroad, if she could bear to part with him. That thought made Meg hurt and hate again. She squashed the next pill too flat and had to carefully remold it.

"If 'n Bett'd get her carcass back in here to watch the place, I'd give you a quick tumble upstairs," Ben said, his big, hard hand cupping her bottom right through her skirts.

Despite the fact that she'd been bracing herself for some such tactic, Meg jumped, then covered her alarm with a girlish giggle. She worked hard never to let Ben know he cowed her or had her at a disadvantage.

"We'd better not," she said, her voice steady. "Dr. Clerewell might be by for his lupin and theriac, and we don't want him buying it anywhere else." Theriac was a new panacea which contained many rare ingredients and cost a small fortune. And though the apothecaries' profit was minimal, the doctors upped their cost sky high for prescribing it, just so folks would know they were getting something new and special—and to fill their already fat physicians' purses, Meg fumed.

"At least, *there's* a bird worth snaring," Ben said, giving her bum a smack before he leaned both elbows back on the counter and lolled there. "Not many doctors you got coming in here reg'lar. Clerewell said he likes our shop best of all, 'specially since I let on you used to work for the queen herself and she still favors you."

Meg wanted to bang him over the head with the pewter tray

of pills, but she bridled her fury. She picked up the tray and walked away to drop her small creations into paper packets and then those into a labeled wooden box in one of the many narrow storage drawers that lined the wall.

"But the queen doesn't favor me," she said quietly, when she got hold of herself again. "And I told you we're doing well enough without your tales to impress customers," she went on in a rush, fighting back tears. "God's truth, the queen wants nothing to do with m—"

He banged his fist so hard on the counter that her scales jumped and swayed. "You promised me you'd work on changing that!" he bellowed. "Like I told you, we need something that'll rattle her good, make her want your cures again. Hell's gates, if 'n you went back to her, the word'd get out, the coins'd roll in then."

"We had a high-paying, well-spoken customer about a fortnight ago who wanted ground unicorn horn," she protested, "so it's not just Dr. Clerewell and a few other courtiers carrying us." She went over to her display of elixirs, syrups, juleps, decoctions, and cordials sitting on the sill and on the three shelves above it Nick had built for display. She rotated the bottles to turn the other sides to the sun in the bull's-eye, thick-paned window.

As she stretched to reach for the top row, she ached, just remembering Ben's hamhock fists the last time he got overmuch beer and lust in him at the same time. With Ben, maybe like with too many folks, love and hate got twisted up sometimes, and they committed demented, daring acts they didn't really mean. But then it was too late.

❧   ❧   ❧

T HE SMALL POX," ELIZABETH WHISPERED TO ROBIN AS they stared down at the ornate figure. "This depicts the Queen of England with pox scars all over her face and hands!"

She pulled her feet back from the effigy, which seemed to crowd the coach between them. She pressed her trembling hands over her eyes to shut out the sight of the plaster face with its ravages of deep, rounded pits and smears of scars. In her mind's eye, she saw the horror of the dread disease again.

She had been a gangly, young girl that summer and was so thrilled to have the continued affection of her father's sixth queen, the kindly Katherine Parr, who had been recently widowed by King Henry's death. At her stepmother's house at Chelsea west of London on the Thames, a garden of hollyhocks and roses grew, surrounded by a wall and locked gate that opened on the narrow lane behind the house. Beyond grew fragrant fields of meadowsweet and woodruff which smelled like new-mown hay. Perhaps that place, that memory was why she loved those strewing herbs yet today.

But the garden was a haven, and Elizabeth, up to that point, had been sheltered from the ugliness of life, from people who were not attractive, for that was what her father favored.

That long past day, slipping away from both the Queen's Grace, and her companion, Kat Ashley, Elizabeth took the key, hidden in the chink of the brick wall. Outside the gate the entire world was splendidly beckoning—until she saw them.

At first she told herself it was only a mother and her two little ones, the girl still in leading strings, the babe held in arms. Even when the princess saw they were ragged beggars, no doubt scurrying from back door to back door in the rural village, she was not afraid and rummaged in her small dangling purse for a stray coin to give.

But then she saw their faces fully in the sun. The mother's, perhaps once comely, deeply pocked and ravaged, the children's, too, a marred mass of scars and pits—

Princess Elizabeth's courage and charitable heart failed her.

Gasping, she backed away and tripped to bounce her bottom in the dirt. The toddler came to stand over her, looking down, holding out a dainty hand, also poxed and pitted.

"Tell the young lady yer name now," the mother prompted as if the precious day and world had not just turned upside down.

"Me 'Liz'beth," the child said in the sweetest voice.

That other 'Liz'beth, Princess of England, had scrambled to her feet and scurried in the gate like a craven coward. But ever since, even when she saw her brother, young King Edward, waste away from the great pox, which the physicians called syphilis, even when she once glimpsed lepers, even when she saw the grotesque neck swellings of scrofulous folk that the monarch traditionally blessed each year, she always saw the face of that mother and her two little ones and hated how she'd run from them. Yet she ran still in nightmares that plagued her in her sleep.

Now in the coach the queen pulled her hands from her hot face and thrust them unladylike under both armpits and clasped them there to steady herself.

"I can have this counterfeit corpse covered and carried into the doctors' hall," Robin said, evidently heedful of her agitation. "You can command them to destroy it or store it, then we will be on our way and put out the word that you simply stumbled getting in the carriage, scraped your hand or face, and cried out, or—"

"Enough!" she told him, seizing her cloak from him and throwing it over the figure. "The queen must not stumble or cry. We are taking this wretched thing back to Whitehall where it can be studied, probed, and whatever I must do to discover who put it here and why. And we must be sure," she added, sitting up straight as the thought struck her, "that it was put in the coach here and not at the palace. Summon Boonen for me."

Robin whispered to Jenks, who produced the driver. Rotating his flat cap in nervous hands, the burly man squinted into the dim coach to see her. Elizabeth leaned toward him in the door so he could not catch a clear view inside.

"Boonen, did you look inside here when you hitched the team this morning?" she asked, careful to keep her voice down so the others would not hear.

"Oh, aye, Your Majesty, that's part of my charge and duty, it is. Swept it out good and all. And the window flaps were down. We were moving all the way, so no one could of throwed refuse in—not till we got here—if that's what happened, Majesty. Begging your leave, but what's that thing there I can see right—"

"That will be all, and tell no one aught of this—refuse."

As Boonen bowed himself back into the crowd, the queen told Robin, "Get out and tell the guards to announce that the crowd should return early on the morrow because they will receive a token of their kindnesses to me today."

"What?" Robin said, his handsome face crumpling in a frown. "You start doing that to crowds and you'll have bedlam next time you so much as show your face at a window."

Elizabeth could tell she was thinking way ahead of him, but then she usually did. "I say that, Robin, so that I may have a few trusted men here tomorrow to question people about what they saw today. Otherwise, we'd have to somehow track them all down. Do as I say."

But he still could not move fast enough for her. The queen slammed the door after him when he climbed out to do her bidding. "Let everyone mount for the ride back," she called out to Jenks through the still partly opened window. "Driver, on!" she cried and slapped down the leather flap.

The entire way back to the palace, Elizabeth did not look out again. It was dark and stale in here, and that thing at her feet shifted and shuddered as if it were alive. The queen felt sick to her soul, but she'd be damned if she wouldn't uncover the villain behind this, and quick.

⁊   ⁊   ⁊

G RACIOUS, CREATING THIS TOOK TIME AND TALENT," Kat observed as she watched Jenks and Robin Dudley lay the effigy on the table in the queen's privy chamber and remove her cloak from it. They had brought it up the servants' stairs from the stables. The queen had ordered the room cleared but for the four of them—and that thing. "Would you believe it?" Kat marveled, evidently missing Elizabeth's baleful stare. "It's really quite good."

"It's appalling," the queen corrected her. "Accursed! Look at that poxed face." If it would have been anyone but Kat, still looking unsteady and wan, she would have rounded on her. "Thank you, Lord Robin, that is all," Elizabeth went on with a dismissive nod, "but I would deem it a favor if you would send Secretary Cecil to me. He cannot be far," she added pointedly when he still hovered. "And do not broadcast to others what—and who—this looks like."

He hesitated as if he would argue, then evidently saw the foolhardiness of that. He opened his mouth, then shook his head and kept going.

"Jenks," she said the moment the door closed behind Robin, "go find Ned and Lord Hunsdon and bring them up the back privy stairs. And fetch Gil, too, as I shall want several sketches of this thing. Kat shall relock the door behind you, but we shall hear your knock and let you in."

As ever, her dear Jenks hastened to obey without question, taking the private back way her father had ordered constructed in almost all of his palaces and lodges. Its entry in her bedroom was hidden by an arras. At the river gate of the palace it was guarded by yeomen, but Jenks could get out and back in.

Returning her gaze to the thing on the table, Elizabeth jolted anew at the sight of it, so cold, lifeless, yet lifelike. It was mostly the skin and hair, she surmised, for they were well done: the complexion seemed to give off a warm glow though it was cold to the touch. Seeing it laid out like this as if at a state funeral rattled her to the bone, but she refused to let on.

"Now, my question to you, Kat, before you take your afternoon respite, is do you recognize the gown on this creature?"

"Oh, that I do," Kat replied, fingering the tawny branched brocade overskirt, appliqued with dainty, daisy blooms of topaz gems and embroidered leaves. "One you haven't worn for months, but the skirts—yes, bodice and both sleeves—the pieces are yours. I must needs consult my records, since I can't recall if this was the assemblage of them the last time you wore it. It must have been nigh on two years ago."

Women's gowns, both plain and great, were a compilation of separate bodices, skirts, pairs of sleeves, and accessories, so that they could be completely mixed or matched by fastenings of laces, pins, or fancy flapped ties called points. At least, the queen thought, the gown bore none of her precious pins to hold the parts together nor scattered about as she was wont to do.

"I would like you, as Mistress of the Royal Wardrobe," Elizabeth said, "to do all you can to trace how these garments could have disappeared from under lock and key in a supposedly guarded building."

"I'd be able to tell you when you wore it last for sure, but my past ailments have fogged me up a bit, you know that, lovey."

"I do not blame you, Kat, but someone is to blame, and I mean to find out who and why. Something is afoot here that reeks of insult, injury—"

"Or plot?" a masculine voice inquired. They turned to see at the door to the hall, William Cecil, her principal secretary, Master of the Wards, and trusted adviser. He quickly closed behind him the door to the gallery that linked this privy suite of rooms to the more public presence chamber beyond.

"Dudley told me I could come directly in," Cecil explained, approaching them after a smooth bow, "but I was already on my way when I heard. And this is the amazing replica everyone is buzzing about. . . ."

" 'S blood, I knew I'd never keep it quiet!" Elizabeth cried and stamped her foot. "Now it will be noised all over my realm, and every whoreson lickspittle Papist spy will write his royal master in Madrid or Paris—or tell Mary, Queen of Scots, in Edinburgh—that someone in my realm wishes me ill, with pox if not worse, and is mocking—if not threatening—me!"

"Then we must put a better face on it," Cecil said as he bent over the effigy, "and I mean that not as a pun. We shall have it told that someone, an artisan of some sort, an anonymous sculptor or lovestruck subject, as all your subjects are, Your Grace, made and shyly presented this as a gift to his *serene* royal highness. We shall baldly deny any rumors about the poxed skin as a trick of the light—or say the face and hands were scratched or marred in being carried or placed in the coach."

"Aha," the queen said, clasping her hands before her mouth. "What would I ever do without you, my lord?"

Cecil's brown eyes lit at that compliment, and he made another slight bow. The queen and her most loyal man had worked together and struggled with each other through numberless difficult situations. Their bond was closer than ever of late, except when he took the perilous path of suggesting she must make a foreign marriage match, and soon.

William Cecil was a brilliant, if ambitious lawyer who had served her well for years, even when she was in disgrace and lived in terrible times with two other royal lives between her and the throne. Now forty-two years of age, he looked older, with his long, shovel-shaped beard and solemn face, but his eyes could sparkle and his wit was sharp as a sword. Cecil was both a devoted family man and a skilled statesman, just the sort of adviser she could build her kingdom on. She worked him hard but rewarded him well, and he was ever up to any task she set before him.

"I shall hastily convene the Privy Plot Council," she said, beginning to pace, "whose members I have already summoned, and we shall ferret out what wretch stands behind this. If it is one of our eminent physicians who has dared to try to challenge me, I shall have him dismissed at best and imprisoned at worst," she went on, gesturing broadly. "If this comes from my political enemies, especially my cousins, who have defied me already, I shall let them rot in the prisons they already inhabit."

The queen's gaze met Cecil's over the figure between them, and she stopped walking so fast, her skirts swayed. "I swear this means something dire," she whispered to him, as a knocking sounded from the next room and Kat went to open the Thames-side privy entrance. "This face, even the hands, are so real . . . it could almost be embalmed. . . ." Avoiding the pox marks, she touched the chin of the effigy, marveling again at the suppleness of the skin.

"I'm afraid it must be from someone who knows you well," he replied, "someone who is aware you dread the pox. Best I don a thick pair of riding gloves for protection and have a look up its skirts, if you'll forgive the impertinence, Your Grace," Cecil suggested, as Jenks, Ned, and Harry came in, with Kat explaining things to them as fast as she could talk. "Who knows," he concluded quickly, "what sort of viper or harmful substance could be hidden in its petticoats, up its sleeves, or even in this red-wigged head?"

Chapter
THE THIRD

Saffron causes headache and is hurtful to the brain, for
the too much use of the brain cutteth off sleep, through
want whereof the head and senses are out of frame.

JOHN GERARD
The Herball

"M Y HEAD IS SPINNING WITH ALL WE MUST DO,"
Elizabeth Tudor told her assembled band, with the effigy laid out before them on the table as if in repose or death. "And I'll not sleep until we discover who is behind this. Even if we do suggest to others that someone is trying to compliment and laud their queen, I am *not* flattered!"

Silence reigned as they gazed at the effigy. Of course, Jenks had seen the thing before, and her cousin Baron Hunsdon was a man of few words. But her chief fool and principal player of scenes—and one of her best sets of eyes and ears about the court—the curly-haired, green-eyed Ned Topside was seldom silent.

And yet, Elizabeth noted, something was slightly askew about it, some facial details not quite hers. If it had been stripped of the hair, cheap attempt at a crown, and the ornate garments, would it look like her at all? Nonsense, she chided herself. Any lackbrain could tell it was a good enough likeness, and the royal trappings showed it was intended to be her.

"Pray tell us what you would have us do," her cousin Harry Carey declared, perching his hand on his sword hilt in a swaggering stance as if ready to do battle for her.

Harry was the queen's first cousin through their mothers, who had been sisters. Now thirty-six, he looked as much Tudor as Elizabeth with his chestnut-hued hair, though his once-fair, freckled complexion was burnished by the sun and ruddied by manly, out-of-doors pursuits. Sporting a close-cropped beard, he was of middling height; the two of them saw eye to eye in more ways than one.

Harry, who had gone into exile on the continent during her Catholic sister's reign, had been ever loyal to her, and she had created him Baron Hunsdon and Master of the Hawks at the time of her accession. Lately, she had given him and his wife, her lady-in-waiting Anne Carey, fine lodgings in Blackfriars so they would be near their children even when serving at court. Like Robin, Harry was a man of action who chafed under a sedentary life, and she could see him champing at the bit even now.

"I would ask certain favors of each of you," Elizabeth began.

"At least we don't have a murder on our hands this time," Kat said. "But will this secret assembly function as we did the other three times you had need of covert actions, Your Grace?"

"Indeed, we must," Elizabeth admitted as she turned from one intense countenance to the other. Cecil looked as grim as she felt. At least Kat seemed animated for the first time in days. Jenks, like Harry, looked ready to take on the world with fists or swords. And Ned Topside, above all the others, seemed utterly fascinated by the replica.

"My favorite player of parts and staged counterfeiting," she addressed the handsome man grandiosely, for Ned loved fine speeches, "what think you of this playacting likeness of your queen? You have been oft skilled with wigs, costumes, and false faces."

"Yes, Your Grace, but only to amuse and please—and you are neither now," he murmured, still studying her second self on the table. Since too many men had let her down, Elizabeth tried to read his expression. Was it dismay that she implied he had the skills to produce this effigy? Shock at seeing what a fine job it was? Wanting to leave nothing to chance, she studied Ned the more as he finally cocked both brows and looked up.

"I think, for a molded mask, someone's done a fine job of it, Your Grace, though never," he hastened to add, "could a work of art capture the rare essence of your beauty. Yet this portraiture would make an audience suspend disbelief whether they sat in the great hall at court or in the gallery, cockpit, or—"

"But it was not meant to fool anyone, my favorite fool," she countered, feeling relieved he was back to his bombastic self again. "It was meant, I believe, to intimidate and threaten, to warn, and even to harm me through unease or fear of the deadly pox or death itself."

"Then," Ned declared, "the maker of it doesn't know you at all, for you will not take this lying down—I mean—"

The queen cut him off with a slash of her hand. The truth was she felt deeply, repeatedly shaken by it. Not only that some-one had laid this thing out as if dead in her own coach, but that it had appeared as magically as if it had materialized from empty air, with a council table full of brilliant physicians, her own ret-inue, and the street full of people close by. Still, it was that rav-aged face and hands, that hellish pox that made her go cold in the pit of her stomach.

"And where would you have us look for the villain or villains, Your Majesty?" Ned asked with a sweeping gesture that seemed to encompass the entire city.

"Here's my plan," she said, "though of course, as always, when we meet in a Privy Plot Council, you may speak your minds." But immediately, giving no one else space or leave to speak, she began to assign each a task to be done on the morrow.

"Ned and Jenks, you are to take small saffron cakes from the royal larder to Knightrider Street at morning light and pass them out to people who returned from today's crowd."

"Saffron cakes?" Ned asked. "Wasn't there something bad about saffron Meg used to say—like it made one's head hurt?"

"Stuff and nonsense. It's a good protectant against measles and smallpox. Besides, my new herbalist tells me that saffron crocus elixir makes one's head feel better and the senses quicker and livelier. Though," she muttered, pressing her hands to her temples, "I had a cake this morning, and my head is hurting now. But saffron cakes it is, because I mentioned I'd had a craving for them and the cooks went overboard turning them out."

She was irritated to see Cecil rest his hand on his chin and his index finger over his pursed lips, which she had come to realize was his sign to her to keep calm when they were in public. It angered her even more that the man could predict a coming show of her Tudor temper. "And I'll not have chatter," the queen went on in her most ringing, bell-clear voice, "about Mistress Milligrew to get me to miss her and take her back. She is banished, as is anyone who misleads or lies to me, hides a spouse, as she did, or takes my garments without permission as she did two years ago when we were at Windsor!

"Now, as I was saying, Ned and Jenks," she plunged on, instantly annoyed at herself for the outburst, "the two of you are, as circumspectly as possible, to question anyone from today's crowd you can find as to whether they saw something strange: someone carrying a covered form the size of the effigy, lurking in an alley, or toting a barrel or large box—anything suspicious."

"Even, I warrant," Ned put in, throwing an arm over Jenks's shoulders to tug him close in a demonstration, "several people walking close who could hold this realistic woman up between them."

"Precisely. Now when Gil arrives," she continued, "I intend to have him sketch this thing, though I am going to hide it in my library and have the door guarded. Meanwhile, I will search this form well. I am going to use my falconers' gloves, for they are thicker than riding ones, Cecil, to protect my hands when I search this effigy for clues to who may have secreted it in my carriage. The link to who sent it and what might be concealed on its person—that is, within its construction—can be the clue we need. Yet I will move as deliberately and carefully as a good physician on a diseased body, because we have seen before how hasty actions at the location of some crime can do us in."

"Haste makes waste," Kat added, nodding sagely.

"Exactly. Kat is going to try to trace how this thing could be wearing one of my gowns from the Royal Wardrobe storage, which is supposedly secure at Blackfriars," Elizabeth continued. "And, though Mary Sidney has not helped us in investigations ere this, she stood close to me and glimpsed this effigy, so I might as well ask her to assist us."

"To fill in for Meg being miss—" Jenks said before he realized his mistake and shut his mouth.

"Not to mention the fact," Cecil put in, "if Lady Mary didn't see this thing, her brother has told her all about it. The man keeps secrets like a sieve does water."

Elizabeth flashed him a narrow glance. Cecil and Robin got on like bears and dogs in the baiting ring, though they had tolerated each other of late, publicly at least, for the sake of queen and kingdom.

"I was going to say," Elizabeth continued, "that I will ask the Lady Mary to try to find the source for this fashionably frizzed red wig, though, of course, that may be a dead end. Difficult, I mean," she amended the way she'd put that. She had vowed to herself that this search would lead to no dead ends.

"The Lady Mary," Jenks put in, blushing slightly and perhaps trying to make up for his faux pas, "would be good for that with her sweet nature and all. She's kind to everyone and never raises her voice . . ." he got out before even he realized he'd done it again.

"It's possible," Elizabeth said, bridling her temper, "that anyone with lovely red hair could have donated it for misguided reasons and knew not how it would be used. But someone had to work it into a wig that resembles my own hair."

She gave her tresses a toss and felt the bejeweled headpins pull at her scalp. Realizing she had been so overwrought that she had not even removed her hat, she slowly did so. Kat scurried to help her.

"All of you look at the hue of my hair," Elizabeth said, shaking it loose to the style of maiden tresses she hardly displayed anymore. "Then look at that wig and tell me truly how close you think the color comes to my own. My hair has not been cut in months, so I wager that wig hair cannot be mine."

"The wig has none of your infinite, starry shine and lustre," Ned began.

"Leave off," Elizabeth ordered. "The color. And this is dire business, actor of fantastical parts."

"All right, then," Ned said, crossing his arms over his chest. "The wig's damn close."

"I warrant it is," Kat admitted.

"I'm afraid so," Cecil concurred. "Someone selected and styled it who at least is a close observer, as I said before."

"Harry?" she asked, though she knew full well such comparisons were not on his horizon.

He cleared his throat. "I like yours better, but it's set like what you've made the style, Your Grace, like my Anne wears now, frizzed and curled. And the wig-maker has aped that, for certain."

A flutter of knocks rattled the privy door in the queen's bedchamber, and Jenks went to open it for Gil Sharpe, Elizabeth's young artist. No one else knocked like that. The tall, thin lad had been mute since he was a youngster, but his mind was as nimble as his fingers and he could hear normally. He spoke only by hand signals and exaggerated facial expressions his mother, Bett, had taught him as a lad. None but Bett and the queen could communicate with him as fast; their talk often looked like a blur to others.

"Gil has the artist's eye," the queen declared. "He will be a good judge of color."

Though Gil was fourteen with one foot on the threshold of manhood, he still had the deceptive face of a cherub under a shock of fawn-hued hair. As ever, he exploded into the room with energy and verve, his velvet sack of charcoal sticks in one hand and a sheaf of parchment in the other.

"Gil, is this a close copy of me, the coloring especially?" the queen asked, gesturing at the effigy.

Gil gasped, then gaped at it. He walked carefully closer, then circled it, forcing the others to step back as he passed each. The lad looked wary, as if the thing would rear up and grab him. Finally, he touched it tentatively with one finger on its wrist, then, wide-eyed, pulled his hand back.

He handed his things off to Kat, then said with his quick gestures and lively expressions: *not enough breasts, though yours are small too.* He cupped both hands on his own chest, then pulled and pushed at his nose. *It has nose too short, not beaked, like yours. Maybe a mixture of wax or plaster.* Here he made motions as if he were rolling or smoothing something. *But an artist did the face and matched that hair color. A person with a steady hand for small tasks and details, just like me—*

"All right, then, Gil," she interrupted. She translated what he'd said as, "The shape of the bodice is too flat and the nose a bit unlike mine, but the villain may be some sort of artist, because the hair color and face is close. We are dealing, everyone," she pronounced, "I believe, with someone of means for payments or bribes to bring all this together—artist, plaster, gown, hair—and the covert conveyance and delivery of the thing."

"But who is going to try to trace the plaster, Your Grace?" Ned asked. "I know it's used to build walls and for medicated dressings for physicians' plasters and heaven knows what else."

"Yes—for physicians and heaven knows what else." She then went on to admit the idea she'd been hatching. "I am going to look into the plaster image myself by visiting some other effigies, royal ones too. Like all of you, I shall report on that at dusk tomorrow when we assemble here again. Suffice it to say for now that we must put out the story that some unknown admirer left this replica in my coach—and should someone ask or speculate on its complexion, say the skin somehow became scratched and scraped a bit. I want no word or idea of the pox to gain purchase."

She looked around at each of them again, waiting for more questions, but she saw only nods. "I thank God for each of you in this endeavor," she told them. "And my Lord Cecil, I would have you visit the physicians of the Royal College to see if they saw aught or can suggest who might have put this thing in my coach—in their own bailiwick, so to speak. And heed with care their words, because they are as good at dispensing them as pills, and I trust them much less than I wish I could."

"Consider it done, Your Grace," Cecil said. "The members of the Royal College are suspect indeed, since the effigy was obviously placed in your carriage by someone who knew your schedule and could somehow maneuver the form quickly from a nearby hiding place while you and your entourage were distracted."

"Indeed, though Robin had remained outside and should have seen something," she said as an afterthought. "And John Caius had just asked me for corpses to dissect!" Kat cringed, and the others jerked alert. Cecil alone didn't budge.

"I've heard, Your Grace," he said, frowning, "Caius is a bit of an artist himself and sketches diseased bodies, palsied faces—"

"Aha!" she interrupted. "Then digging to the bottom of this insult may be easier than we think. But now I'll ask all of you to disperse but for Kat and Gil while we search and sketch our best and only evidence, just as Dr. Caius evidently plans to do with real bodies."

A FTER ELIZABETH HAD SUMMONED MARY SIDNEY TO explain her task and give her a snippet from the wig, the queen, Kat, and the busy Gil, who was making sketch after sketch, were alone. "Now to examine this counterfeit at close range without taking it totally apart," she said as she tugged on the hawking gauntlets.

But the gauntlets were totally unwieldy, thick with suede and leather to protect skin from the hawks' talons. She soon threw them on the floor and donned riding gloves as Cecil had first suggested, though she'd not tell him he'd been right on this.

Carefully, she removed the circlet of crude crown and lay it aside; it was all wires with a few paste and wax mock gems on it, the most shoddy part of this dreadful display. She peeked under the wig. The head was carved wood with the facade of the almost pliable plaster face laid over it.

"Do you think the fiend who made this is implying you're a blockhead?" Kat queried, and Gil snorted his silent laugh.

"This is deadly serious, both of you," Elizabeth scolded.

The wig was sewn to a silk base and stuck into the wood with flat-headed metal pins. They were mayhap the sort that dressmakers used, or some physicians to draw a small sample of bad blood when they didn't want the gush a lancet brought. Then too, she'd heard artists who desired multiple copies of a portrait would draw a master sketch, then make pinpricks in the outline and smear charcoal through the tiny holes onto another paper. That faint outline would then be inked or painted in.

The queen felt through the wig with the tips of her gloved fingers, to be certain nothing was secreted in the curled hair, then lifted the wig off. "The work here is quite fine—small stitches in the silken skullcap. And no opening into the head," she said and replaced the wig, even taking pains to straighten it so it looked right again.

She pulled the narrow ruff aside and set to examining the neck of the thing—an extension of the wooden head—and then worked her way down the body. Kat untied the small bows attaching the tapered sleeves to the bodice and pulled them down the arms. While Kat turned the sleeves inside out, the queen carefully squeezed the arms. Finding nothing amiss, they rolled up the lower skirts to observe that the legs were much like the arms.

"Linen skin stuffed with something soft," Elizabeth observed. "Something a bit stiff and crunchy too."

"Straw?" Kat asked, carefully squeezing the limbs too.

"I don't think so. You're just picturing the country scare-the-crows that used to stand in the wheat near Hatfield or those dummies-at-the-quintain that jousters took their lances to in practice. This is far finer work than that."

"I recall, lovely," Kat said, "you once watched Robin Dudley make passes at the quintain with his sword and lance for hours at Windsor. His squire used to crudely dress his dummy like Catherine de' Medici, even with a wig and crown, and you laughed and laughed."

"I'm not laughing now. That was long ago I hung on Robin's every word and ploy to get in my good graces. No more!"

"Whatever the stuffing is, it smells good, like your favorite strewing herbs," Kat observed. Also wearing riding gloves, the old woman poked at, squeezed, and sniffed the effigy's arm above the lifelike plaster hands—long-fingered, graceful hands, just like hers, Elizabeth marveled. She saw Kat glance at the floor of the chamber with its herbs swept into corners by skirts and feet. Elizabeth knew what she was thinking. When Meg Milligrew was here, the floors were kept sweeter and fresher. The queen heaved a huge sigh, and saw Gil start as if the effigy itself had made the sound.

"No, Kat," Elizabeth insisted, returning to their task, "that's not this thing you're smelling. The meadowsweet and woodruff's on the floor, and the hint of lavender's in our pomanders and garments."

Gil stopped drawing again and gestured to her, *I think this thing also smells just like you. If Bett was here she could tell you what's inside with one sniff, and you wouldn't even have to cut into it.*

"I'm not sending for Bett now," Elizabeth said. "Go sit over there and work until I call you back." She let him think he was just getting in her way when she actually did not want anyone but Kat to see her disrobe the effigy. Gil shrugged and shuffled away to perch on the curved, padded bench under the oriel window where the fading outside light was better.

"Now," Elizabeth whispered to Kat, "let's look all the way up under my stolen skirts."

The petticoats were hardly as full as her own, but her mocker had not skimped on them, mayhap to keep the tawny brocade gown from dragging if the effigy was stood straight up. Each holding a side of the outer skirt, Kat and the queen lifted it up to cover the figure's head, as if it shouldn't see its own intimate examination.

"That top petticoat's one of yours, I warrant," Kat judged as she squinted at it.

"How can you tell?"

"If you ever helped dress yourself these days, you'd know. See here," she said and pointed a gloved hand at a white embroidered circlet near the hem. "*E.R.,* plain as day."

"There's nothing wrong with your eyes, my Kat," Elizabeth told her, pleased at the proof and yet even more annoyed at her petticoats being pilfered too.

"It's just I knew where to look," Kat said as they peeled up the next layer of linen, then one of taffeta, then the next, until they came to the bum roll. The sausage-shaped, stuffed bolster was knotted flat across the belly but bulged on the sides and back to push out the skirts. It was much more old-fashioned than the current cagelike farthingales, but bum rolls were still in use.

"We'll have to cut into that, too, but right now let's see the rest of her," Elizabeth said as she exposed the linen hips and midriff, which looked rather lumpy with their stuffing. But as she got a knife and prepared to cut into a thigh, she hesitated. What if something dangerous was hidden within? Even if it wasn't, she half expected this thing to bleed.

She steeled herself, then touched the knife to the cloth and drove it in, before they both startled at the rapping on the hall door. She'd given orders she was not to be disturbed. But 'S blood, she was disturbed by all of this!

As the queen stayed her dagger, Kat went to the door and said through it, "The queen's resting. Who's there?"

"It's Cecil, Lady Ashley. I shall just step in a moment, then, and leave these important papers for Her Majesty to tend to in the morning."

Kat glanced at Elizabeth, who nodded and moved to meet him just inside the door rather than have him see the half-denuded form. But when he stepped in and closed the door, he discarded his sheaf of papers on a chair and peered over her shoulder.

"I see," he said, gesturing at a discarded hawking glove on the floor, "you've thrown down the gauntlet."

She knew he did not intend a jest. No one smiled or laughed. Everyone stared now at the dagger she held in her gloved hand. Silence hung heavy in the royal rooms.

"I am determined," she told him, annoyed at herself for blinking back tears, "to ferret out the villain."

"Or villainess," he countered, his brow furrowed. "I fear we might have more of those who wish you ill than we want to admit. Your Majesty, I returned not only to see what you have found. I believe we must indeed follow clues to uncover links to someone unknown. But we must also make a list of certain dangerous persons who are your blood kin, those we know would like not only to dismay or harm you, but also—"

"Who would like to take my life and throne," she finished for him.

Chapter

THE FOURTH

Both the leaves and roots of bistort or snakeweed have
the powerful faculty to resist all poisons: the venom of
the plague, the small pox, measles, purples, and any
other infectious disease.

        NICHOLAS CULPEPER
The English Physician

T HE MOMENT MEG MILLIGREW UNLOCKED HER SHOP
door the next morning, Marcus Clerewell appeared in
the dim dawn.

"Oh, doctor," she said, cloaking her surprise, "there you are,
and so early too. I thought you'd be by for your goods yesterday."

"Forgive my tardiness, Mistress Sarah." He shook her hand
as he always did. His fingers and palms were warm and soft, especially for a man. Warm hands, warm heart, Kat Ashley used to
say, and Meg knew that was true of this kindly man.

"Please, after you," he said with a sweeping gesture and followed her into the shop. His deep, musical voice was pleasant to
her ears, especially after Ben's constant carping. She was glad her
husband had not rolled out of bed yet and probably wouldn't till

midmorn. Marcus Clerewell was not born or bred a gentleman, but he seemed one, ever polite and charming. And, for a physician, modest and humble. He didn't talk down to her or put on airs. She had to admit the man was her favorite customer and not only for the amount of coin he spent.

"It smells wonderful in here as usual," he told her. "No doubt from that meadowsweet you put on your floors, which I believe your husband said you used to strew in the royal privy chamber too."

"Ben brags too much of my days with the queen."

"I have no doubt you were of great help to Her Majesty and will be again someday when she realizes how much she lacks your good services," he assured her as she walked around the back of the work counter and he paused before it.

"Your lupin and snakeweed are ready, your precious theriac too," she told him, gathering the herbs from behind the counter.

"Good old treacle, as the common folk always call it," he mused. "But not you, mistress. Sarah Wilton, ever on her toes."

"I'd have to be to keep up with you," she said, and they shared a little smile. Indeed, she'd have to stand on her toes in more ways than one, for the man must be nigh six feet tall and carried himself proudly, never stooping or slumping like Ben did.

"I believe what you are endeavoring is noble," she added as she placed his herbs in a hemp sack that would keep them safe but let them breathe. She was especially heedful of handling the theriac in its horn container with a piece of parchment tied across its mouth. It was concocted of near fifty special ingredients he'd specified.

"Anyone," she went on, "who is bold enough to work with people scarred by the pox, let alone strive for a cure for them— why, noble is the only way I can think of it." She flushed as she beamed at him, but from his left side she could not glimpse his expression.

She'd never seen Dr. Marcus Clerewell remove his cocked, big-brimmed, plumed hat, though the breadth of it made him always turn his head to see. At first, she'd thought it strange he didn't wear the brimless, ear-flapped cap that was the proud sign of a learned doctor. And she'd not understood his always keeping his hat on until she'd glimpsed his face in the slant of window light and had nearly fallen through the floor one day.

Worse than if he were poxed, he had puckered, stretched, and thickly layered reddish skin—like dried mud that carter's wheels had driven through—covering half of his once-handsome face. Scarred skin hung a heavy fold of lid over his left eye. Even his other arched brow, classically chiseled nose, firm mouth, and strong chin could not save an observer from shock. From his right side, Marcus Clerewell, Norwich doctor come to London but two years ago, looked a princely man, but from the other . . .

Besides admiring this man, Meg had to admit, she pitied Marcus Clerewell, though she never let on. There but for the grace of God walked all men. Besides, she sensed his disfigurement had inspired him to do great things, and she was thrilled to be a small part of that effort.

"I have a surprise for you, mistress," he told her. "Steady yourself and gaze upon my scars, for I know you have glimpsed them afore. Then tell me what you think, for I would sue for your assistance, more than you have already bestowed so generously upon me."

Slowly, he removed his hat and turned his left side to her.

"Oh," she said, surprised by the pale if slightly swollen smoothness of his skin there. "You—dear heavens—you've cured your scars!"

"Not cured, mistress, but covered and treated in the process," he said solemnly. "With this."

She tore her gaze from the miracle of his skin as, from his leather satchel, he produced with a flourish an alabaster box and opened it. A thick, creamy substance lay within.

"You'll make your fortune with pox survivors!" she cried. "If it does that for your scars . . ."

He held one finger to his lips to quiet her. "My scars are burns, mistress, not pock marks. Its use for that is yet to be proved. Now, one must not rub this in, but carefully layer it on and let it set a bit. Sarah, I never told you how I became so flawed, did I, and I bless your sweet nature for never asking as others always blurt it out."

"I didn't want to hurt your feelings."

"You've done quite the opposite. You see, my mother's skirts caught fire from the hearth when I was but four years, sleeping in a trundle near the fireplace to keep warm. 'Tis not uncommon," he added, and she saw his eyes mist. "I mean, of course, disfigurement or even death from such a cause."

Meg blinked back a prickle of tears. "True," she rushed to reassure him. "I've heard and seen such and mixed medicines for accidents like that. You should have told me before. Her skirts caught your bedclothes on fire, didn't they?"

"I was ill, you see, with a fever that made me delirious, and she'd tucked me in tightly. She tried to beat out my flames and so died in agony from her burns, but I . . ." He cleared his throat. "You can imagine the rest, my suffering as a lad, reared by a father who felt her death and my face were God's just punishment for—for what I know not. A bookish man, a hard man . . . But I believe your kind heart knows how much I've grieved from taunts and cruelties as I grew up. Pox scars, indeed, folks expect to see, but this stigma is so much worse."

"Glory to God you're not a bitter man. That you want to help others."

"Yes, well, I had once only hoped to help burn victims, but there are so many poxed. Don't misunderstand me, Sarah. I know full well there would be financial profit in such a cure. I could expand my library and have a work printed about my belief in the vapor theory of various disease and pestilence. But as to your help . . ."

He stopped speaking as Meg's second customer came in, Pru Featherstone, a tavern keeper's wife. Dr. Clerewell must have heard or sensed the woman, as he swept his hat back on and whispered, "Please, see to your customer."

Meg tended to the goodwife's needs, but her eyes and mind kept focused on the doctor. A miracle! A medication that could save hearts and minds if not lives. And he was counting out a pile of coins, more than he owed her, even for the expensive theriac. She couldn't wait until the woman left the shop.

"So you've tested the cream on yourself, and it's perfect," she exulted the moment they were alone again.

"But hardly perfected. It needs more trials and not only on me and the few patients I have access to." He sighed and shook his head. "It isn't easy for a provincial doctor, no matter that Norwich is the realm's second largest city. Here am I, just beginning a London practice where the learned doctors of the Royal College rule and reign."

"Don't they, though," she commiserated. "They keep an eagle eye on the apothecaries and herbalists too, I can tell you that."

"And yet I implore you that I might leave this goodly sample for you to try on whomever might dearly need its benefits. I've noticed that your assistant Bett has a puckered scar on her chin."

"I could try it on her. But if I'd sell such and it got out, I could be closed down and worse."

"Not sell, mistress, but use gratis on persons who might need a godsend, like Bett. I've seen how she helps you and how much she loves her son, the queen's mute artist, as you described him. Indeed, perhaps I can work to cure his muteness too."

"Oh, Dr. Clerewell, we'd all be so grateful."

"But let's keep that our secret now too, not to get people's hopes up. And I'd ask only that you—and they—keep quiet about the source of this emollient till we are certain it would work well for others too. I cannot be besieged for it, not now. And if they ask you what is in it, that I cannot tell at this time, to protect my work. Will you help? And do not fret that this is underhanded, for I intend to drop off a second petition for its legal sale to the Royal College of Physicians on my way home." He lifted his surcoat so she saw a wax-sealed letter stuck in his belt.

His eyes were as warm as his voice and hands. The fact he'd admitted to her that this letter was his second petition to those unfeeling, pompous physicians made her sympathize the more. Their fingers touched as he slid the box toward her and she nodded.

"You have my word I'll help and keep your secret," she whispered. "May I know what you call it, then?"

"Venus Moon Emollient. Named for the goddess of beauty and the white-faced moon. And I give it into your care, fit for a goddess."

Meg blushed, unsure if he'd meant to compliment her or not. She took the box from him almost reverently. For one moment she had thought he was going to say "fit for a queen."

꿈 꿈 꿈

I DON'T KNOW ABOUT YOU, BUT I'M ABOUT OUT OF cakes, questions, and patience," Jenks muttered to Ned as the morning wore on in Knightrider Street. They had set themselves up several doors down from the physicians' hall. "No one's seen one damned thing out of the ordinary, and Bess won't like us coming back empty-handed—without information, I mean," he added, stuffing a piece of broken cake in his mouth.

Ned Topside rolled his eyes and shook his head. He'd never gotten used to how dense Jenks could be with his blunt, naive approach, when Ned was certain using various voices and personae was a better tactic of discovery.

"I'm not surprised," Ned muttered as they dumped their sacks of crumbs for the ravens that scavenged in the streets. "The crowd only had eyes for Her Grace and, according to what people have said, the coach was down a bit out of their line of sight. But I think we should suggest to her we return to knock on doors farther down the street, since folks there might have had the coach in their view, especially if they were peering out an upper window."

"Maybe we should do it now and surprise her."

"Let's just tell her what we found—or didn't find—and suggest it, and don't forget who came up with it first. Halt there!" Ned called to a man with a large hat as he strode down the street. "Were you in the queen's crowd yesterday?"

The man was tall and stately and seemed in a rush. Ned would have given a fortnight's salary to get his hands on that dramatic, French-looking hat.

"No, as I'm just visiting the doctors. The queen's crowd, you say? What's amiss?"

"Nothing's amiss," Jenks put in, elbowing Ned.

"You mean," the man said, looking sideways at them and shifting his big package and the wax-sealed missive he held to his other hand, "you're queen's men?"

Ned was going to give a grandiose answer, but Jenks elbowed him in the ribs again. "If you weren't here yesterday, go on about your business then," Jenks ordered. "Good day to you."

As the fellow hurried on and knocked at the front door of the physicians' hall, then stepped inside, Jenks mounted, and Ned followed suit.

"He could easily find out what we were doing here," Ned

grumbled. "It doesn't pay to lie or be secretive in this instance. We've even tipped off the eminent physicians. I noted more than one of them staring out at us when we first came, though I haven't seen a face at a window for a good hour."

"Probably part of her plan, to rattle them," Jenks said smugly. "Wait till they see Cecil on their doorstep later, eh?"

As they headed away, their horses nearly knocked down a young, blue-coated apprentice as he ran pell-mell from one of the narrow alleys into the street. "Ho, can you tell me if I'm too late for the queen's kindness then?" he called to them. "My master wouldn't let me go two days in a row, so I sneaked out."

They reigned in, and Ned leaned an arm on his pommel to bend down to regard the man at closer range. "You saw the queen here yesterday, did you?"

"Aye, first time 'cause he always keeps me working. Pewtersmith's man I am, down on Cheapside next to the Rose and Thorn. Say," he said, looking up at Jenks, "you were in her procession. You the guard wedded to that cloaked maid in the crowd, the one with sunset hair like Her Majesty's?"

Ned and Jenks exchanged quick glances. "Hair the color of the queen's, you say?" Ned asked.

"Certes, in a cloak and hood. Standing in the alley, she was. And then run off when I said she looked like the queen."

"Not just hair hue, but the maid's face too?" Ned prompted.

The lad frowned and scratched his head right through his cap. "Aye, that's the way of it though none's so fair as our fair queen."

"Well said, man," Ned said and flipped him a groat. He caught it easily and bit it to be certain it was real. Ned thought that one piece of information just might make up for the wasted saffron cakes they'd passed out to the rabble. This man had given them something to go on, though Jenks might not have caught the import of it.

"That girl in the street could have been Meg," Jenks blurted out to dash his hopes, "though I suppose other maids have the queen's coloring too. But our old friend would never do a thing to hurt Her Grace. Meg yet loves her dear so there's no motive, as Cecil would say."

"Of course not," Ned clipped out and turned away before he rolled his eyes at the man's stupidity. When the apprentice hurried off and Jenks spurred his horse, Ned yelled, "Stay!"

"Me? Stay why?" Jenks challenged, pulling up.

"I believe you should stay behind and knock on a few of those house doors. It was a good suggestion you had—to do it now."

"*I* should? And what of you then?"

"Her Majesty would certainly trust that task to you alone, and I am certain you will do a fine job of it. I'll ride a bit down these narrow alleys to see if there is a discarded trunk or large sack in which that effigy might have been carried. I'll meet you back at Whitehall."

Before Jenks could protest, Ned wheeled away. He'd make short shrift of the alleys all right, because he had a visit to make he didn't want Jenks or the queen to know a thing about.

❧   ❧   ❧

K AT ASHLEY, WITH ANNE CAREY AS COMPANION, RODE toward the vast manors and privy apartments in the enclave called Blackfriars, once a massive monastery. After the dissolution of the Catholic Church's vast holdings in England, the crown had taken over such church property for its own use.

Westminster Abbey, on the far side of Whitehall, had become a Protestant church and a secular college. To the east, prime Thames-side land once boasting the chapel, cloisters, gardens, and dormitories of the black-garbed friars was now the elite environs of important court personages like the Careys. The monks' former supply rooms, infirmary, and sanctuaries also provided extra storage for royal barge trappings, masque and pageant properties, and, as was Tudor tradition, the great royal wardrobe. Though the queen's seasonal gowns and accessories were kept in her palace of current residence, that was too meager a space for all she was coming to possess.

With their treasures bundled within, daily wardrobe carts trundled back and forth from palace to wardrobe, a brick building off Thames Street which had housed the black friars' sewing and mending shops before the Tudors took it over. Kat felt so tired she'd almost taken one of the carts today, settled down amidst the royal attire. She could have ridden a barge, too, but you might know all of them were out fetching goods or people.

"Are you quite certain you won't mind if I stop round to see my children before we head back to Whitehall?" Anne asked, as she drew her horse up within Blackfriars' once-hallowed precincts. Despite being Lord Hunsdon's wife, Anne didn't know why the Mistress of the Royal Robes was really here. The queen insisted that her Privy Plot Council keep secrets, even from spouses. As far as Kat knew, no one had broken their pledge of honor yet—hopefully not even the disgraced Sarah Wilton, alias Meg Milligrew, who had known her share of them.

"I expected you to see your little ones," Kat assured Anne. "Go on then, and I'll meet you here at the wardrobe in an hour." Kat figured it wouldn't take her long to cross-question the guard and give the wardrobe girls a good going over about the missing gown and petticoats.

The old woman dismounted with difficulty, then stomped over and cuffed the dozing guard, slumped on a bench in the sun by the wardrobe door. He lunged to his feet, cursing until he saw who had smacked him. He swept the door open for her with, "First Lady here unannounced!"

"Next time you'll watch that door proper and help me dismount too!" Kat muttered as she entered the cool, vast building.

"Queen's First Lady of the Wardrobe here!" the guard bellowed a second time, then beat a hasty retreat, closing the door behind him.

Seeing no one down the shadowy rows of suspended garments, Kat nonetheless heard scurrying, as if she'd stirred up a nest of mice in a larder. The mingled scents of lavender, rosewater, and lime curled around her to calm her nerves.

Finally, the two men who drove the delivery cart and the two women who did the mending and scenting fell into a line, dropping ragged curtsies and bows as if she were the queen herself. Though the main laundry, where most things were boiled and bleached, was in the outbuildings of Whitehall, two light-soil laundresses came running, wet to their elbows. She'd forgotten about them. She supposed she should separate this lot and go at them one at a time, but she had not the patience nor strength for that.

Though Kat wasn't expecting her, one of the queen's cobblers, actually a slipper-maker, came running too. Foolish lass, she held a long needle in one hand and could have accidently jabbed herself or any of them. Finally, the two who embroidered or stitched on jewels and pendants, as well as the haughty old dame who was the royal lace-maker appeared, with her new ruff girl in tow, so it looked as if Kat would get them all in one fell swoop.

"I've been ailing of late," Kat began, "but I'm back now and my being indisposed is no excuse for your laxness."

"No, milady," echoed in various voices down the line.

"I consulted my book, and I want you to fetch a gown the queen hasn't worn for some time but wants to see now," she went on, setting in place her plan to make them search for that which was not there. "A tawny, branched velvet skirt, matching single sleeves, and boned bodice. The skirts have flowers appliqued on, made of matched topaz, and—"

"Oh, I know the one," Melly, who was the brightest of the bunch, piped up. Kat hoped she would not be implicated, because the girl could sew on a gem in any pattern and have nary a thread show. "I spent all night putting those golden daisies on that gown, and went near blind as a bat. I know where it's kept too, back with the golden or canary ones what have sprinkles of jewels."

She darted out of line before Penny, the oldest of the staff, could grab her back. "Here now, you're not to fetch and carry gowns!" Penny cried and ran after her. "I'll get it. I shifted the befurred gowns and the embroidered smocks on the other side of the bodices. Here now, you just come back!"

But they both returned empty-handed with their caterwauling ended, and that gave Kat the excuse to go down the line and grill each one of them. She kept Lady Anne waiting an extra hour before they headed back to the palace, because it took that long before the new lace and ruff girl, Lucinda, finally broke down in tears.

She admitted she'd let a fine foreign gentleman who spoke real fancy lease those pieces for a fortnight just to show his friends, and he'd never brought them back. At that distraught display, Kat pulled the guard off the door and ordered him to take the sobbing girl straightaway to the queen at Whitehall.

⁂

THE QUEEN SHIVERED AS SHE ALIGHTED FROM THE royal barge at the Thames water gate and climbed the steps toward the old Palace of Westminster. As her companions fell in behind, a late afternoon mist closed off the city and river like a vast gray curtain.

Elizabeth Tudor's destination was Westminster Abbey, the

place of her joyous coronation. But it was also the solemn site of a Tudor cemetery, where her paternal grandparents, one of her stepmothers, her brother, and her sister were entombed. She shuddered and went on, anxious to have this quest over and angry with herself that she had lost her temper at Kat before she had set out.

"I've found a link," Kat had crowed when she'd returned from Blackfriars, "to who stole the effigy's gown, and I'm having the wench brought in direct for questioning!"

Delighted, the queen had delayed coming here while they waited for the lace girl Lucinda to be delivered by the wardrobe guard. When no one arrived, the queen had sent her own men to fetch them. It was they who learned that Lucinda and the guard were more than fast friends. Further inquiries revealed that both servants had disappeared into the teeming city with the queen's questions for them unasked and unanswered. Who was the man who supposedly leased the gown? Or if his name was unknown, what was his appearance? Now standing in the mist-swept gray shadows of Westminster, Elizabeth was not even certain what her questions here must be.

She had brought four of her ladies and a covey of guards. But, telling her women she wished to be alone to pray, she sent them into the palace nearby to wait for her and went on foot toward the Abbey with but two guards. It annoyed her that Jenks and Ned had not returned from Knightrider Street yet or she would have brought them, but perhaps they at least had turned something up.

She did not enter through the main west door to chance meeting the deans and canons of the college who had replaced the abbots and monks. The protectors of this place would be put out she had not announced her visit so they could make a fuss for it, and they would ask a thousand questions of their own.

She pulled her sable-lined hood and cape closer and walked

around to go in through the north door. Fortunately, it was not locked, or she would have had to send one of her men to open it from inside while she waited. The metal hinges, however, protested their entry with a shrill, scraping sound.

It was even more dim and chill inside with the day's wan light washing in through high stained-glass windows. Silence hung heavy under the lofty ceiling's soaring vaults, vast arches, and stone carvings. The Abbey's musty breath seemed to seep into her bones from floor stones, chapels, and carved effigies of long-dead kings and queens.

Seeing several of the abbey staff clustered before the high altar, Elizabeth skirted behind it, her footsteps whispering, her two guards hurrying to keep up. Here, where distant, disembodied voices echoed, she strode by the recessed chapel of John the Baptist. Pulling her cloak closer, she remembered how he had been beheaded, with his head then brought in upon a platter. She pictured again the head of her effigy, wondering if the maker of it wanted her real one on a platter too.

Weak-kneed, she heaved a huge sigh. Gripping her hands as if in prayer, she paused at the coronation chair, set behind the high altar when not in use. She vowed she must do all she could to keep herself and her kingdom safe.

She quickly passed the vault under which her sister's body lay, but slowed her steps at the chapel deepest in the nave. Here stood the grated, gilt resting place that the founder of the Tudor dynasty, King Henry VII, had built for himself and his queen, Elizabeth of York. A single, flickering lantern illumined its sheen and etched its shadows deeper. Behind the altar, above the ornately enclosed tombs, her paternal grandparents' gilded forms, guarded by cherubs, lay side by side, staring up toward heaven. But these glorious, golden effigies were not the ones she sought today.

Passing other chapels, she crossed the south transept and

passed through to the cloisters, the old grounds of the monks who had once tended this sacred place. Elizabeth nearly jumped out of her skin when her guard spoke, even though he whispered.

"Do you not wish this lantern lit now, Your Grace?" the taller guard, Clifford, asked, producing it and a flint box from under his cloak.

"Yes, all right. This cloister is always dim, even during midday."

She waited, looking nervously about, as they lit one glass-paned lantern and, when she nodded, the other. If this took too long she was going to be late for the Privy Plot Council meeting she had called.

"It seems darker than it really is in here," Clifford observed as if sensing she needed encouragement.

It was an astute comment, but she did not answer. Indeed, where she was going was called the Dark Cloister, for it lay beyond this arched, more open section where the monks used to take their air in bad weather. She only hoped the effigies she sought to examine—lifelike ones of some earlier monarchs that had been paraded in their funeral processions—were still kept downstairs in the Undercroft, which had served as the monks' common room. Once she viewed them, she would decide whether to privily summon their caretaker or maker to Whitehall for questioning.

Her guards each holding a lantern, they walked a ways down the Dark Cloister until they reached a narrow stairway down that loomed like an open mouth. "Wait here," she told her men, taking one lantern. "Come if I call, but call me only if you are challenged for your presence here."

One hand holding up her hems, the other lifting the lantern high, she went slowly, carefully down the stairs. She had only been here once years ago with her three Grey cousins, Jane, Katherine, and little Mary, on a lark during the days of her father's fifth queen, Catherine Howard. It was long before Lady Jane found herself a figurehead in a revolt against Elizabeth's sister, Mary Tudor, long before Jane was beheaded in the Tower of London where her younger sister Katherine was now imprisoned for her treasonous deceit against her current queen. Ah, those were happy days when they were young and sneaked down here to see the effigies and jested about them as if they were great dolls they could toy with. And yes, Elizabeth realized, Katherine Grey knew all about these royal effigies, and she—along with Margaret Lennox, their cousin—were women Cecil had suggested could be behind all this.

Elizabeth shook her head so hard her pearl earrings rattled. The girls had been caught and scolded that day, then thoroughly lectured by the Duke of Norfolk about how the effigies were carved here, painted, garbed, and made ready to be displayed on funeral hearses or tombs.

As she descended, the queen's heart began to pound even harder. She neared the bottom of the stairs before she realized it was not just her lantern throwing shifting light upon the walls. Someone else was here already.

Prepared to call for her men, she peeked from the stairwell into the pillared and vaulted stone room. What she saw made her mute. She lurched backward and dropped the lantern, which exploded to glass shards at her feet. In blinding torchlight thrust close to her face, the ghost of her dead sister lunged at her.

Chapter

THE FIFTH

*The oil which is pressed out of flax seed is profitable for
many purposes in physick and surgery, and is used of
painters, picture makers, and other artificers.*

           ❧ JOHN GERARD
The Herball

T HE APPARITION SOUNDED LIKE HER SISTER, MARY,
with its rough, masculine voice. Elizabeth couldn't catch
the words over the banging of her heart. Nor did its
mouth move or wide stare change.

"I said, sorry, milady, but you gave me a real fright," the
thing repeated when she just gaped at it.

She felt like a ninnyhammer, though it took her but a moment to realize that this was no ghost of her sister but a fully
garbed effigy which could compete with the one of herself. The
gown of crimson velvet, the replica of the scepter it held all
seemed so real. Whoever had done that face had captured Mary's
bland features and sullen stare. And the limbs of the short, squat
form had moved with such lifelike suppleness, and its head had
turned.

Elizabeth's guards, who had evidently heard the shattering of her lantern, came thundering down the stairs, but she held up her hand to stay them. In half stride, swords drawn, they waited.

This time when the effigy spoke, a man's blond head popped out from behind the wigged, crowned one. "Oh, no!" he cried as his torch illumined Elizabeth full in the face at the bottom of the staircase. "It cannot be—Your Majesty?"

"Stand away with that torch and figure," she commanded, but her voice shook. A quick glance around made her realize this man was alone. Thinking she'd do better questioning him without her men here, she motioned them back up the stairs. Slowly, they retreated.

"Forgive me, but no one warned—informed me you would be coming, Your Majesty. I was just moving this image of your royal sister Bloody Ma—I mean Queen Mary—to the table to dust it when I saw your shadow and grabbed a torch. I really had no idea, so perhaps the dean or canons forgot to tell me."

As he spoke, he fumbled one-armed with the figure to lean it against the wall, then backed away, bowing so low to Elizabeth, though it looked like his obeisance was to Queen Mary, that it seemed the torch would singe his hair.

"Your name?" she inquired.

"Percival Oldcorn, Your Gracious Majesty, assistant to the dean, at your service," the man introduced himself with another bow.

Over the grit of broken glass, she stepped into the room and glanced around. Two other torches in wall sconces cast fitful light into the deep recesses of the barrel-vaulted chamber. One chair, a long table, and a set of deep wooden shelves were the only furniture. Other effigies, as she correctly recalled, lay on the shelves, wrapped in sheets like winding cloths as if waiting for someone to call them forth from the tomb like Lazarus.

Despite Percival Oldcorn's low voice, he seemed a mere lad, she thought, with his beardless, smooth skin, and protruding ears. She was not used to men with no sun color; he looked as if he lived underground year-round.

"And your business here, Master Oldcorn?" she inquired, thinking he was yearning to ask the same of her.

"I see to the needs of these memorials of our realm's royalty, that is these funeral and tomb artificial personages," he told her proudly, gesturing toward what must be the newest effigy, the one of her sister. He placed the torch in its sconce, then, as if to make the slumped figure presentable, he darted over to brush dust or cobwebs from Mary Tudor's velvet sleeves.

"Indeed, then I am pleased to find you here, for there are some things I would know," Elizabeth told him, striding toward the effigies at the end of the room, where he hastened to follow. "I was told once how these are made, but I would see them and hear it from you, Master Oldcorn. Tell me all you know, especially about their heads, of what they are fashioned and who does such clever artifice."

The man knew a great deal, so Elizabeth suffered him to lecture her about how the ancient Greeks and Romans first modeled the heads of revered family members to keep in their homes. "Though most of those were of stone, metal, or wax and these are painted wood or plaster," he explained as he located the figures of King Henry VII and his queen. Oldcorn unwrapped them for her as he talked.

Elizabeth was amazed to see her grandmother's slender figure attired in a mussed but exquisite gold satin, square-necked gown, edged with red velvet. A fine fakery of a crown was wired to her wig, much more realistic than the crude one on the effigy in her coach. These painted wooden hands, one clutching an imitation scepter, were graceful, long-fingered, and so like Elizabeth's own.

"Even the limbs look real," she observed, pressing the effigy's supple wrist.

"The Tudor images are jointed at the shoulder and elbow, and Queen Mary's that gave you such a start even turns her head. Their skins are leather or canvas stuffed with hay and herbs," he added.

"To mold or sculpt, then paint these faces takes great skill," she observed to prod him further.

"Oh, yes," Oldcorn said smugly, as if he'd done the work himself. "See here on the king's face, the sunken lips, mouth gone askew, even the hollow cheeks and hard-set jaw. Features of a cadaver. Like these two, the best ones are from death masks."

"Death masks?" she gasped as a bolt of fear shot through her.

"Indeed, though masks can be modeled from life too. With the assistance of the subject, of course, and breathing straws in the nostrils while the plaster hardens."

She shuddered at the mere idea of her face being encased in a stiffening mask, whether she was dead or alive. But that reminded her of something else: Ned Topside had mentioned last evening that the poxed face on her effigy was a *molded* mask and she had not heeded him. Perhaps she'd best speak with Ned again about all he knew of how actors fashioned such a mask.

"But of course, it's much easier to make a death mask," Oldcorn was saying. "Plaster is smoothed on the corpse's oiled face, then, when that hardens and is removed, a second batch is poured into that oiled mold to get the features true before it's painted. But I've heard that, on the continent, the future of such modeling lies not in plaster, but in a return to the old way of wax, which has the flesh color poured directly into the molten mixture instead of painted on."

She was hardly listening now as she stared at, then touched, the copies of her grandparents' dead faces. They felt hard, whereas the poxed face on her effigy had seemed slightly malleable. Mayhap it had not quite set yet. And this false flesh seemed not so real and luminous as on her figure.

"Do the plasters harden and paints fade over time?" she asked.

"I've only tended them for several years, but I believe so. 'Tis said the coloring is mixed from the same pigments and flax seed that oil painters use on wood or canvas."

She watched Oldcorn rewrap the form of her grandmother Elizabeth, for whom she had been named. Suddenly, the entire room closed in on her. The stone ceiling holding up the Abbey floor seemed a huge, cold plaster mask stopping her breath. She hastened to the door, taking one of the torches.

"I need the name of the man who did the plaster and paint of this one," she informed him, pointing to but not looking at her sister's effigy, which seemed to guard her escape up the stairs. "And of its wig-maker," she added, turning back.

"The wig-maker I can tell you," Oldcorn said, annoying her by coming over to brush at Mary's gown again, "but the man who did this face of your royal sister—"

"Half sister."

"—half sister, Your Majesty, fled to the continent, they say, when you ascended the throne. Whether he's come back, I know not, nor his name because I've asked around before, just for the record, of course. I heard he was trained abroad as a doctor or some sort of surgeon."

Elizabeth's knees went weak again. She prayed Cecil would find something she could use to tie Caius, Pascal, or their continent-visiting ilk to that effigy back at Whitehall.

"But the wig-maker lives out in Chelsea still," Oldcorn went on, "a former prioress, who used to procure her supply of hair from novices and nuns. She may not be yet alive, for I hear she was aged when she did Queen Mary's wig, and that, of course, is nigh on four years ago."

"I shall have someone look into it."

"Forgive my curiosity, Your Majesty," his words floated to her as she started up the stairs, "but surely you are not personally planning your own funeral effigy, and you so young and healthy?"

She stopped and turned back to him. "Inquire again most circumspectly as to who molded and painted the former queen's face and send word to me if you learn aught," she ordered, clipping out each word. Then, desperate to escape this catacomb chamber, she nearly ran up the stairs.

≈   ≈   ≈

CECIL'S MAN BANGED THE ORNATE BRASS KNOCKER ON the front door of the Royal College of Physicians, then stood back as he'd been ordered. Cecil straightened his shoulders and spread his legs to a wider stance. When the door was swept open by Dr. John Caius himself, Cecil didn't budge nor speak.

"My Lord Secretary," the doctor said, sounding not one whit riled, which, in turn, riled Cecil even more, "what an unexpected visit, though, of course, not an unwelcome one. No doubt you've come to explain more fully about some effigy discovered in the queen's coach that we've been able to glean from rampant rumors and street gossip."

"Do you always answer your own front door, doctor?" Cecil countered, rather than answering. He swept past the man with his two secretaries in tow. Two other men stayed with the horses in the street as the fog thickened and daylight fled. At least Cecil saw that lamps were lit in the front room.

"I happened to be in the council chamber and glanced out to see you," Caius countered, following him in. "How fares our dear queen after that unfortunate incident in the street as she took her leave yesterday, and what might we do for you—or her?"

Cecil turned into the council chamber Caius had indicated

and sat at the head of the long table. He brazenly gestured to his men to take chairs on either side of him. It was then he noted Dr. Peter Pascal in the dim corner of the room, where he'd been either trying to hide his great bulk or had been squinting sideways out the window to watch the street.

"Pascal," Cecil intoned, "I haven't seen you for years and would hardly recognize you with that shiny pate."

"Lost so much hair, I shave it now."

"Ever thought of wearing a wig?" If Pascal thought he was making light conversation, Cecil thought, so much the better.

"I used to, but it's not worth the bother—and I am not a vain man."

"Have a seat, won't you, while Dr. Caius sends someone for the college account books. No good purpose served by lurking in corners."

"It wasn't that," Pascal declared defiantly. "I misplaced something dear to me. It's simply vanished."

"So that the remnants of my patience does not follow suit, sit here," Cecil said, pointing across the table.

"But—the college account books?" Caius parroted, making Cecil turn to study him again.

"Aye, man. 'Tis by the queen's goodwill you have your charter and your power and by my goodwill you aren't all marched to prison to be questioned for what you know about what she found in her coach outside your door."

Pascal grabbed the tall, carved back of a chair, while Caius blanched at that frontal assault. Over the years Cecil had learned that might did not make right, but it could produce fright and that made even wily and wicked men blurt out the truth. He had nothing against these two—yet—but that they'd dared to treat their queen shabbily and had both means and motive to try to scare her with that damned, poxed dummy. He worked hard to keep Elizabeth Tudor on an even keel and didn't need her being distracted or distressed.

"Outrageous," Pascal sputtered. "We only do our duty against disease and death. As Sir Thomas More put it," he went on, hooking his thumbs in his broad belt, " 'We never ought to look on death as a thing far off.' We, Lord Cecil, the queen's loyal physicians, should not fall under any sort of suspicion for merely trying to help Her Gracious Majesty and her people."

"Very grand, doctor, but fetch the books. Geoffrey," he told the clerk on his left, "take down Dr. Pascal's comments. After all, that effigy in the queen's coach seemed a harbinger of 'looking on death as a thing not far off,' not far off indeed from this very council room and college."

"Now, see here," Pascal insisted loudly enough to drown out the noisy scratching of Geoffrey's quill, "I oft quote my beloved mentor, Thomas More, so I meant naught. But what has that to do with our books?"

"Let's just say," Cecil said, picking his words as carefully as he chose his quills, ink, paper, and sandpot from the satchel his other secretary offered, "that when one wants to know what people are plotting, one looks at their books or the refuse they throw out, and I prefer books to refuse. John," he said, addressing his younger assistant, "please accompany Dr. Caius as he calls for all the college's latest accounting records, say going back one year."

"We are plotting naught but our God-given—even queen-given—duties to cure and heal. And we would be happy to come to the palace and speak with Her Majesty about anything she wants to know," Pascal insisted, all the while looking as if he'd swallowed some vile elixir.

"I fear we may have upset her," Caius put in, "with our request for corpses for study to improve our—"

"Some sort of inquiry on that may come later," Cecil interrupted. "And to quote Sir Thomas More's well-known words when he was climbing the steps of the scaffold, 'Help me up with your hand. As for my coming down, let me shift for myself.' We all must shift for ourselves, doctors, and I am always shifting to be certain the queen comes to no harm. Questions about that effigy will come apace, but for now, your books of purchases and payments quickly," he said, calmly folding his hands over his papers on their table.

He saw the two men shoot each other helpless glances before Pascal sat and Caius hastened to obey.

～ ～ ～

E H, NICK, I TOLD YOU TO KEEP STIRRING THAT WHILE it boiled! It'll stick to the bottom if you're not careful. Laws, I'd better do it, even if I can't stand the smell."

Listening to Bett scold her husband, Meg smiled as she cut different shapes of thin linen for the skin of the grace plasters. Nick Cotter had vowed he'd stir the medicinal plaster of betony, verbena, and pimpernel leaves mixed with wax and sheep's suet, but his wife, Bett, was a stickler for things done right. That, Meg thought, and Bett's sharp nose, were two things the woman had in common with the queen.

Meg envied Bett that the big, muscular Nick willingly did as his petite wife bid him, turning the wooden spoon over to her care. Ben would have probably smacked his own wife with it for ordering him around like that, but Nick, big bruiser that he was, seemed always amenable. Besides, he and Bett were still far gone in love and that cut Meg to the quick.

She sent Nick out on two deliveries, which Ben could have done since they were both down by the river, but she didn't want to even ask him to lift a finger. It didn't take much for him to lift a fist against her anytime she irked him, the sot.

"All right," Meg told Bett, as she laid out the first linen piece on the counter and smoothed it open, "put a spoonful of that here, and I'll show you how to spread and roll them. Then when the customer steams them, the grace plaster is moist again to cure anything from the ague to chest cough."

Bett Cotter, nee Sharpe, was of slender but sturdy frame, with flyaway blond hair and pale eyes. Whenever her temper flared, like at Nick just now, the jagged, puckered scar on her chin reddened, and the bigger scar on her thumb where she'd had her "T" brand for thief burned off by a surgeon several years ago was always hurting her. Bett indeed might just be the first recipient of Dr. Clerewell's Venus Moon mixture.

Bett laid a good dollop of the thick medicinal plaster on the linen, and Meg adroitly spread it over and through, however much mess it made on the counter. "You've got to work quick with this or it hardens fast," she explained, "and then you have to heat it again."

"Mm," Bett said, as she hung over Meg's shoulder, then jumped back to stirring. "Gil signaled something about wanting to learn to paint on plaster, but it couldn't have been this mushy kind. He was a bit secretive about making some gift for Her Grace."

At that scrap of knowledge, Meg forced herself to roll up the linen carefully, then spread out another. She tried not to cross-question Bett overmuch about the queen because she didn't want her to suspect how sad—and furious—she was about being dismissed.

"Her Grace hasn't been sick or out of sorts, has she?" she asked, keeping her voice calm. "Here, you do this next one, but get that pot off the flame first."

As Bett plopped another glob of plaster between Meg's caked hands, a shadow filled the doorway. Meg jerked so hard when she saw who it was that she ruffled the linen into sharp folds. Why in heaven's name did she always have to look out of sorts the rare times Ned Topside came calling? At least Ben wasn't here, but who knew when he'd be back?

"Good day to you, Master Topside," Bett sang out as she took the mixture off the small cauldron fire and plunged her hands in the mess Meg had made.

Meg tried to scrape off what she could and plunged her hands into the bucket of water, hoping to wash off the rest. Working with plasters always dried her hands. She thought longingly of Dr. Clerewell's soft skin, but then Ned never so much as took her hand.

"Ned, how are you—and everyone?" she inquired, hoping that sounded nonchalant as she rolled her sleeves back down in place.

"I'd like to talk with you privily," he said only and didn't smile.

"I guess I don't mind," she replied, hoping he wouldn't note her bad case of trembling. She dried her hands on her apron and walked as slowly as she could to the door. Damn the rogue. She'd never yet seen a man with such a fine turn of leg, ruggedly handsome face, and clever mouth to boot, and he knew it.

"Gracious, it's gone foggy out," Meg said, peering past him into the street. Weather was always a safe topic.

"Take a little walk with me, then, to cool off."

"Cool off?" she challenged.

"You were working hard in there, weren't you? I thought I saw steam coming from the counter."

She breathed a bit easier. Always fond of wordplay, he could easily have meant that she was angry with the queen or him, or that he made her go hot as a brass kettle when he looked assessingly at her like that. "I could use a bit of air," she said, grateful to get away from the shop in case Ben came back. Bett knew not to squeal about her being with Ned.

They strolled down the Strand toward the palace, past Ned's horse a hired neighbor boy was holding. "How is she then?" Meg blurted, unable to hold back.

"Her Grace?" the jolthead asked, knowing full well that's who she meant. "Better now that Kat's cured, but busy as you know, going hither and yon to keep folks' spirits up and keep a sharp eye on things. But then you know that too, especially with your knowledge of her trips by barge or horse, maybe coach too."

"Meaning what?" she asked as they walked around a puddle of refuse someone had just heaved out of an upper window. Instinctively, they moved closer to the shops and houses, beneath the overhang of second and third stories.

"Meaning Jenks and I see you now and then as you are seeing her."

Tears burned her eyes, but she blinked them back. "Everyone likes to see her. Oh, Ned, I wish things hadn't exploded so bad between Her Grace and me. I'd risk all to have her take me back."

"Would you now?" he said as he studied her askance.

They stopped before a group of children playing a game with pig knucklebones, then turned around and started back toward the shop. "But taking her clothes like that, Meg," he protested, "then impersonating her with—"

"What do you think you trained me to do and she asked of me more than once?" she demanded so loudly he glanced both ways and tugged her back into a narrow alley.

"You'd never do such a thing again, would you?" he demanded, "I mean, borrow one of her gowns and such?"

Her stomach flip-flopped. Could this mean he'd been sent to ask her to return?

"I may be some knock-headed girl she took in and you taught to read and write proper, but do you think I'm demented?"

"Fine, fine," was all the usually loquacious actor would say.

Her hopes of a palace reprieve shattered. "I've got to go," she said, however much she cherished each moment with him. Each time he turned tail to return to the world and woman she cared so for, it nearly killed her. "No good to be seen in alleys with the likes of you," she added, hoping that sounded lighthearted.

"It's a good place to observe others from, though, isn't it?" he countered as he glanced up and down their narrow hiding place, his voice dark with unspoken accusations again.

She stared him down. "Spit it out, Edward Thompson, alias Ned Topside, queen's fool and favorite player. I'm no fool, so don't play your clever games with me."

"I have it on good authority you were in an alley on Knightrider Street yesterday morn, covertly watching Her Majesty."

Caught, she thought, but she spit out, "On whose good authority? Jenks's?"

"Meant to stay hidden, did you?"

"I was part of the crowd there and crowds don't covertly watch Her Majesty. They do it loudly and publicly. Yes, I was out in the area doing deliveries because Nick Cotter took sick, and you can ask him about that. And I don't need you playing inquisitor any more than I need Ben Wilton doing it!"

She turned on her heel, but he seized her arm and spun her back hard against his chest. She pressed both hands flat to him until he let her go. They stared deep and long into each other's eyes while her stomach turned another flip-flop or two.

"Yes," she said, her voice nearly breaking, "I watch her when

I can. I love to watch her, be near her. Like you, like all of us, I *love her*."

He but nodded when she was expecting a bitter scolding or long speech. "It's just that someone in that crowd put something in her coach that shouldn't have been there," he said, his voice more kindly now. "Were you present when she screamed?"

"Screamed? Elizabeth Tudor screamed? No. What caused it?"

"Suffice it to say it was something stuffed with your—and her—favorite sweet-smelling herbs," he told her, and she saw he was again watching her face for any reaction. But if the man was too much of a lackbrain to know how she adored him, she wasn't worried he'd uncover her passion for him or much else.

"Then that's all?" she asked, hand on hips. "If you're going to blame me, you're barking up the wrong tree, royal lapdog."

"By the way," he said, "Lord Robin's not even that anymore, so she's taken a turn from all men. The queen uses Mary Sidney as a sort of escort, a chaperone when Lord Robin's around, and it irks him to no end, however much he doesn't let on. And, by-the-by, speaking of herb stuffings, I was in a discussion the other day as to whether saffron is good or bad for one's health—headaches and all," he inquired in an obvious change of topics.

She studied his shifting expressions with a keen eye. "Saffron is good for many cures," she told him, relieved to be on solid ground again. "It seems to help in diseases like measles and yellow jaundice, not that a mere herb girl grown to an apothecary is allowed to prescribe a thing these days with the vulture doctors hovering over our shoulders. But, as in life, too much of a good thing can be bad, even fatal. If you take more than ten grains of saffron at once, it can hurt your heart. . . . "

She stopped talking. His allure was so great she almost tilted into him. "Ned," she blurted, before she lost the courage to say it, "I'm asking you not to come to the shop again. Not because you came with questions today, but because of Ben. He's real jealous, not just of you but of—"

"Of Nick Cotter too?" he asked, frowning, one hand gripping his sword hilt so hard his knuckles turned white.

"Well, no, not since he thinks Nick's so thickheaded, but . . ."

"Which brings up Jenks."

"Ah, Jenks—just a little."

"Surely he's not disturbed by Gil's dropping by. Or do you mean he's jealous of customers?"

"Ned, leave off. A pox on it!"

He seized her arms hard, pressing her back against the wood-and-plaster wall. His sword hilt hurt her hipbone, his leather jerkin flattened her breasts. For one wild moment, she thought he meant to kiss her.

"Don't say that—a pox on it," he ordered, giving her a little shake. "And, yes, I'll stay away unless I need to come back with more questions or even accusations about your trying to get even with Her Grace for sending you away in disgrace."

She was so appalled that she burst into loud sobs. To her amazement, he pulled her into his arms, rocking her slightly. "I'm sorry, Meg—Sarah. I didn't mean it like it sounded," he murmured, his mouth in her hair against her flushed forehead. "I know you long to come back to serve her, and if I had a way to achieve it for you, I would."

"Truly?" she asked with a sniff and wiped her nose on her sleeve as he set her back. He fished out of his jerkin a linen handkerchief, fine as any courtier's. She took it and blotted her nose, then tucked it down in the folds of her gown, hoping he'd forget it. In case he heeded her plea and never came back again, she'd have something to remember him by beyond her crazed dreams at night and daydreams by morning light.

"I've got to get back," she said. "Fare-thee-well, Ned Topside.

And if you see me staring from the crowd someday, don't you go thinking the worse of me."

"I won't," he promised. "I understand. But Meg," he added as she started away, "would you mind then if I take a lock of your hair to—just to remember old times?"

She almost cried again. Ned did care. He wanted a keepsake, a token of their friendship. Afraid to trust her voice again, she nodded and stood still while, from her pinned tresses under her kerchief, he adeptly loosed a curl and cut it cleanly with his penknife. His early days of playing women's parts and years since working with lads to paint and primp and dress them like ladies for the stage made him smooth as silk with things like that.

She grasped his fingers as he took the tress, and brushed a kiss on his hand before she rushed from the alley. At the door of the shop, she nearly ran right into her husband coming up from the river.

꙰   ꙰   ꙰

I HAVE A SURPRISE FOR YOU, YOUR GRACE," MARY SIDNEY said with a gleam in her bright blue eyes as she sat next to the queen on the oriel window seat. Her other ladies were grouped about the presence chamber playing primero, giggling, or fussing with their lapdogs or parrots, for the queen had sent the men away early after supper. "You've been overly distracted with all this worry, and I want to cheer you," Mary insisted with a pretty pout.

Elizabeth forced a smile. Who could not respond to Mary's graceful and generous gestures? "What sort of a surprise, dearest Mary? Lately surprises are not as amusing as they used to be. But I thank you for your help," she added, leaning closer to her friend, "in trying to trace the red hair. I intend to discover if that old woman is still making wigs."

Glancing askance at the other ladies, Mary whispered, "But since you had already heard of her from another source, how did I help?"

"I did not know she was still working with wigs, or exactly where she lived, so I have you to thank for that. Nor did I know her name was Honoria Wyngate before you told me so."

"And I have you, my queen, to thank for being my beloved friend—mine, my lord's, and, of course, Robin's," Mary said as she produced a small, velvet box from up her sleeve. "See, this is only the first part of the surprise."

"And is this gift from you or from Robin too?" the queen inquired cautiously, as she took the box.

"From my lord and me, though Robin's seen it and approved."

"Very prettily said, worthy of Cecil's political answers," the queen remarked as she lifted a finely tooled, gold and gem-encrusted pin from the box. "Ah, a mermaid! How exquisite!"

"I knew it suited you, for like you, a mermaid is beautiful and luring and yet men know her not," Mary said. "But you must come outside to the fountain in your privy garden now and see the rest of the surprise we have planned."

"Mary, I thank you, but I've called Cecil, Lord Hunsdon, and a few others to a privy meeting—a discussion of policy."

"But this will only take a moment, Your Grace," she wheedled. No wonder, Elizabeth thought, Sir Henry Sidney had wed Mary and made her Countess of Pembroke and lady of the great estate and house of Penshurst. Henry had declared Mary the most beautiful woman in the kingdom, after his queen, of course.

"All right then," Elizabeth said, pinning the mermaid on her bodice and rising. She waited until everyone stood so she wouldn't have to pick her way through the puddles of skirts to the door. "The Lady Mary Sidney says a surprise awaits us in the privy garden," she announced to the others.

Knowing smiles, rolled eyes, and titters told Elizabeth that they were all in on it. Probably, she thought, some little play or masque about mermaids, or a new madrigal for all to sing around the fountain. If they thought she would abide another water battle like they had staged a few weeks ago where everyone ended up laughing and drenched, they were much mistaken. If so, they had misread her mood. She wanted no part of frivolity this night, for she was dying to know what her Privy Plot Council had uncovered.

When she saw her male courtiers awaiting them in the gallery, she realized they too were in on the covert charade. They trooped down the grand staircase and outside together into the large, walled garden with its grassy lanes, fruit trees, and thirty-four high, painted columns topped by gilded, mythical royal beasts and flapping pennants.

Ned Topside appeared and, as she emerged into the evening air now greatly cleared of fog, began to recite a poem about Venus emerging from the sea. *But e'en Venus is ne'er so fair as our fair queen,* went the chorus as everyone joined in. Passing the sundial they approached the central, triple-tiered fountain.

Reading their minds, she refused to go closer. After all it was she who had oft secretly signaled her gardener to turn up the force of the water to douse courtiers and even Cecil when it pleased her. Did they think she would fall for her own trick, especially when they were deeming her a mermaid this night?

But two half-walking, half-swimming human mermaids emerged from the crowd, both Mary's servants, if Elizabeth recalled aright. Lightly draped in gauze and most comely, they made graceful, undulating motions with their bare arms, but they had trouble walking, encased in satin fish tails from their waists down.

As the mermaids broke into song, everyone began to laugh and clap while Ned recited the same words loudly so everyone could hear. The water did indeed spout stronger, though not full force, to play airborne rivulets above their heads. Six other Dudley and Sidney servants emerged with torches to light the scene as others flapped long bolts of blue, green, and white fabric to mimic the waves of the sea. Entranced, Elizabeth came closer as the mermaids sat upon the slick lip of the fountain, still singing.

The crowd edged closer. Evidently on some sort of cue, the mermaids lifted their tails into the fountain and stood there as if they would sink into the depths. Torches held aloft on either side of her, the queen stepped forward to thank her dear Mary for this double gift. To her surprise, Mary's husband, Sir Henry, took one of the royal hands and Robin quickly seized her other.

"I knew you had a part in this," Elizabeth mouthed to Robin. "But if you think to throw me in with them, you had best think again."

"I live only to adore and protect you," he whispered.

His smile was so ravishing she almost slipped on the damp paving stones where the mermaids had sloshed water out. Mayhap, she thought, she'd been wrong to hold Robin off so, to punish him so long for the scandal they'd barely survived when his wife had died so mysteriously. She knew he longed for her to rely on him as she had once, turn back to him and—

"Hell's gates!" Robin shouted, looking down into the torch-lit, roiled waters of the fountain between the two mock mermaids. He loosed Elizabeth's hand and threw out his arm before her as if to keep her back. "Mary, was there a third one?" he demanded, pointing between the mermaids. "What's this?"

Surely this, too, was part of the fantastical surprise, Elizabeth thought. She leaned over Robin's restraining arm to gaze down through the shifting surface at a naked woman drifting, faceup,

eyes and mouth wide in the halo of her gold-red hair, as if swimming, floating forever free.

For the second time in three days, Robin stood at her side in
a crowd to pull her back when she found what appeared to be a
corpse.

Chapter
THE SIXTH

Violets admonish and stir up a man to that which is comely and honest . . . for it would be an unseemly and filthy thing, for him that doth look upon and handle fair and beautiful things, to have his mind not fair, but filthy and deformed.

JOHN GERARD
The Herball

T HIS TIME THERE WAS NO WAY ELIZABETH COULD keep everyone from seeing the prone female form. Pushing forward, then jumping back in horror or awe, ladies shrieked and men cursed. The queen did not scream as she had when she saw the effigy, but she struggled not to show the fear that racked her.

"Guards," she cried, not trusting Robin with this, "to me!"

Six big yeomen, halberds in hand, came clattering through the cluster of courtiers. "Send everyone inside except the Sidneys and Lord Dudley but keep the torches here. We need more light."

As the guards hastened to obey and the two mock mermaids

were assisted from the water, Elizabeth forced herself to gaze down upon the body again.

A complete stranger. A slender, young blonde, so pale and— dear God in heaven—with tiny, round pox marks on that face, each limb, and over all of her body.

Elizabeth shoved past the hovering Mary, Henry, and Robin and was sick upon the grass with her back to the fountain. As she wiped her mouth with her handkerchief, Mary came to her aid, but the queen shook her off. Her friend had led her to this with everything so planned. Could she trust even Mary Sidney now?

"Your Grace," Mary said, her voice choked with emotion, "I swear by all I hold dear I had naught to do with this. My Lord Henry and Robin—none of us did."

"They will have to answer for themselves," Elizabeth insisted. "Another poxed body—this one real."

"But this one is not tricked out to look like you," Mary protested. "What if someone heard about the other, then with cruel intent and forethought aped the first perpetrator's filthy work?"

Elizabeth rounded on her. "In other words, these two bizarre events were not masterminded by the same villain? No, Mary. Too few saw the other, and this one mimics the effigy, which mimicked me. That dead woman is of an age with me and fair of face—or was!"

"Your Grace," Robin said, sidling closer and taking Elizabeth's arm, "you must not let this shake you."

"A woman's poxed corpse appears in my fountain in my walled, privy garden you three lure me to as if on cue, and I should not let it shake me?"

"But, my queen," Robin went on, "the entire court knew of this—of our plans for a little masque to cheer you. It is naught we alone planned or knew of."

"And you, my lord," she told him, pulling her arm free of his grasp, "just happened to be at my side when I found that dreadful image of myself in the coach, did you not?"

"I long to ever be at your side, my queen! I beg you, never suspect nor punish me for that."

"Your Grace," Mary said, her tear-streaked face slick in torchlight, "my Lord Henry and I—Robin too—wish you only well."

"We shall sift this out later," Elizabeth declared. "I warrant this act is the doing of a deformed mind, and I want from the three of you by sunset Monday a complete listing of everyone—courtiers, servants, seamstresses, gardeners, musicians, whomever—who knew of my coming to this fountain this evening. If the three of you had naught to do with this, you will find who did. Now leave me!"

"Here with that—that drowned soul?" Mary cried. "I'll not desert you."

"Go!"

Mary fled in sobs with her lord hard on her heels, while Robin dared to linger. "Go from me," the queen repeated, almost afraid she would break down and throw herself into his arms. She suddenly longed for someone else to shoulder her burdens, to take on this threat to her composure, health, and life.

Finally, Robin obeyed even as Elizabeth turned to her guards, grateful to see one had fetched a sheet to wrap the poor wretch in.

"Put the sheet in the water to fetch her out wrapped so none will directly touch her pox sores nor gaze upon her nakedness in the open air," Elizabeth ordered them. As they did so, she stood back in the shadows, her gaze skimming the palace windows and seeing there silhouettes of her curious courtiers. Surely none of them could be behind the appearances of the effigy and the body, these implied deadly threats to her person. Not those with whom she mingled freely, daily. Not those she trusted, who needed her even more than she needed them.

She turned to gaze at the dark line of fruit trees standing before the outer brick wall. That was the only side of the garden not enclosed by buildings. If someone had invaded her palace grounds from that direction, could that someone still be watching? Racked by an icy shudder, she wrapped her arms around herself as if to buffer the chill night wind.

"Clifford," she summoned the guard closest to her, "go inside and find Stephen Jenks, Ned Topside, and Gil Sharpe and send them to me forthwith."

He hastened to obey as four guards lifted the ghostly, shrouded form. It dripped water as they shuffled toward the palace. Like a hired mourner in a funeral cortege, Elizabeth walked behind them, followed by other guards with torches.

%. %. %.

G LAD YOU HAD US STAY TO SUPPER," NICK COTTER told Meg and gave a hearty belch. "Good chine of beef."

"Bett shopped for the food and prepared it so I could finish the grace plasters before the mix went hard, so no reason you shouldn't enjoy it with me," Meg assured him.

She rose wearily from the table in the largest room above the shop. "Besides, Ben's long overdue and has probably settled into some tavern for the night with his old bridge shooter companions." She'd sent him on a very special errand, one he'd readily agreed upon for once. And she knew he'd taken enough coin to get over his distasteful task afterward.

She touched Bett's shoulder as she rose from the table, and Bett patted her hand in return. Bett saw Meg's predicament with Ben and, Meg knew, felt deeply for her. The thing was, did Bett know how deep the pain cut of losing her former life at the palace? Did she sense to what lengths Meg was willing to go to get that life back? Though Nick and Bett worked for her, they were sent out now and again to gather information for Her Majesty. That was a good one, Meg thought, perversely amused: Meg Milligrew and Bess Tudor sharing servants.

"Bett, could I talk to you downstairs before you head home?" Meg asked, stacking their pewter plates to take with her. As long as she was going down, she'd clean them out proper in the shop wash water instead of just wiping them with a crust of bread up here.

While Nick leaned back in Ben's chair, putting his feet up on the bench the women had shared, Bett lit a fat tallow candle and lighted Meg's way downstairs.

"You can talk in front of Nick," Bett said, sounding a bit annoyed. "I mean about Dr. Clerewell's mention he'd consider a cure for Gil's muteness."

"I know," Meg assured her. "Though Nick is not truly Gil's sire, he loves him like he was."

Meg sighed silently. She did not want a baby with Ben Wilton, yet she sometimes longed for one to love. Though Gil was hardly a child anymore, Meg had come to care greatly for him. Too bad, she thought for the hundredth time, that apothecaries were legally banned from prescribing cures. But now she had hopes for Gil, thanks to Dr. Clerewell's suggesting he could help.

"What is it you want to say then?" Bett asked, interrupting Meg's agonizing. "Or has Ben been at you bad again?"

Meg shook her head as she dropped the plates in the wash water and lit a second candle. "I have something special for you here, just so you can tell me how you think it does."

Handing Bett her candle too, Meg motioned her over to the

cabinet of deep drawers that lined the wall behind the counter. In the one where she usually kept dried spring flowers, she had hidden the precious box of Venus Moon Emollient.

"How something smells, you mean?" Bett asked. "If it's medicine for me, I'm healthy as a horse."

But when Meg produced the alabaster box, Bett was all eyes and ears. "Even looks pretty," she said solemnly. "What is it then?"

"A skin cream that covers and treats scars at the same time. And you're not to tell anyone where you got it, because it is both rare and—well, being investigated for its effect right now, so you mustn't try it if you're afraid. But I've seen someone who used it with fine results."

Peering as suspiciously into the box as if it were Pandora's, Bett frowned, then shrugged. "If you say so," she said with a sniff at the substance.

"And you won't tell a living soul about this, not even Gil, because he chatters so," Meg insisted.

"Chatters, that's a good one. My mute boy chatters," Bett said, and they exchanged smiles.

While Bett held both candles, Meg put a bit of the thick cream on her index finger and smoothed it over the jagged mark on Bett's chin, caused by a gunpowder explosion years ago, the same accident that had thrown Gil into a wall and made him mute. The substance felt both smooth yet slightly grainy to her touch, but it went on well. It was even closer to Bett's pale skin hue than it had been to Marcus Clerewell's complexion.

"There!" Meg pronounced as if she'd done an entire portrait fine as those Gil produced. "Don't wash your face till I get a good look at you in the morning, and if anyone but your family asks, don't trust them. Just say it's evidently starting to fade after all these years, praise God."

"Praise God for a friend like you," Bett said with tears in her eyes as she stared into the small square of polished bronze mirror that Meg held before her face. "Laws, I just knew I'd be scarred forever, but I didn't figure on this."

⁂

KEEPING HER DISTANCE FROM THE BODY, ELIZABETH paced back and forth in the large anteroom down the hall from her state apartments, where she had ordered the corpse laid out on a table. It was all too eerily reminiscent of what she'd been through with the effigy, and she was certainly not taking this into her privy chambers. No matter that the best medical knowledge declared that pox was spread either by the wrath of God or by foul air from a living, infected person. She was taking no chances touching or getting overly close to this victim, so she needed others to observe it.

It—she—lay covered to her armpits with the soaked sheet in this well-lighted room. She almost looked asleep as water dripped on the parquet floor, which the queen had ordered covered with a second sheet.

"I just don't want my court doctors privy to our investigation," Her Majesty rambled on to Ned and Jenks, while Gil sketched the dead woman's face from his perch on a windowsill. "They might let something slip to their illustrious colleagues over on Knightrider Street. So I'm forced to have you, Ned, fetch that irascible German Doctor Burcote who tended Kat. Well, hie yourself after him now!" she shouted, smacking her hands on her skirts. "And where is Cecil? He should have reported to me an hour ago for our scheduled secret meeting. And Kat? Lord Hunsdon?"

Ned seemed only too glad to escape. The queen kept pacing, not touching anything. If this woman had died from drowning and not the pox, her disease could recently have been in its virulent stage. The small, round sores had not yet turned to pockmarks, and the winding sheet looked speckled with tiny drops of blood, so the onset of pox—and death itself—must be recent.

Besides, she knew bodies went stiff after several hours and this one was still pliant, unless floating in the water had done that to it.

"I also need to find out how whoever left her got in my privy garden!" Elizabeth went on to the nervous Jenks. "If he or she can breech that, what else is safe?"

"He or she?" Jenks asked. "You mean mayhap this girl wandered in when she was sick with delirium fever, took her clothes off, died, and just toppled in?"

"Don't be simple! Of course that's not what I mean!"

"You want me to check the grounds now?" he said, all too eagerly edging toward the door.

"By dawn's first light. Oh, Kat," she cried when the hall guard opened the door to admit her, "where have you been?"

"Fell asleep and lost track of time and all else I hear went on." Elizabeth could see the truth of that, for Kat's coif had gone flat on one side and the underpinnings of her farthingale had slid awry to make her skirts look lopsided. Elizabeth suddenly cursed herself for letting Harry Carey go home to Blackfriars, but he said he'd felt nauseous. 'S bones, so did she! She hurt all over and had a good notion to send for him to come right back, ill or not.

As Jenks slipped out, Kat shuffled a bit closer to the body. "Lord have mercy, no!" she cried, pressing her fists to her mouth. Gil's charcoal stick stopped whispering on the paper.

"You know her then?" Elizabeth asked. "It isn't that lace girl Lucinda, is it? But poxed?"

"Never saw this slip of a thing before, but ugh, I see what someone's done to her."

"Drowned or dumped the poor poxed thing in my fountain!"

"No, that's not what's all over her," Kat explained, walking boldly closer to the corpse. "Someone's overbled her, that's what happened here."

"You see lancet scars somewhere?" Elizabeth demanded, holding her ground ten feet away. "You mean she's been stabbed too?"

Shaking her head, Kat came over to Elizabeth and put her arm around her slender shoulders to draw her slightly closer to the corpse. The queen could feel Kat trembling too.

"This woman may look poxed, lovey," Kat said, "but I think some mountebank or quacksalver passing for a physician has bled her near dry with a legion of leeches all over her skin. Don't you recall that time my leech bites wouldn't heal for days? Next to the pox itself, not much you and I hate more than leeches."

⁓   ⁓   ⁓

J A, LADY ASHLEY IS RIGHT," DR. BURCOTE PRONOUNCED after viewing the corpse two hours later. "Not the pox but far too many leeches." He shook his head and stroked his chin. "Any *dumkopf* should have known it vould kill a female of this size."

Elizabeth stared at the little man through the haze of her exhaustion and horror. "But if it was leeches, they were placed so regularly on her—all over," she stammered, "instead of at some specific site to drain bad blood for a particular malady. Was it intentional—to overbleed her, and she was too ill or weak, or perhaps given some sleeping potion so she didn't resist?"

"I'd say she did resist, or at least her leecher feared she vould," he muttered, "even vit that broken arm."

"Broken arm?"

He pointed to her right arm, swollen and at a slightly strange angle, then at both wrists. Elizabeth could see what he meant. "I don't hold vit tying patients down," he went on, "especially ones vit a bone that should have been set, *ja.*"

"Tied down, with a broken arm," Elizabeth marveled at his deductions. Shuddering, she squinted at the slightly rough, red marks around each wrist and at the crooked elbow-to-wrist bone. She saw now that the skin was discolored each place he pointed. Also the body bore a walnut-sized strawberry birthmark at the base of the throat.

"As to the wrists, mayhap she had bracelets or sleeves that were too tight," Elizabeth suggested. "It is simply that I cannot bear to think the worst, but I must learn to. Can you tell if she was gagged to keep her from crying out during all this?" she asked as an afterthought.

He shrugged, frowned, but looked closer at the mouth and cheeks, even her earlobes. "Not vit a gag that vas tied around her head with her mouth open or closed. But she could have had something stuffed in her mouth, then pulled out—after."

Elizabeth was trying to discern if this girl must have been tortured and killed in a place where there was privacy from witnesses overhearing, but that seemed a dead end. All her ideas were too much of that lately, but she wasn't giving up.

"Doctor, do you think she was deceased before being brought to the palace, or could she have somehow been brought or escorted in, then drowned? It was dark a good half hour before my retinue went outside."

"Her face seems calm as if there was no final, fitful death throes—at least ven the leeches began to do their slow, steady vork. Yet she is newly dead, for rigor mortis is only setting in now. Bled to death first vit leeches applied in the pattern of the small pox, *ja.*"

Elizabeth seized a tall chair back to steady herself. Some desperate or demented mind was behind all this. And to exactly what horrid purpose had this corpse been delivered, almost ceremoniously, to the Queen of England?

"Besides," he said, lifting the sheet from the body and peering under it, "the girl was unclothed ven the leeches vere applied, and I don't think garbed after that."

"But certainly not carted through my palace or over the garden walls stark naked!"

"Ask the one who wrapped her up ver he found this sheet," he said. "The blood specks on it seem to match her vounds, so I vould say it came vit her. After her being dead and in the vater, the leech sores vould not dot the sheet like this."

"Yes," she whispered. "The guard I questioned before you came said he saw the sheet on the ground and did not fetch it from the palace as I had first thought. So—she was brought in wrapped in that sheet. That's how," she said almost to herself, "I pictured the other being delivered too."

"Vat other?" he asked, looking sharply up at her.

"No—nothing. If you would discover if there are any other telltale or identifying marks on her besides that birthmark, I will leave you to your task. We will hold her body for a few days to see if it is claimed, then see she is properly buried. My Lord Cecil is instructing my courtiers only to say that some half-witted girl wandered in and drowned herself here—not the rest of it."

"As you vish, Majesty," he said and turned away as if he were dismissing her. As she put her hand to the door latch, he said, "In the morning, have someone take a good look at the fountain vater to see how much she bled in it. Some leech vounds ooze for hours after."

"I know," she said. "Years ago, a country doctor leeched Kat for a migraine, and it was—terrible. I vowed then, only quick cuts from lancets, not this ugly, lingering . . ."

She thought she would be sick again and stayed her hand on the door, partly to hold herself up. "Tell no one anything I've said or asked," she ordered. "And if I have need, I shall send for you again."

※   ※   ※

ACCOMPANIED BY TWO GUARDS WITH LANTERNS, Elizabeth returned to her state apartments and through them to her privy chamber. With her yeomen opening doors for her as she went deeper into her secure world, she tried to tell herself she was safe here, but she felt the barriers had been breeched.

"Post double guards to seal the back river entrance," she ordered Clifford. But as he hastened to obey, she realized she should have waited for that command until her covert Privy Plot Council left this night, if they were still waiting for her after all this time. They would just have to go out the front entrance and damn what people said. They would chatter that she had sent for her longtime guard Jenks because she was afraid, that she had summoned her fool Ned Topside to cheer her. They would whisper that, because she was besotted with her own beauty, she kept the boy Gil up all hours to draw her. Gossip was going to gallop everywhere about this night.

Instead of going directly into her presence chamber, she had the sudden urge to see the plaster-faced effigy again. Would the pattern of pox marks on it indeed resemble the leech bites on the corpse? After all, though the dead woman's face did not look like her own, the corpse's size and coloring were much the same. Mayhap someone was trying to drive her to a doctor. What profit to make her fear for her own health, when she did so already?

The queen had ordered the effigy stored in her library because so few entered there, and guards stood at both corridors giving access to it. Two doors, the one from her rooms and one from this blind corridor, opened into it. Yet when she peeked in though the latter, Ned Topside stood there, bent over the effigy with a knife in his hand as if he would stab it.

"Ned!" she gasped out. "Sheath that knife this instant in my palace and my presence!"

He spun, all too obviously shocked to see her. "Oh, Your Grace, you gave me a start." Quickly, he stowed the knife. "I was simply—ah, going to take a small snippet of the effigy's wig for when we visit that Chelsea wig-maker Cecil, Kat, and I were just discussing. You know, Honoria Wyngate." Nodding in the direction of her chambers, he rushed on, "I could compare this to any hair swatches she has. I assume that's how she would have things set up there, as that's the way actors who make wigs do it."

"First of all," she said, stepping in to see he had a red tress in his hand already tied with a black ribbon, "have you dared to begin that council meeting without me? And I thought you said you were *going* to take a tress."

"Oh, of course we haven't begun the meeting without you, Your Grace. We were simply sharing information, that's all," he explained as he smoothly dropped the tress in his pouch.

"But only Mary Sidney and I knew so far about the Chelsea wig-maker, especially her name," she pressed him.

"Mary must have told Kat, and she told us," he admitted.

"I have been meaning to ask where such skilled artificers as you actors obtain the wigs, paint, and occasional plaster masks that are your stock-in-trade."

"When I was with my father and my uncle's traveling troupe, we made them ourselves," he blurted out, shrugging as if her question meant naught. He seemed overly casual about it all now. Still, she trusted Ned. He had no motive in the world for upsetting or threatening her. She'd plucked him from a life of rural obscurity and set him high—something, she recalled, in a far grander way she'd done for Robin Dudley. She must not become a victim of this horror by fearing to trust those closest to her.

"You know, Your Grace," Ned said, his voice much quieter, almost beseeching now, "I think there may be a link to the doctor at the Royal College who Lord Cecil says keeps quoting Sir Thomas More."

"Cecil's been speaking to you of that already too?" she demanded, sweeping through the second door, which led directly to her privy chambers. Ned followed in quick pursuit. "You have been thrashing it all out about wig-makers and doctors without me?"

"But, Your Grace," he said, "it all fits like pieces of a puzzle. Dr. Peter Pascal lives in Sir Thomas More's old home in Chelsea, and, according to Kat, that's nearby where the royal wig-maker lived under your father's and sister's reigns!"

"That proves naught by itself. Sir Thomas More's old home is also near a house where I lived once with my stepmother, Queen Katherine Parr!"

Her blurting that out gave Elizabeth pause. That was the house where she'd seen her first pox victims up close. Chelsea was a place with painful memories she had no desire to visit again, but neither did she want to send someone who could foul up a meeting with this almost mythical wig-maker.

Things seemed to be spinning out of her control, and she would not have that. She turned back to face Ned in the narrow passageway. "It's not only Dr. Pascal who bears watching. Dr. Caius was Queen Mary's doctor and wanted to be mine until I sent him packing. But, whatever any of you have discussed, *I* realize that a little sojourn to Chelsea is called for, and *I* would speak to this old woman of the wigs myself."

The others of her Privy Plot Council must have heard that tirade, for they were all standing like silent sentinels at their chairs around the table in her presence chamber when she entered.

"Is the meeting over, all things decided, and you are ready to disperse?" she inquired of them, her voice dripping sarcasm.

"Not at all, Your Grace," Cecil dared. "I, for one, have much to tell. Not only does it appear that the physicians of your Royal College are not to be trusted, but I've discovered through their accounts that said doctors have definite ties to two of your most pressing problems and that they wish the best to the third."

"The doctors, of course," she put in, "are Caius and Pascal."

"Indeed. But as we briefly touched upon before, Your Majesty, then decided to set aside until there was more solid proof, there are three women possibly involved, all kin to you, ladies of lofty rank."

"You mean of royal rank and my most dangerous rivals. Curse those three greedy, Catholic furies. I hate to admit it, but they are powerful and vicious enough to be plotting against me, never mind that one is in Scotland and the other two in prison—one in the Tower itself!"

Chapter
THE SEVENTH

Build not your faith upon tradition. 'Tis as rotten as a
rotten post.

NICHOLAS CULPEPER
The English Physician

T HESE EVENTS HAVE TOSSED ME TOPSY-TURVY,
Cecil," the queen admitted. "I thought my next trip
must be to Chelsea, but this is of a sudden more important. And I swore once that I would never be rowed to the Tower
again, but here I am, of dire necessity," she groused, shaking her
head. "Still, I am not going to enter through that damned water
gate!"

Knowing full well that that entry was traditionally called
Traitor's Gate, Cecil shifted on the bench next to her. Through
early morning mist, they had set out from Whitehall in a plain
working barge, though six of her regular men-at-oars and four
guards were aboard in civilian garb. The queen and her principal secretary sat under a three-sided, roofed canvas canopy, partly
to seek shelter from the wind and partly so that others on the
bank or in river craft would not recognize them.

"I quite understand, Your Grace," Cecil assured her. "Those were not good days for any of us when your sister sent you there."

"At least I lived through it. My mother was taken in that way and never came out. My stepmother, Catherine Howard, the same. And poor Lady Jane Grey . . . Well, I need not rehearse all that to you."

Blinking back tears, she leaned out of their shelter to stare at cattle grazing on the south bank of the Thames. The choppy water seemed to mirror the cloudy sky and thrashing trees. Memories almost capsized her calm.

But now, she thought, here she was, under the guise of taking to her bed with a migraine for a second day. After church yesterday, claiming illness—indeed, she was greatly disturbed—she had passed the day consulting only with Cecil and her Privy Plot Council. She'd slipped away from her duties this Monday morning for a few hours to interrogate Katherine Grey, Lady Jane Grey's younger sister. Because the Grey girls stood in close proximity to the throne, they had always been thorns in her royal sister's side and now hers too.

Indeed, she even fretted over Robin's loyalty to her. After all, he was the son of the man who had tried to place the Greys—and through them, Robin's brother, who had wed Lady Jane—upon the throne. Or did Robin merely hope to make her realize her femininity or mortality, to admit she needed an heir, and to agree at last to wed him and bear his child to inherit the throne someday? He had been chafing under her strict handling of him lately, but would he stoop to actual plots involving effigies and corpses? He still had that squire who used to dress his dummy at the quintain to look like Queen Catherine de' Medici, so mayhap Jenks should sound out that clever servant.

"No, it cannot be, not Robin," she muttered, her fist pressed to her lips.

"What's that, Your Grace?" Cecil asked, trying to peer around her. "Which way will you go into the Tower then?"

She sat back and looked straight ahead again. "We shall both alight at the public stairs at the foot of Thames Street and walk in the gate of the Middle Tower," she told him. "You shall handle the Earl of Lennox as we discussed, and I shall cross-question my cousin, who has already betrayed me more than once ere this. And we shall both keep calm at our distasteful tasks to make them give themselves—and their ties to Pascal and Caius— away."

"I fear affairs of the heart mix dreadfully with affairs of state, Your Grace." They both held on to their seats as a wave from another craft rocked them. "I believe Katherine Grey eloping with Edward Seymour against your express wishes and bearing him a son has more to do with passion than politics."

"That lying, insolent chit knew full well a woman with her royal blood must wed an approved man from a trusted family, Cecil. I would never have approved of the Earl of Hertford, not a man from another brood of serpents in our bosom, not a Seymour!"

"Precisely why she acted so rashly, Your Grace."

"You sound like a lawyer defending her at the bar. But, Cecil, she kept the marriage a secret for months until her breeding belly betrayed her, and all the while her Catholic leanings and rebellious character entice both Scottish and Spanish traitors to rally round her deceit and treachery! I will not have it!"

"What I cannot abide is the tilt the stories take on as your people bandy gossip about," he groused, throwing out an arm that seemed to encompass all of London. "Hell's gates, the rabble gets taken in by the romance of sad stories and lost loves, never mind the hard, cold facts of the necessity of securing this realm!"

"Bett and Nick have told me of public sympathy for the Hertfords, for everyone else seems afraid to let me know. Katherine and Edward so young, so in love," she repeated what she'd been told, "pining away in prison, separated by the cruel queen. 'S blood and bones, those two have made their own bed and now they must lie—well, I meant not to say it that way," she amended, looking off into the distance again.

Cecil, for once, kept his mouth shut. Even he dared not expound on the fact that Lady Jane Grey had borne a healthy male heir with the Grey strain of Tudor blood in his veins while the queen was a virgin and unwed. That's why, though Katherine's husband was prisoner in the Tower too, the queen had ordered them kept apart. She needed no more plotting between members of powerful families and no more new male heirs that were not hers.

"But we shall do our best today," she told Cecil, "to focus on the visits they have had from Drs. Caius and Pascal, supposedly to treat their ailments, in the Tower. What you found in the doctors' accounting book points the finger, yet we must close the fist of accusation around them—all of them—in this plot."

Cecil's report to the Privy Plot Council late last night had been enough to seal the doctors' fates with the queen, at least for severe questioning. Yet she bided her time for having them arrested, because they could not have personally deposited the effigy in her coach and perhaps not the corpse in the fountain either. She must cast her net wide and catch whoever worked for them—or for whom they worked. The queen knew she had misjudged those she had trusted before, so she might misjudge those whom she did not trust.

Yet Cecil's fine barrister's brain had turned up three clues that they could use. First and most negligible, both doctors had recently purchased herbs from a Cheapside apothecary that could be used to cure pox, so they were interested in the deadly disease, which the effigy's markings had mimicked.

"But I would expect my doctors to buy such herbs," Elizabeth had pronounced last night in her chambers. "I've pressed them to be prepared to treat both personal disease and public pestilence."

"Secondly," Cecil had told them all, "Pascal's run up a big bill for Papist votive candles, outrageous numbers of them."

"I have made it clear to my people they may worship as their consciences dictate as long as they are loyal to their Protestant queen," Elizabeth had countered. "But you say huge numbers of them?"

"Mayhap," Ned had put in, "he's supplying all the Catholics of London and you can lock him up on graft or embezzlement of Royal Physicians College funds or some such. That would at least take *him* out of commission."

"We knew both physicians were staunch Papists," Elizabeth had said, not heeding Ned's idea. "Say on, my Lord Cecil."

"I saw a scribbled note in the margin of their account book," Cecil explained, "that candles would be burned in the Tower in honor of *both* St. Thomases."

"Both St. Thomases!" Jenks had cried. "I thought there's only one."

"Pascal nearly worships his former mentor," Elizabeth said, ignoring Jenks's outburst. She was so exhausted she only wanted this to be over. "He has probably made some sort of memorial to him. But why in the Tower?"

"Mayhap because that's where Thomas More was imprisoned before he went to his death, Your Grace," Kat had muttered.

"That is possible," Elizabeth said, pleased her dear friend seemed to be following everyone's conversation. "Aught else?"

she had asked Cecil and held her breath when she glimpsed the expectant look on his usually inscrutable face. Cecil was a genius at keeping the best—or worst—till last.

"And thirdly, both doctors have been paid for their services to two prisoners in the Tower of London, unnamed patients. But their sexes, ages, and maladies were noted with the fees, quite handsome ones, compared to similar service to others with the same afflictions."

"Which are?" Elizabeth demanded as everyone held their breath and leaned forward.

"The man, aged forty-six, has the common gout. The woman, married with one son, is aged twenty-two and being treated for a malady which is too blurred to read. But I warrant the word was either *unknown* or *untold*."

"The exact ages," Elizabeth had reasoned aloud, "of the troublous Scottish Earl of Lennox, husband to my greedy cousin Margaret Douglas, whom I have under house arrest at Sheen. That she-wolf wants my throne either for herself or her son, Lord Darnley."

"Exactly, Your Grace," Cecil seemed to egg her on. "Even if it means sharing the throne—and strengthening their claim to it through Darnley's marriage to another of your dangerous cousins, Mary, Queen of Scots."

"The three furies who would take my throne," Elizabeth muttered. "Mary, Queen of Scots. Margaret Douglas, Countess of Lennox. And—"

"And," Kat had interrupted, "that snide little snippet Katherine Grey, who was ever treacherous down to her toenails."

❧   ❧   ❧

"D R. CLEREWELL, I'VE BEEN WAITING TO TELL YOU," Meg said, then lowered her voice as he came closer to her work counter, "that I've had some success with your special project."

"The Venus Moon?" he asked with a smile. "And you've kept it quiet?"

"I've sworn the two patients, or should I say subjects, to utmost secrecy. I did use it on Bett Sharpe as you suggested. So far it's worked wonders to cover her scar, but I don't know if it's changed it."

"Time, Mistress Sarah," he intoned almost solemnly, tapping his knuckles lightly on the counter. "Time and repeated treatments will tell."

"The other patient is a customer, a man who was kicked by a horse, even as I once was. I always sympathized with him, though the accident merely left a scar on his cheek while mine took away my senses."

"Then why is it, Mistress Sarah, I believe you have more sense than most apothecaries I have met since I've been in London?" As he smiled broadly from the depths of his hat, she felt herself blush. It wasn't that he was really trifling with her, she told herself, but his praises were sweet to her ears.

"I'm waiting for you to say the rest of that," she told him coyly. "You know, that most apothecaries have no sense to begin with, so more than nothing isn't much."

"Ah, you've been taking to heart the strictures and criticisms of the physicians of the Royal College," he said, shaking his finger as a tutor would. "Indeed, those learned men believe I have no sense either, mistress, not so much for my petitioning to sell Venus Moon Emollient but for my espousal of the infectious water droplet theory of pestilence. No doubt they have laughed me to scorn behind my back more than once."

"But belief in the four warring humors and the heavenly constellations' power over human health has been the custom since the Greeks," she protested, proud to be able to demonstrate her knowledge. "Infectious water droplets flying through the air—well, unless someone throws sweat or sneezes, it's just not fact or tradition."

"Damn tradition. Progress is what's needed, as with my Venus Moon, eh?"

"I can't argue with that, doctor. Oh, that reminds me, I was thinking about the possibility of your curing young Gil Sharpe's muteness, like you said."

"Ah, were you? Do you think the queen would allow it, perhaps let me treat him at the palace? Or if not, he could be brought to my shop in Cheapside."

"Would you use valley lily distilled in wine? That's the herbal lore I recall is good for the dumb palsy. Her Majesty used to employ my herbal cures, especially when we lived in exile, before she was queen. She was afraid both of physicians and being poisoned then, but she trusted me. I've longed to try to cure Gil, but I know apothecaries are not to prescribe or treat whatever ails—"

"Mistress Wilton," he interrupted, "amateurs—doctors' cooks, as they call you—could get things wrong and do harm. To wit, it is rosemary, not valley lily, which restores speech to those possessed of the dumb palsy. I warrant your simple herbal cure would turn out to be just that—simple."

Surprised that, for the first time, Marcus Clerewell sounded exactly like one of the other doctors, and had switched his tone so fast, Meg didn't argue. She wasn't sure why, but she had the strongest memory that her parents had used valley lilies more than once, back in the days when apothecaries held some sway.

"I'm sorry, but I can't act as intermediary to the queen about Gil's being healed," Meg answered the question she'd pointedly ignored before. "Gil's parents must decide, and then ask Her

Grace if need be, as they—they run the occasional errand for her."

"Do they? Then let's arrange it," he went on, smiling at her again, evidently when he saw how crestfallen she looked. "Have the boy's father bring him, for Nick knows my shop from his occasional deliveries. And let's not tell the queen in case it doesn't work, for who knows if the boy's damage is permanent or curable."

"And charge at least most of the reckoning to me without telling his parents. Will you?"

"If the child is so important to the queen, perhaps she herself will pay, if I effect a cure, eh? At any rate, it will be a great honor to treat one of Her Majesty's household servants, even as it has been an honor to know you, a former one," he said and took her hand.

"You don't mean you're not coming back?"

"Of course I don't mean that," he whispered, lifting the sack of supplies she'd packed for him but not loosing her hand. "I—"

"Not much traffic in the shop today, eh, Meg?" Ben's voice blared on the staircase behind them. He must have just come downstairs; he wasn't there a moment ago. Meg yanked her hand free.

"But," Ben went on, "I heard someone with a deep voice lingering, talking low, and here it's Dr. Clerewell. Bet you got a great deal to do today, busy man like you and all."

"Ben . . ." Meg began in warning as the telltale vein in her husband's forehead began to throb.

"I do at that," Marcus Clerewell said, depositing a stack of coins on the counter, touching his hat brim with a flourish, and backing away from them as the best-schooled courtier might from the queen herself. "Master Wilton, mistress," he said at the door and was gone.

But as Meg rounded on Ben, she almost thought she saw her husband give a brisk wave to the departing doctor. Knowing Ben, it was some sort of obscene gesture.

"Ben, why on earth would you insult our best—"

"*Mistress,* that's a good one," Ben interrupted as he came behind the counter and swept up the stack of coins.

"Meaning what?" she dared.

"Meaning there's more than one meaning to that."

Meg just turned back to her mortar and pestle, but Ben grabbed her arm and spun her around so hard that the pestle thudded to the floor. "Leave me be," she ordered. "You come in late last night and just flop in bed and expect me to welcome you with open arms—"

He hooted a sharp laugh. "Open arms wasn't what I was looking for, *Mistress* Sarah. But I see now I'd better be here day and night like some kind a watchdog. I used to think that fancy foreign doctor—"

"Marcus Clerewell is from Norwich. He's not foreign—"

"—was here buying our goods just because I'd told him you used to serve the queen and he liked the palace connection. I thought he was hoping you'd put in a good word for him with Her Majesty or some such. But now I'm thinking there's some other reason. Maybe I been wrong you're pining for that slippery player Topside. Maybe you're set on Dr. Scarface, eh? Not wed, is he?"

"Don't be ridiculous. And if you want to know, we were discussing Gil's muteness, because he used to talk before that gunpowder blast sent him flying into a wall. It's got to just be his throat that's the problem, because it's not his ears or head."

"Oh, just whispering with him about poor Gil, huh, having him hold your hand for poor Gil, who's sitting pretty in the queen's lap where you ought to be."

"Just leave off."

"Now I know why Her Mighty Highness really tossed you out. 'Cause she can't trust you behind her back, that it? It all went to your head, still does. I can see you're always trying to look down on your own God-given husband, the way you're wishing you could just shuck your wifely duties and play virgin just the way her great and glorious majesty does."

When he fixed his hand in her hair to tip her head back and pressed her hips hard against the counter, she almost brained him with the marble mortar. But there was only one thing worse than this, and that would be going to prison and then being burned alive for her husband's murder. So Meg let him drag her up the stairs and bit her lower lip until the bitter blood in her mouth nearly gagged her.

⁂

T HE WALLS OF THE TOWER OF LONDON LOOMED HIGH and gray as if rising from the river. Clots of morning fog still hung the air.

"Put in before you reach the water gate," Elizabeth ordered her men-at-oars, though she'd told them the same earlier. "The public steps will do."

The barge bumped the busy wharf. Pulling her plain gray velvet hood over her head, she let Cecil help her out. With her guards scrambling to surround them, they quickly made their way to the street entrance called the Middle Tower, then over the moat to the Byward Tower. Elizabeth had not been here since her recognition parade had gone through the city the day before her coronation. And she had hoped never to be here again.

Cecil banged on the narrow wooden door, though the big portcullis gate next to it was kept up for daily deliveries. "Ho, there!" he called. "On queen's business to see the Lieutenant of the Tower."

The door opened immediately, and the guard bid them

enter. A chill shot through Elizabeth as she walked up the slanted cobbled walk, at least, thank God, surrounded by her own guards and not her sister's this time. Passing beneath the stone skirts of the Bell Tower, where she had been housed in those nightmare days, she glanced up at the ramparts where she used to walk to take the air. It always seemed she was short of breath in here. As they entered the grassy stretch within the walls and series of surrounding towers, her gaze jumped to the Wakefield Tower, where her mother had been tried and condemned. And then, the other direction to the now bare spot where her scaffold had stood. Gripping her hands against her belly as if to quell its roiling, the queen turned away.

Someone must have run for Sir Edward Warner, Lord Lieutenant of the Tower, for he emerged from the lieutenant's house and hurried toward them, strapping on his ceremonial sword. The man was near sixty and spare of body though his face and jowls were flaccid and his turkey neck bounced as he ran. He had enjoyed this sinecure of royal trust and remuneration for years. When he saw it was her in person, he went down on the dank cobbles on one knee and swept off his cap.

"I had no idea, Your Majesty. You should have sent me word."

"I did not want to send word, Sir Edward. I am simply here to ask you some questions and then to visit my cousin Lady Grey."

"Oh, of course, and my Lord Cecil here too," he said, looking even more green at the gills.

"I would speak with the Earl of Lennox while you escort Her Grace," Cecil clipped out. He went his way with but one guard, while the other three trailed behind the queen and her host toward the Bell Tower.

"I suppose because you are no stranger here," Sir Edward said, his voice and gestures both jerky, "that is why you have assigned your cousin and her family to this very tower."

As they entered the squat stone edifice, Elizabeth suddenly fell as mute as Gil. On the first coil of the stairs, she stopped to gaze out a slitted window as if she cared for the gray-on-gray view. She shut her eyes to steady herself. The belly-clenching dampness from the river, the distant clank of keys still rattled her. The city bells were distant here, but the piercing shriek of a raven or the clatter of delivery carts in the courtyard could echo in one's soul. The stones seemed a heavy burden, like the weight of water pressing down to drown her. . . .

Her eyes flew open. "Before I see my cousin, I meant to ask which cell was Sir Thomas More's," she said.

"Sir Thomas More's, from in your f-father's day?" he stammered.

"Obviously. Take me there straightaway."

She followed him up one level. He took overlong fumbling with his keys until she nearly seized them from him to open the door herself. "No one within, but so carefully locked?" she inquired.

"Just tradition, for safety's sake," Sir Edward muttered and, reluctantly it seemed, swung wide the door. She stepped into a long, narrow, vaulted room with its shutters closed. Yet the chamber was bathed in the soft light of banks of flickering votive candles surrounding a makeshift altar on which sat a crucifix and a framed painting of a man she did not recognize but knew full well.

"Sir Thomas himself," she observed.

"I believe so, Your Majesty."

"Since you were here in his day, I warrant you *know* so, sir. Who has placed this here? Catholics you allow to meet secretly in my royal Tower?"

"In truth, 'twas Dr. Peter Pascal, one of your physicians of the College, who admired the man and has recently arranged this as a personal remembrance—for himself, privily."

"And for a fee? To you?"

He cleared his throat, and his jowls quivered. "I did not think Your Majesty would mind a man's remembering someone who was imprisoned here and died so sadly."

She glared at him, then slowly approached the portrait and examined it more closely. A bit crude yet quite detailed, a pen-and-ink drawing. She could not recall More herself, though she'd once seen a Holbein portrait of him and his family. This drawing bore no signature. She reached across the rows of candle flames and plucked it from its perch, then turned it over. Nothing on the back of the stretched canvas.

She handed it to Sir Edward by smacking it into him. "Pascal set this up during his visits to tend my cousin Katherine?" she asked as she made for the door. Her lieutenant had to run to keep up, thudding on the stairs behind her, the portrait under his arm until he set it down in the corridor.

"Ah, yes, though another doctor sometime comes instead to—"

"To treat not only my cousin but my other cousin's husband, the Earl of Lennox," she finished for him. "And that physician is Dr. John Caius."

For one moment he gaped at her like a beached fish. "Yes, that's right, Your M-Majesty. But surely there is no harm in either of them, as they are among the elite of your College of Phys—"

"Is this the very chamber?" she asked as she stopped at the too-familiar door, one she herself was once certain she would exit on her way to the scaffold.

"Of the Lady Katherine, Countess of Hertford, and her son, the Viscount Beauchamp? It is. I put them here because this chamber is the best—"

"No chamber in this godforsaken place is best. This was

mine, and I know it like the back of my hand. Now let me in and do not announce me."

But she had forgotten how voices carried through the peepholes. As the wooden door swung inward, Katherine Grey stood facing them with her young son held tightly in her arms. Imperious as a queen, she glared down her nose as if she were the visitor and Elizabeth Tudor the prisoner again.

Chapter
THE EIGHTH

*The distilled water of the flowers of rosemary being
drunk at morning and evening first and last, taketh
away the stench of the mouth and breath, and restoreth
speech to them with the dumb palsy.*

         JOHN GERARD
         The Herball

EVER SINCE HE'D NEGOTIATED A TREATY WITH
England's northern neighbor two years ago, William
Cecil had hated the wily, stiff-necked Scots. And
Matthew Stewart, Earl of Lennox, husband to Elizabeth's cousin
Margaret Douglas, was one of the worst of that dyed-in-the-wool
ilk. Lennox was forty-six years old, but looked ten years younger,
as if that raw climate to the north somehow preserved the
wretches.

"*Och,* if it isna the queen's own secretary come calling in the
flesh," the strapping, sandy-haired earl greeted Cecil when he entered his Tower cell without the ado of announcement.

Amazing, Cecil thought, how this blackguard could make a
greeting sound like a drubbing. And he detested their guttural

Scots burr, as if they had caught in their throat those prickly this-
tles they so venerated as their prideful symbol. Lennox no doubt
only rose from behind the small table where he'd been writing
because he was tall enough to look down his nose at Cecil. As if
this chill cell suited him, the earl wore only an open-necked laced
shirt, hose, and breeks of crosshatched muted hues that Highland
rebels always favored.

"I was in the vicinity," Cecil said with a small shrug, "and
thought I'd bring you a bit of news."

"Naught amiss wi' my lad?" the man blurted. "He isna ill?"

"Not that I've been informed. Nor your wife, since, of course,
you have a care for her health too."

"My countess is of braw constitution, so I dinna inquire after
her."

"Even in here, I've no doubt that someone slips you word of
how she's faring, as you two have always been skilled at covert
communications." Cecil let his eyes dart to the letter the man had
been writing, then looked briefly ceilingward.

"*Och,* mon, you should not listen to vile rumors. Her
Gracious Majesty must surely ken we dinna wish her but goodwill and a long reign," Lennox insisted, gesturing that Cecil
might take the only chair in the spartanly furnished cell. When
Cecil didn't budge, he added, "And Her Grace kens full well
how forces swirling aboot one close to the throne can be mistaken
to be rebels by the monarch's counselors."

That little rejoinder, Cecil thought, was less a slap at him
than an allusion to Elizabeth's stay in the Tower for supposedly
encouraging a Protestant plot. Though the earl and his countess
had lately professed Protestantism, more than once, the
Lennoxes had been put under close watch for plotting with
Catholics against her. But the queen had a long memory: Cecil
knew she would never forget that Margaret Douglas Stewart,

Countess of Lennox, had once tried to garner proof to send her to and keep her in this place.

"Must I lecture you on the vast differences between you and Her Grace, Lennox?" Cecil countered. "Her Majesty was proved innocent of malicious, slanderous accusations, whereas the bedrock facts against you and your countess . . ." Cecil rolled his eyes yet again. "But I came to inquire for your health, my lord. How goes the treatment for gout in the second joint of your left big toe?"

Only for a moment did surprise almost betray the man. Cecil could see him thinking: If the crown knows that small detail, what else do they know? But the earl soon vexed him again by laboriously explaining how badly his toe pained him and made him walk shoeless with a halting limp he demonstrated ad nauseam back and forth in the small cell.

But then, Matthew Stewart had never been a simpleton, however much his wife actually seemed to overshadow him when they were together. Even if he had not wed Margaret Douglas, Henry VIII's niece through the former king's sister, Lennox had his own convoluted family claims to the throne of Scotland. However, it was now held by Mary, Queen of Scots, Margaret's second cousin, to whom the Lennoxes were obsessively if covertly loyal.

And the Stewarts were canny enough, as the Scots themselves would put it, to know that, since it would mean a bloody war to claim the throne themselves, a marriage between their son, Henry, Lord Darnley, and the young widow Mary must now be their righteous cause. They'd even sent the boy, aged seventeen, to France to court Mary when she was newly widowed there, before the English managed to fetch him home and put him under house arrest with his mother at Sheen while the earl languished here—or limped here.

"Enough of this damned demonstration," Cecil insisted, though he had a good nerve to let the man keep walking since it did seem to pain him. "Is this particular malady of yours being treated fully?"

"Didna your sources pry that from Dr. Caius too?" he parried, sinking in his chair.

"What is he treating you with?" Cecil asked, ignoring the man's latest jab. "I've a touch of that too."

" 'Comfrey for gout and for all inward griefs and hurts,' " he recited. "The mon's a canny healer and much misused these days, it seems."

"Dr. John Caius counsels you about how to alleviate your inward griefs and hurts, does he?"

Cecil sensed that remark hit home. Lennox's left eyelid began to twitch; he rubbed it quickly, as if it would betray more than he already had. Cecil had every intention of questioning Lennox about hiring and inspiring Dr. Caius in some plot to terrify or unhinge the queen with effigies and corpses. But that interrogation would come later when the trap was better baited and sprung—and the queen had the Stewart family in her clutches at court.

" 'Twas just a wee bit of some medical book the doctor quoted, Lord Cecil. *Och,* I ken too he said hemlock was a surer cure for the gout, but dangerous if taken inwardly. He said he'd ne'er get past the guards wi' it, being poison and all if ingested. And he's a stickler for doing things by the book, and you can tell Her Gracious Majesty such. Meanwhile, you just take a care you dinna get any hemlock in your craw if a doctor lays paste of hemlock leaves on your gout, master secretary."

The man dared to smile, like a beast ready to spring, baring its fangs. Despite the palace guard outside the door, Cecil shuddered. And this was the man, with his she-wolf and handsome, spoiled whelp in tow, whom the queen thought should be brought back to court to keep an eye on them the better?

"Hemlock's out at court too," Cecil said, "so you'll have to stick to your comfrey cure, Lennox. And I wager you'll have to change to one of the queen's court doctors."

"What? Why's that then? What about Dr. Caius?" the Scot demanded.

Cecil turned rudely away, though he'd told Elizabeth he would not betray her scheme. But he half turned back, watching the man out of the corner of his eye. "Her Majesty," Cecil clipped out, "in her wisdom and great generosity, is bringing your count-ess, son—and you—back to court, where you can all become one family again."

He almost choked on that line the queen had asked him to use, but his last comment had, at least, shocked Lennox to silence. Mayhap, after all, Her Grace did know how to handle the treach-erous feral pack with Tudor blood always baying for her own.

⁂   ⁂   ⁂

COME ON THEN, BOY," NICK TOLD GIL AND HUSTLED him along busy Cheapside, a main city thoroughfare lined with shops and clogged with traffic. The wide, paved street of which Londoners were so proud ran east and west, so the morn-ing sun both warmed and lighted it. The street was most famous for its huge open market, but it was also lined with sedate shops leading to one crowning block of houses and commercial estab-lishments known as Goldsmith's Row. The fourteen shops there stretched between Bread Street and the Cross, four stories high, all decorated with the goldsmith's ornate, gilded arms, for they were not only jewelers but bankers.

Though Gil had said he'd had a hearty breakfast at the palace, Nick thought the boy seemed a deep, empty pot waiting to be filled. Dragging back against Nick's rush, Gil looked more interested in the oyster stalls and the lures of street vendors hawking hot sheep's feet and pies than in this chance to have his muteness cured.

"Come on then!" Nick insisted, pushing him past food stalls and carts.

Gil rounded on him and signaled with flying hands and fingers, *I go to queen's doctors if I need talk.* Or at least Nick was pretty sure that's what the boy dared, when Meg had been so kind to arrange this and Dr. Clerewell was willing.

"Meg says this man has a good heart and wants to help," Nick explained as busy shoppers shouldered by them.

What if queen wants me draw, not talk, Gil signaled, slapping out his motions so fast Nick could hardly follow. *What if I talk she send me away for go behind her back?*

"Deuce it, boy!" Nick shouted, stopping at the door they wanted. "You should of told your mother all this, not me. We're going in here to see Dr. Clerewell, and that's that. 'Sides, Meg thinks your muteness will take lots of treatments. You won't be just jabb'ring away. So you can ask Her Majesty if need be. Now, hie yourself in there when he comes to the door."

Nervously, Nick knocked on it once, then again, louder. Huffing for breath, a plump, pink-faced woman opened it. Nick was surprised not to see Marcus Clerewell in this shop where he'd always met him at the door for deliveries. And he'd never seen this woman before, so he looked at the doctor's painted sign above the door to be sure he was in the right place. He was.

"Here to see Dr. Clerewell," Nick told her, keeping a firm hand on Gil's shoulder.

"Oh, the physician who tends the place when Dr. Pribble's out," she said in a singsong voice. "He's s'posed to be by this morning for a spell, but . . . Oh, *there* he is," she sang out as

Clerewell rushed toward them down the street with his satchel in his hands.

"You're late," she told him, "and you've missed Dr. Pribble." She opened the door for all of them. "Good, now I'll go back to tidying things upstairs. That's what I do for Dr. Pribble, just tend to the upstairs and never mind what goes on down here."

As she hurried back upstairs, Clerewell shooed them into the front room and seated them across a small table from the only chair with arms, which he took. This low-ceilinged, beamed chamber was sunny and furnished with table, chairs, and three corner cupboards, the one that was open full of stoneware jars and boxes.

Nick was glad to finally see the man take his hat off. His scars were covered but the bad side of his face still look bloated. And, 'course, that one drooping eyelid showed. But mostly, the mess Meg had described on his face was hidden, but for blotches of different-colored skin where the curing cream was. Bett and Meg had made Nick and Gil swear to keep all this secret, so Nick didn't even mention it now.

"Well, Nick, Gil," Clerewell said, producing packets and a flask from his satchel, "you've caught me at my game."

"What's 'at?" Nick asked.

Clerewell looked surprised. "The fact that, during deliveries and as today, I treat this physician's shop as mine. I've only come to London two years back and found it quite an expensive place to begin my practice, at least in a decent place."

"Sure 'nough, it is that—expensive," Nick agreed, and Gil stopped studying the face long enough to nod.

"I'd take it as a favor," Clerewell continued, "if you don't tell Mistress Wilton or Bett—and certainly not Her Majesty—that I watch another man's place and am allowed to see my patients here while he's out. My rooms are up Gutter Lane not far from here, but I am hoping for grand things—a home in the country someday, a shop along this fair expanse of Cheapside. Well . . ." he left off as if he was out of fancy words, "a man's got to start somewhere."

"Aye, he does," Nick said. "And how 'bout you start today working on Gil's throat? Some sort of potion, Meg says?"

"Meg?"

"You know, the name Sarah Wilton had when she worked for the queen. Meg Milligrew. She prefers it, but if you don't tell her I slipped it out, Gil'n me will keep your secret too."

"I do like a man who knows how to strike a fair bargain, Nick Cotter. Now, distilled rosemary tonic, no matter what any mere apothecary says, is best for what ails the young man here, of course, with a bit of powdered licorice for dry cough and hoarseness which may follow."

"Laws," Nick said, frowning. "Give him something to help, then something to help that?"

"In a manner of speaking," the doctor said testily and turned his eyes on the fidgeting Gil. "The queen's young artist, eh? Ah, Gil, if you could only talk, what tales you could tell."

Gil tapped Nick on the arm then signaled words Nick translated as, "The queen likes I don't tell tales."

"So this cure could be a grand surprise for her?" Clerewell asked the boy.

Gil shifted in his seat and nodded.

"A pleasant one, I'm sure, because no doubt Her Most Gracious Majesty only wants the best for you. And what a blessed gift from God to be able to draw. Some doctors are skilled at that, you know, drawing herbs or anatomy, the former so that apothecaries don't confuse similar leaves and such. I wish I could draw, but I don't have a drop of artistic talent in me—facts, just facts and new ideas, that's my stock in trade. Come over here by the window, Gil, and let me get some light to peer into that throat of yours."

Gil got up, looking, Nick thought, as if he'd been commanded to mount the gallows. "Oh, by the way, Nick," the doctor said as he turned Gil to face the window, "I'm hoping you'll take a note to Mistress Wilton for me. You see, I propose to treat Gil completely gratis."

"Gratis?"

"For free. I wager you will be able to run this errand for me privily since I hear you run errands for Her Majesty at times."

"Oh, Meg tell you that?" Nick asked. "It's kind of a secret."

"And I will keep that secret. I usually ask a patient to say 'ah,' but can you even say that, my boy? Ah—ah!"

Gil only made a hacking then a retching sound when the doctor stuck a flat wooden stick down his throat. He bit it clean through, spit it out, then signed to the doctor a string of foul names. If Her Majesty would have seen it, Nick thought, she might have laughed, but Bett would have washed out that poor mute mouth with tallow soap for sure.

꩜   ꩜   ꩜

ELIZABETH SLOWLY ENTERED KATHERINE GREY'S chamber. It was larger than most cells, indeed larger than she had remembered it. Though Katherine dropped her a half curtsy, for one moment they stared at each other in silence. Then from the ceiling, the small, shrieking demon dropped on the queen's head.

"Ugh!" she managed as she struggled to get it off. It yanked her hair; it chattered and shrieked.

"Oh, dear, oh no!" Katherine cried. Through a shifting web of hairy arms, feet, and tail, Elizabeth glimpsed her cousin hand her year-old son to her maid. "Marchie, bad boy! I had no idea he'd do that when he climbed up on that ceiling beam, Your Grace. Marchie, no, no!"

A pet monkey! It jerked her hood off, clung to her neck, crushed her ruff, and tore her hair free from her upswept coif. It screeched directly in her ear before her guards bounded into the room and pulled the thing off, even as Katherine tried to unwind its wiry limbs. The baby began to wail, and two little dogs emerged from somewhere to nip and yelp at the queen's feet.

"Consuela and Miguel, shush right now! Please don't hurt Marchie, please," Katherine cried to the guards as they took the monkey away and shoved the dogs out with booted feet. The lord lieutenant motioned the nurse to step out with the child. Tears in her eyes, Katherine wrung her hands. At least that look of defiance was gone, Elizabeth thought. It had said so clearly, *No matter your power over me, I have an heir and you do not.*

"I said the Lady Hertford could have furnishings," Elizabeth clipped out to her distraught lieutenant, "but I did not give permission for a wild menagerie!"

He opened his mouth, then obviously thought the better of whatever he could say. As he bowed his way out and the door closed to leave the two women alone, the queen shoved her hair back and stood staring at her cousin again. It had hardly been the auspicious beginning she had planned.

"Oh, Your Majesty, dear coz, I had no idea you would visit us, or I would have tied Marchie's collar to his chair," Katherine told her. "Marchie, short for marchpane sweets since he's so sweet and, with our dogs, are my little Edward's only delight."

"You mean Consuela and Miguel?" the queen inquired, trying to keep calm as she and Cecil had decided. "Quaint names."

"Ah—Spanish."

"I believe I noted that. A gift from someone Spanish, someone who must have visited here?"

"I am allowed no visitors, Your Majesty," Katherine retorted and glanced around the room as if a foreigner hid here even now. "I just thought the names were fanciful, that's all. Please do not have my pets—or my dear son, Edward—taken because I so long for companions here. You surely know how that is in this place."

"I do indeed. But I tell you, the queen who sits the throne now has been more generous in the furnishing of this chamber than the queen who sent me here." Elizabeth slowly walked the small circuit of the room she used to pace, noting the Turkish carpet on the floor, the velvet padded chair and footstool from the storage rooms at Blackfriars.

"And I do thank you," Katherine said, her voice low, "that my son resides with me and my Lord Hertford nearby."

"Though you have not cohabited with him."

"Oh, no, Your Grace," Katherine assured her, wrapping her cloak closer and walking to the single window with its leaded casement set slightly ajar as if she suddenly needed fresh air. "Forgive my question," Katherine blurted, "but why have you come in person when I know you cannot abide this place?"

"To inquire after your health, cousin."

"My health?" she asked, blanching. "You know?"

"Were you tended by Dr. Pascal or Dr. Caius?"

"You have spoken with them?"

Elizabeth nodded, studying the girl. In the short time she had been here, Katherine Grey had gone from defiance to distress and now absolute panic, though she sought to hide it.

"They both tended me, Your Grace, and both confirmed the—the diagnosis. I supposed, if pressed, your kindly lord lieutenant would tell you they both visited me."

"Kindly, is he? But let's not stray from the doctors. Did they come together or at separate times?"

Katherine had begun to tremble, though she held her cloak

closed in a vain attempt to hide any sign of it. The girl had always been of overindulged, volatile temperament, but she had a Tudor backbone of steel. Mayhap she was simply afraid for her gaoler, who had obviously summoned and admitted the doctors and risked allowing pets. Or now that she had a young son, mayhap Katherine feared for his sake.

"They are both approved men of your Royal College of Physicians and came when they could, and I was—in need," Katherine said. Her eyes did not meet Elizabeth's, and she was all too obviously picking her words warily. "And, of late, I have been sore in need. Please, Your Most Gracious Majesty," she cried, her voice rising, "punish me if you must, but do not harm my children!"

"But I have seen to it that your heir was christened and titled Viscount Beauchamp," Elizabeth began to argue before what the woman had said sank in. *"Children?"* she demanded.

Katherine nearly fell back against the wall. Again she shifted her cloak closer. And then the queen knew. Knew the so-called unknown or untold malady from which this deceitful wretch was suffering. Knew that the "kindly" Lord Lieutenant of the Tower had let more than dogs and a monkey into these rooms to amuse and comfort the pretty and beguiling Katherine Grey. After all, her husband's cell was in this very tower.

"It—cannot be!" the queen whispered, more to herself than to the cowering girl. "I came to inform you that you may come back to court—if you would promise to behave—and you have not behaved but have defied and betrayed me yet again!"

She leaped at the girl, ripping her hands and cloak wide. Katherine wore but meager petticoats in here. Her belly was barely showing, but it was more than what overeating or a disease like the dropsy would do to a twenty-two-year-old, one nearly as trim as the queen herself.

"You stupid, little fool!" Elizabeth shouted, pounding her fists on the windowsill instead of on Katherine. "You're with child again when that was what gave you away and caused all this before. Do you never learn or think? You're breeding another heir when one is sorely needed elsewhere! Now traitors will doubly flock to you."

Despite the royal raving, the girl looked so much a Tudor at that moment—for of her three Grey cousins, Katherine had always resembled her most closely—that Elizabeth almost pitied the chit. But had she not fathomed yet that Tudor blood in one's veins meant duty and denial, not giving into one's passions, and especially not with men?

Wanting to both cuff and cuddle the stupid girl, Elizabeth shoved her back into her seat and hovered over her, leaning slightly forward with her hands on the arms of the chair.

"I want answers from you, Katherine, and now. Since both the Papists Pascal and Caius have lived abroad, did they act as your go-betweens with foreign or Catholic contacts?"

"N-no, Your Grace, but who am I to read what was in their hearts?"

" 'S blood, forget hearts and think with your head! When Pascal and Caius were here, did they suggest that you cohabit with Edward Seymour? Did they urge it? Bribe the lieutenant to allow it?"

"No, of course not."

Elizabeth slapped her once across the cheek. "Look into my eyes when you answer my questions and recall that I am your queen. I am not your sweet coz anymore, not some fond, romantic soul you can convince with tears and sighs and meanderings. I am sick to death of public talk I should loose you and Lord Hertford because of the sad story of your love. And yet I came here to do just that, to bring you back to court."

"You did? Truly?"

"All the better to keep an eye on you, but now you've ruined even that."

"I insist you take us back. You must!"

"I intended for just you and your son to return. But Katherine," Elizabeth countered, her voice deadly cold, "we both know, for those who continually defy and endanger their queen, that the view outside this window used to include a scaffold for others of our blood and their husbands too, and orphaned heirs can be fostered out or even reared at court."

Katherine gulped audibly and slumped back in the chair. She gazed into the eyes of her queen as if facing a hovering hawk about to swoop for the kill.

"I—I believe that the doctors," Katherine whispered, "perhaps Dr. Pascal, spoke with the lord lieutenant about how distraught I was, Your Grace. The doctor said that my husband's company would be a far better tonic for me than any medicine ever would."

Tears like a fountain ran from the girl's cornflower blue eyes and dripped off her chin. But Elizabeth hardened her heart as she always had when it meant her survival, even when she most wanted to comfort. Her throne, her life, her realm could be at stake if there was a plot afoot.

"And," Katherine choked out, her words half smothered by her sobs, "it was Dr. Caius who suggested the molding be made of me for a statue, ere something happen to me in here, so my son—now two heirs—would have a remembrance of me . . . and . . . What? Why are you looking at me that way?" she cried, cowering even more. "I am telling you God's truth, so you have pity on me and my own."

"A molding made? Explain yourself. A—a plaster death ma—a life mask?"

"Yes, I guess so," the girl admitted, nodding wildly as she teetered on the edge of hysteria. "Dr. Caius had a friend of his visiting from somewhere in Italy do it. Someone who knew that clever Italian doctor who taught anatomy there—Dr. Caius's teacher—the one who stole the bodies to make death masks and take them apart."

"Take them apart? The masks or the bodies?"

"The bodies. To learn more about the human form to make better treatments and cures. I think he called it dissolution."

"Dissection," Elizabeth said. "But stealing bodies is only one step from killing them first."

"What?" the girl cried, looking totally appalled. "I swear by all that's true, he said nothing of killing anyone, only healing. And I thought a painted mask would be a sweet and charming thing, like at the masques with music at court, even like that one your fool Topside staged before I was sent here. And who would not want a fine sculpted bust made of themselves?"

" 'S blood," the queen clipped out, bracing herself on the carved arms of the chair. "Caius may," she whispered to herself, "have used that life mask for the effigy mask. You resemble me closely enough, but I knew there was something slightly off in the face."

"My face? Death mask? Please, Your Grace," she cried as the queen straightened and stepped away, "I swear I shall never defy you again, nor allow foreign elements to cling to any hopes that I might heed—"

"Foreign elements indeed—Papist ones! From Italy perhaps, such as Dr. Caius's visitor, or from Spain, someone who brought pet dogs as a little gift. Or that deceitful dog that is your husband!"

As Elizabeth started away, Katherine threw herself at her, going to her knees, then her stomach, but catching only her hems. "I beg you, Your Majesty, do not harm my husband or those I love! Though I bore a son and would bear another heir, do not blame me for being just a woman—"

The queen stepped back and pulled her skirts free, though Katherine's nails ripped her hem. "You, like me, cousin Katherine, can never afford to be *just* a woman. You are of royal blood but have not learned yet that the price of your willful desires and conniving must be paid. Do not fear I will take your life nor harm your husband or your children, though you and he must go separate ways, far away from London this time. You may keep the new babe with you, as the heir goes with your husband. And you will answer every question put to you by a cross-questioner who will be here on the morrow. So, stand up for your babe and for your Tudor blood, for we will never meet again."

Katherine's gasp and smothered sobs were the only sounds in the room as Elizabeth turned away and knocked once on the door. Her guards opened it immediately. She lifted her skirts to avoid tripping over the dragging hem. On the stairway down she saw Cecil coming up. Mayhap he had heard their raised voices, but they exchanged a glance that said it all: *Nothing goes as planned.* Her guards fell in behind her as she passed Sir Edward Warner, who bowed so low she could barely get past him on the stairs.

"For allowing dogs, monkeys, husbands, and spies through that door, you are now the retired Lord Lieutenant of the Tower of London," she informed him. "Be ever grateful you are not the newest tenant here. Be gone to your rural home by nightfall and never return."

"And Lady Hertford?" Cecil whispered as he followed her down the twist of staircase.

"She's fingered John Caius, Pascal too, to a lesser degree.

Send for them both to be brought to Whitehall—separately. As for the lady, I shall never see her again. Never."

She could tell by the sound of his steps that Cecil had stopped walking for a moment. Then she heard him hurrying to catch up as she left the Bell Tower and cut across the cobbled courtyard.

"And I shall never see this godforsaken place again," she shouted so loudly that her voice echoed off the cold stone walls.

THE NINTH

You must not think, courteous people, that I can spend
time to give you examples of all diseases. These are
enough to let you see so much light as you without art
are able to receive. If I should set you to look upon the
sun, I should dazzle your eyes and make you blind.

NICHOLAS CULPEPER
The English Physician

T HE SIDNEYS AND LORD ROBERT ARE HERE TO SPEAK
with you," Kat announced as she entered Elizabeth's
privy chamber late that afternoon.

"Send them in," the queen said and threw down her quill.

Cecil and three of his secretaries yet hovered over the table
strewn with bills, grants, warrants, and decrees, which she'd been
reading and signing. Though rattled from her visit to the Tower
earlier today, Elizabeth had sat through two meetings with am-
bassadors and one with Parliamentary advisers to accomplish the
nation's business this long afternoon.

But her mind was not on her labors. If she didn't diagnose
the strange symptoms of this effigy plot, she feared she might not

even survive to do the nation's business. Indeed, malicious intent toward her lurked behind that mocking effigy and the body in her fountain. She was thinking of escaping to Hampton Court earlier than planned, just after an annual public healing ceremony at the Abbey in two days.

"My Lord Cecil, please stay," she said, gesturing his secretaries away. "I had ordered Lord Dudley and the Sidneys to report what they discovered about that body in the fountain during their mermaid masque, and they'd best have answers for me."

After stilted greetings and overmuch bowing and scraping from the three of them, Mary Sidney said, "We have spoken with nearly everyone at court, Your Grace, servants too, even the Cheapside jeweler who fashioned the mermaid pin. But it seems no one who knew of the timing for the masque looks guilty of abetting or committing murder."

Both men nodded but kept their peace, and that from Robin was most unusual. Elizabeth sensed that they'd had a family council and made Mary their speaker. They were, no doubt, harboring hope that her close friendship with the queen would smooth things over.

"But we did locate ladder marks," Mary went on.

"From the feet of a ladder, deep-set marks," Robin put in.

"I am getting to that, my lord," Mary remonstrated. "Deepset marks, we surmise, because someone carried that unknown woman's body up and over the wall, behind the orchard—precisely between those two pear trees you favor, Your Grace."

"And footprints?" Elizabeth asked as her pulse quickened.

"Yes, a single pair, a man's boot soles, quite deep too."

"I hope they have been preserved, as Gil's been out with his parents today, and I would have him sketch them. We must judge the man's size, whether the boots were worn or not, and—"

Robin cleared his throat and exchanged a wary glance with his brother-in-law.

"Say on," the queen ordered. "Tell me flat, Robin, for I didn't use to call you My Eyes for naught."

"We fetched a gardener's ladder to go up and look over the wall ourselves," he said. "Ah, Jenks was there poking about too, but we told him we had it under control."

"And?" she prompted, her voice rising as she stood. "Must I turn torturer to get you to spit it out?"

"We found an abandoned ladder on the public passageway side of the wall," he blurted.

"But then," Mary added, "in coming back down our ladder on the privy garden side, in the soft loam there, the ladder wobbled—with both Henry and Robin on it, trying to duplicate the weight of two bodies—and they had to leap off to keep from falling."

"And somewhat obscured the best prints," Robin concluded when Elizabeth stared him down.

The queen employed one of her father's favorite seagoing oaths and began to pace. "But you did go around on the other side to look for prints and tracks there?" she demanded.

" 'Tis stones and cobbles on the other side, not garden loam," Mary explained. "But we—they—asked folks in the area if they'd seen anyone carrying two ladders or even one. They said they were searching for someone trying to pinch late apples, so they didn't stir up a hornet's nest of suspicion or start rumors."

"Pinch late apples from denuded pear trees?" Elizabeth asked, uncertain whether to laugh or cry.

"But, Your Grace, we came up with a clue—in a way," Mary said, coming closer and holding out her hands beseechingly to her royal friend. "You know that walkway on the far side of the wall goes to the public water stairs. A bargeman hanging about says he indeed saw someone on a ladder there Saturday evening. He thought it was just a man trying to get a glimpse within, for the man had no one—or thing—with him. Especially visitors, some even foreign, he said, sometimes try to see you within your walls those times no one is invited—"

"Invited to catch a dazzling glimpse of the sun," Robin put in with a hopeful smile. "We all understand wanting a glimpse of our smiling, radiant queen, do we not?"

"You spoke to the bargeman?" the queen asked, ignoring the flattery that used to make her fall headlong for him.

"Robin did," Mary said, with a warning look at her brother, "and it was that man your former Strewing Herb Mistress of the Privy Chamber wed before she came into your service. If you want him brought in for questioning, he's most willing."

"Ben Wilton," the queen muttered. "No, that won't be necessary if Robin spoke with him. But the description of the man Wilton saw up the ladder?"

"A man," Robin said, obviously aching to take over, "all in black with a hat with some sort of flaps over his ears. Actually, it sounds like physicians' garb."

"Why didn't you say so at first?" Elizabeth cried. "See, Cecil, the two men you have sent for are exactly who hold the key to this deadly puzzle."

"What men?" Robin demanded. "You still suspect Dr. Caius or Dr. Pascal? Pascal's fat as a pig and could never get up that ladder, not with a body over his shoulder. And Caius is no new-fledged stripling to be hefting weights either."

"Then Wilton said the man was not fat or elderly?" she demanded.

"He couldn't tell," Robin admitted. "Besides that flapped cap, the climber wore a black robe or cloak, though I must admit that would fit a doctor's garb too."

"Of course," Lord Henry put in, the first time he had spoken in all this, "that's assuming that a murderer—any murderer—would not wear a loose black cloak and some sort of obscuring hat to hide his identity in case he was seen."

They all looked at him. Elizabeth felt deflated and foolish. She was so desperate of late, she was wildly pinning her hopes on any clue, however secondhand. And that reminded her of the lovely mermaid pin Mary had given her on that dreadful night. She would not want to wear it again. Frowning, she dismissed Mary and her lord with brief thanks. Robin stood before her now, looking half hopeful, half fearful.

"I do have one more question for you, Robin."

He eyed both the queen and Cecil suspiciously. Despite the fact he had not been bidden to approach her, he walked around the table and went down on one knee before her chair. "Ask me aught you would know or have me do," he said.

"I believe you still employ the squire who so cleverly created a dummy for your passes with the lance and sword at the quintain rail."

"I not only have him, but just today scolded my man Jenks—"

"*My* man Jenks."

"As you wish, my queen. Scolded Jenks for shoving his nose in to ask my squire to see that old dummy. I take it since Jenks and now you, and who knows who else," he added, risking a glare at Cecil, "seem suspicious, you believe I am somehow linked to the making of that other effigy you found?"

"My, how you jump far afield, my lord," she remonstrated gently. "Not at all, though indeed your effigy was also of a queen."

"Of Catherine de' Medici, an enemy to you and your realm, *my* queen. As Mary, Queen of Scots' former mother-in-law, Queen Catherine is both an Italian and French, Catholic, conniving—"

"A queen, no less, and one whose effigy, I recall, you had richly gowned and crowned with a fine wig—which you got where?"

He had the brains to go white as a ghost at last. She could tell he wanted to stand to not be at such a disadvantage, kneeling at her feet.

"Indirectly, from an old Chelsea wig-maker years ago," he said, his voice rising. "For my mother when she began to fret about losing her hair, if you must know, Your Grace. But you cannot be serious that I would have aught to do with ... with what you found in your coach. And hardly with that body in the fountain." He stood at last; she rose too.

"If I believed that, I would have your squire and that dummy both thoroughly examined and you arrested, Lord Robert Dudley."

"I will fetch it and him up here straightaway, Your Grace. I have naught to fear."

"Do so then, but wait until I summon you again, for I have other visitors to see," she said, dismissing him with a wave of her hand as she turned her back on him. But the moment he stomped out, she turned to the silent Cecil. "Quickly, my lord," she whispered, "pick one of your best men and have him covertly watch Robin's every step. I yearn to trust him, but I fear that I cannot."

⁂   ⁂   ⁂

MEG WAITED UNTIL SHE CLOSED THE SHOP THAT afternoon and could escape upstairs. Only then did she take from her canvas apron pocket Dr. Clerewell's note, which Nick had slipped her several hours ago. Ben was gone. Street noise still rose up from the Strand, but it seemed private and silent here above the shop.

Meg wondered if she'd see the little girl today, Susanna Miller's youngest child, from the house directly across the way. These top stories leaned out so far that, if the shutters were open, it was easy to see in each other's places. Yes, there she was, running hither and thither about the Millers' main chamber. The golden-haired, giggling three-year-old vision made Meg's arms ache for her own babe sometimes.

Before the sun sank over the tightly packed, gabled rooftops, she broke the wax seal and smoothed the note open on her knees.

> *My Dear Mistress Wilton,*
>
> *Because we have forged a working partnership for particular cures and causes, I feel I may be so bold as to sue for your assistance in this matter, as you have helped so in another. To wit, I have a young, once-comely female patient who is sadly disfigured and afflicted with the scrofula or struma, which is also known as the King's—no, I reckon these days, more appropriately—the Queen's Evil.*
>
> *Your former days in service to our queen and your skill with herbal healings must have given you an intimate knowledge of this ceremony from former years. And, I believe, if I can but bring my patient to this traditional royal service on Wednesday at Westminster Abbey, our Gracious Majesty's mere touch may save this girl from a lifetime of misery—and I may accomplish my aim.*

"That's a good one," Meg muttered. "Said he didn't believe in traditions in medicine, now wants to rely on the oldest healing ceremony I know."

But perhaps, she thought, it was his sad, once-comely female patient who begged him to get her into the healing ceremony. Meg wondered how old this comely girl was.

And so, I implore you to let me know if you have attended or seen this age-old service, so that I might know what to ex-pect and how I might position myself for best results.

Meg's mind drifted to that ceremony. As one who fancied herself a healer in earlier days, before all the restrictions put on herbalists or apothecaries, Meg had been dazzled by the beauty of the ceremony and the power of her queen. Standing in the slant of sun through stained-glass windows, the queen touched and blessed each ill person. She presented each with a specially minted coin, a golden angel on a ribbon to wear around their poor, swollen necks.

Gold angel, Meg thought, distracted from her reverie by the sound of giggling. She looked up to see the little Miller girl, waving through her window. Meg smiled and waved exuberantly back. *That girl* was a golden angel better than any queen's coin.

Meg had seen that ceremony four times since Elizabeth had held the throne, twice while in her service, twice after she had been dismissed. Mostly the royal household physicians and those of the Royal College brought their patients to be healed of the disfiguring tumors and scabrous marks of the dread disease. But it was true that other doctors could bring their patients and hope the monarch turned aside to them too.

It was tradition that French and English monarchs touched victims of glandular neck tumors. The affliction was known as the King's Evil, for superstitious folk of yore believed the monarch's touch could cause as well as cure the disease, and the unfortunate name stuck. The Tudors kept up the ancient prac-tice, for the message to the people was a sound political one: God granted to his chosen sovereign, at least upon occasion, the Lord's own power to heal.

Meg had already planned to sneak away from the shop to watch Her Grace this year. It was a marvelous opportunity to see her when she was not sweeping grandly past in a barge or on horseback or hidden in that damned coach of hers.

Meg skimmed the rest of the note, rereading the end where Dr. Clerewell offered to treat Gil's muteness for however long that took and for no remuneration, so that the boy *could regale them with tales of the palace.* Tears prickled her eyelids. Yes, Meg thought, no matter that she risked Ben's throwing a fit if he ever learned she had spent hours on the day after next with Marcus Clerewell. She'd take the good doctor there and show him where to stand. If she could snag Nick first thing on the morrow before she and Ben took care of their unpleasant business in Chelsea, trying to collect a fee, she'd send him back with her reply.

Before she took out pen and ink, Meg reluctantly closed the shutter, lit a candle, and built up the low-burning hearth fire. But at the last moment, she couldn't bear to burn the note that asked for her help and so graciously acknowledged her healing skills and former importance to the queen. Instead, she folded and stuffed it in the toe of her oldest darned stocking in the chest at the foot of the bed.

I T WAS AFTER ELIZABETH HAD DINED ALONE THAT CECIL was announced again.

"My men have brought Dr. John Caius in, Your Grace," he told her, standing at the door to her privy chamber where she sat now alone. "And he's evidently as mad as a wet hen about being summoned so late at night."

"The pomposity of these men *I* have approved in their positions boggles the mind," she told him, rising from the same table at which she'd worked all afternoon. "And Pascal?"

"He's evidently gone home—to Chelsea, to be precise."

"Indeed?" she said, raising her eyebrows. "They used to say 'All roads lead to Rome,' but now I believe they lead to little Chelsea. Then mayhap we shall pass him on the river in the morn, for I am going to see the wig-maker."

The queen was in a foul mood, having put her stomach off her food by another row with Robin after cross-questioning his squire, then taking a quick glance at the most moldy, moth-eaten, and horribly hacked effigy she had ever seen. Its face was painted wood, not delicate plaster. Her memories of it, like her memories of how much she had so desperately desired Robin, were not to be trusted.

Yet the man had admitted that his effigy's wig had come from Chelsea, and worse, that its gown had once been Elizabeth's, borrowed from the Wardrobe in Blackfriars, in another seeming coincidence she did not like. He swore up and down she'd given the gown to him when he'd merely hinted he needed one. It had made her furious that she no doubt would have done so once, that and more for the wretched man.

"Let them fetch Dr. Caius in," she ordered Cecil when she saw he was still staring at her, "but wait a moment until I go tell Ned Topside something. And stay, my lord, though I intend to do the talking."

꧁   ꧁   ꧁

THE PHYSICIAN ENTERED, ALL OBEISANCE AND SMILES. If he was nonplussed, he wasn't showing it. "I was so relieved to hear you are not ill, *Maxima Regina,*" he began, bowing low, "for to be called out so precipitously after dark usually bodes no good news for a physician."

"As you can see, I am hale and hearty," she said and watched his quick, dark eyes assess her.

"Then you wish to discuss our part in the King's—I mean, Queen's—Evil healing ceremony day-after-tomorrow?" he asked, either jumping to conclusions or playacting that he was innocent of what she intended to ask.

"I would never take my time," the doctor went on when she stared back at him, "to discuss diseases with the common people, but, of course, if *you,* Your Gracious Majesty, would like information or advice on anything, I am willing."

"How magnanimous of you," she retorted, her voice steel-tipped as she folded her hands on the table before her. "Give me advice then, doctor, on why you and your colleagues have not yet found a medical cure for that dread disease called the Evil."

"I—why, of course, we have treatments for it, namely the family of herbs called *scrophulariaceae.* And the affliction is properly called *tubercular adenitis.*"

"Quite a series of impressive tongue-twisters," she observed, starting to rise. Cecil hastened forward from his post by the door to pull out her chair for her, then stepped away again. The queen leaned toward Caius on stiff arms over the table. "No doubt the mere mention of that disease scares its poor, untutored victims, but do not play your obscure language and knowledge games with me!"

"Let me explain, Your Majesty," Caius said, raising his hands as if to hold her off. "That grouping of herbs are selected for the glandlike tubers on their roots which mimic the human tumors. Therefore, learned medical minds deduce those must be meant as a sign of their specific curative power. In this instance, to whit, the herbs of figwort, speedwell, and foxglove, which—"

"Which obviously do not heal scrofula and thereby necessitate this ceremony for the worst afflicted. As I have long preached to you, doctor of doctors," she plunged on, rapping her knuckles on the table to emphasize her words, "more work ... must be done ... to heal and help ... my people."

Here he got a coughing fit. She wondered if it wasn't from his bitter memories of being dismissed from her service as court physician in this very room.

"Actually," she said, after Cecil stepped forward to offer him a swig of ale and the doctor quieted a bit, "I sent for you to speak more of that effigy that so strangely appeared in my coach outside your Royal College. Such a cough," she observed when he began to hack again. "You are quite well yourself, are you not, doctor?"

He nodded, but when he spoke his eyes watered and his voice was not his own. "Neither I nor the others at the College know aught of that unfortunate incident, Your Majesty. Nor have we learned more in inquiring of our servants about it, *et cetera.*"

"Then I must tell you that my inquiries so far," she clipped out, "indicate I could both dismiss you from your position and have you sent to the Tower you have recently visited more than once without my express permission."

"The Tower?" he gasped, coughing again. "Merely because I treated those of your blood living there, Your Majesty?"

"Treated them *and* tampered with matters of state."

"With what matters of state?" he whispered, apparently aghast.

"I have it from Katherine Grey's own lips that you urged that her husband be allowed to see her when my wishes were quite the opposite. A fine cure that was, since she is—as you know and I did not until today—with child again!"

"She was deeply melancholy in heart and mind, and it was affecting her health, Your Majesty." His voice was still rough, but his cough seemed to have been scared out of him. "However, I assure you, I had no notion your lord lieutenant would leave them to their own devices. I was shocked to learn that—"

"And saw fit not to tell me she was breeding another heir!" she accused, coming around the table at him so fast he fell back several steps. "And, of course, another heir to whom Catholic conspiracies could flock!"

He jumped back again as she reached beside her to smack the table with a fist, splattering ink and sand from her writing pots. "And, doctor, she told me of the life mask your foreign friend has made of her face," she cried, gesturing and pointing, "a face conveniently enough similar to mine as is the face on the effigy I found outside your door. Ned, now!" she called through the inward door she'd ordered left ajar.

Ned Topside came in, carrying the red-wigged, stuffed effigy upright as if he had his arms around a real woman. Again it looked so real that he seemed to be embracing the queen herself from behind. He held it close before Dr. Caius's stunned face.

"Where," Elizabeth demanded, "is your Italian friend now, doctor, the one so skilled at masks and at dissecting corpses? Were you asking me for bodies so he might practice his forbidden arts here in my realm as he did in Catholic countries?"

He gaped at the effigy's face, then back to her. If she had not known his deceit—the depths to which all men could stoop to serve themselves—she would have sworn he had never laid eyes on the mock queen before.

"But this—this is made to look as if you—that is, as if it—has the small p-pox," he stammered.

"Are you informing me of that as if I am some simpleton? It is mockery at best and treason at worst!"

"I—my friend is Stefano Natus, Your Majesty, a physician and a fine limner and sculptor who trained with me in Padua."

His gaze repeatedly darted from the effigy to her, then back again. He was visibly trembling now. "Our teacher there, the illustrious Andreas Versalius, was a genius in the art of anatomy. He taught all his pupils to dissect—for which he had to beg or steal executed cadavers. And he encouraged us to draw to the best of our ability what structures of the human form we found, muscles, bones, veins, organs, the body's innermost workings—but—but," he rasped, as if he'd run out of breath, "we did not fashion effigies of those diseased."

Still shaking, he drew himself up to his full height and looked her straight in the eyes. "It is what our English physicians—your physicians—must needs do to propel your realm into the forefront of the medical arts, Your Majesty. *Ad astra per ardua.* It is why I implored you and yet implore you to allot us corpses, however much it seems to go against tradition, for no more true progress can be made otherwise. And yes, Your Majesty, I took Stefano Natus along once to see Katherine Grey, Lady Hertford, and knowing he was skilled in sculpting as well as drawing had him make a life mask of her."

"And this is it?" she demanded, pointing to the plaster face.

"I have never seen that before," he insisted, tugging down the cuffs of his robe over his wrists. "The life mask of Lady Hertford is in Padua, Italy, with Stefano Natus so that he might sculpt a bust of it when he has the time. I am innocent of all these dreadful, half-spoken allegations and beg you to simply allow me to do my duty as I see it. And that begins when I examine those who will be blessed at the healing ceremony to be certain that the victims of scrofula you touch have that disease the Lord God gives the monarch to heal and no other."

Now he left her breathless. Either he was indeed the man to lead her London Royal College of Physicians boldly into the future or the most cold and calculating liar she had yet ever seen.

T HE THAMES TIDE RUSHED TOWARD THE SEA THE NEXT
morning. For the first time in two years, Elizabeth admitted
to herself that she wished she had Meg Milligrew in her service
so she could take her place in her supposed sickbed while she
ventured out on a privy task dressed as Meg. But this plain gray
cloak and hood lined with squirrel from her own wardrobe
would have to do.

Chelsea was a small, charming village but four miles beyond
Westminster. Its proximity was a blessing, for the queen planned
not to take long at this task of questioning the old wig-maker.
Had Honoria Wyngate not been reported as so ancient, she
would have sent for her. But then, she admitted she was somewhat curious to see Chelsea again.

Ned and Jenks sat, nearly shoved off the ends of the bench by
her wide skirts, on either side of her under the three-sided
canopy of the same working barge she'd taken to the Tower yesterday. Gil sat cross-legged on a leather cushion at her feet, his
drawing tools and paper in a canvas sack. Six men-at-oars and six
guards completed their party.

"Remember to keep a watch on passing crafts for that crafty
Dr. Pascal on his way back from Chelsea," the queen reminded
them.

"Your wit never fails you," Ned told her. "Not even when
you're scared out of your wits."

"I wish I could quip and laugh my way through this spiders' web of clues and crises," she admitted, hitting her fist on
her knee. "Who knows but it is Dr. Pascal and not Dr. Caius
who is our primary quarry? After that makeshift shrine I saw
in the Tower, I am coming to believe he is truly of unhinged
character. How I'd like a glimpse inside Sir Thomas More's old

home in Chelsea where Pascal now resides. He's obviously never forgiven the Tudors for condemning and beheading his beloved mentor."

"The old wig-maker may have known Sir Thomas too," Ned posited, "and is not just a hireling, but a full-fledged accomplice."

"Let's not jump to too many conclusions," Elizabeth warned. "But if Honoria Wyngate or her staff, if she has aught, can identify who bought the wig"—she glanced down at the bag Ned held—"then we can begin to lay the blame at someone's door. And I'll warrant it's the same someone who bribed the missing lace girl and her lover to hand over my gown from the Royal Wardrobe."

"But didn't the girl tell Kat he sounded foreign and spoke fancy or some such?" Ned interjected.

"Any educated person could flummox a lace girl," Elizabeth said. "Even some medical Latin strung together would do; though, of course, if we are dealing with a group of plotters, foreigners could be involved. I would wager all the gold angels I'm giving out at the healing ceremony tomorrow that someone Spanish sent Katherine Grey those little dogs and that the Lennoxes, who will be reunited with us at court this week, are covertly communicating with the former queen of France, my clever cousin, Mary, Queen of Scots. But I'll catch them at spinning their webs. People who should be watched will be, and those whose conversations should be overheard—"

Gil tapped her foot and signaled wildly. *What if I talk?* the boy signaled. *If I talk and draw, I stay with you?*

"But of course," she said, then signaled the rest of her thoughts to him with flying fingers: *But your finest talking will always be through your art, and I'd not have it any other way.*

"I think, whether or not it is a conspiracy," she went on to her men, "that doctors are involved. Mayhap their prodigious and pompous intellects are fed by taunting me before they strike."

"If not a doctor," Ned muttered, "it's someone who wants us to think so, to point a finger toward a too-obvious scapegoat he—or she—can hide behind."

"Look, Your Grace!" Jenks shouted so close to her ear she jumped. "In that small barge there—that man!"

"Has Dr. Pascal spotted us?" she asked. "Where is he?"

"No. It's Meg with her husband. See?"

Elizabeth did see. Meg was at the tiller in the stern of a small skiff while Ben rowed mightily against the tidal current. Gil began signing something to Meg about *no talking yet*. The queen looked into Meg's eyes in the moment it took to pass their small craft at close quarters. So much for not being recognized, at least by Meg, Elizabeth thought, but the girl sat silent and stoic as a fine lady while that big-shouldered lout Wilton hooted. Meg looked sad—angry too—and hardly happy to see her queen.

"I've noted her before when we've been on the river," Ned said, "but usually when we were in the barge of state."

"Hard to miss us then with all that red and gold, queen's coat-of-arms, and thirty men-at-oars," Jenks muttered as he craned around to see the last of the Wiltons.

"Yes, but what coincidence they passed us now," Ned mused, "and we're supposedly making this jaunt in secret."

"Meaning what?" Elizabeth demanded. "Heading the opposite direction, they can hardly be following us."

"Nothing," he murmured, but she saw his mouth silently move to add, "yet."

"I told you Ben Wilton claims he saw a man peering over the privy garden wall and volunteered to come in to testify," Elizabeth pursued the topic. "No doubt it's a question of his angling for more reward, for I fear the man is lazy but greedy."

Ned nodded, looking surprised, she supposed, that after all these months she was willing to discuss the Wiltons. "I am no longer angry with her," she said, looking straight ahead again. "I simply find it best not to speak of her—of those early days, for they distract me from my necessary business, that is all."

But it was not memories of Meg that moved her as they approached the hamlet of Chelsea. Despite its proximity to her capital city, she had not visited it for years, though she had oft seen it from the river as her royal barge passed by en route to her several palaces to the west.

In sleepy, rural Chelsea, Elizabeth had once lived happily with her stepmother, Katherine Parr, and her husband, Tom Seymour, before everything had gone to pieces. Elizabeth had been sent away for losing her young, yearning heart to Seymour, a man who merely wanted her for what she was, a Tudor princess, then but two lives from the throne.

"Her Majesty wishes to put in at the public stairs," Ned's voice interrupted her agonizing as he called to the men-at-oars.

Chelsea seemed ever the same, Elizabeth observed. The facades of the manor houses that could be seen from the river were set back across gardens and wide lawns, each with its own water gate and stairs. Smaller, thatched village houses hoved into view. Chimneys, tall ones on lofty roofs and squat ones on cottages, peeked above treetops and trailed crooked fingers of smoke into the brisk September breeze.

"There's the house which used to belong to my stepmother." She pointed it out as the barge made for shore. "And that one farther down was once Sir Thomas More's, though he was dead years before I lived here, and one of his heirs had the house then. And, of course, Pascal has it now."

"After we see the wig woman, you still want me to knock on its door and order him to Whitehall to see you forthwith, Your

Grace?" Jenks asked. "If he hasn't returned to the city yet, I mean."

"Let's decide after we hear what old Dame Wyngate has to say."

Ned helped her out. Grateful no crowds gathered as in London, they made their way onto the grassy village green and waited, the queen with Jenks, Gil, and the six guards, while Ned went into the only tavern to inquire after the wig-maker's location.

"Cottage at the end of the village," Ned called to them as he emerged and led their little procession across the green. "They say she's deaf as a stone and has a granddaughter living with her, who's been apprenticed to the trade. In other words, we can either shout our wishes at Dame Wyngate, or the girl will do it for us."

"At least she's still alive and obviously isn't going anywhere," Elizabeth said as they spotted the hunchbacked thatched roofed place on the opposite end of town from the finer houses.

Honoria Wyngate's dwelling was grown higgledy-piggledy all on one floor. Its plaster had grayed, and its wig of thatch looked ragged and balding. A once-tended garden sprawled to riot and ruin, with everything blasted by early frost so that only dead hollyhocks bobbed in the breeze.

"Ned, Jenks, with me," the queen said, "and the rest of you wait here within call." She nodded and Jenks, his hand instinctively resting on his sword, rapped sharply on the door while she and Ned stood back a few paces. Jenks knocked again, his fist rattling the door in its frame, but no one answered.

"I said she's deaf, Jenks, or are you too?" Ned needled him. "Knock harder or just shout for her granddaughter."

"You're the one with all the fancy, foreign stage voices you can throw about!" Jenks shot back.

"Stop carping at each other and look in the windows," Elizabeth ordered. "They are fine glass, so you'd think she'd have the money to keep this place up better than this. Knock on the glass, as the sound may carry better."

The men worked their way around the irregularly shaped exterior, knocking on windows. Elizabeth, trailing four guards and Gil, walked to the back door. An oriel window overlooked a length of lawn to a small, noisy stream, and morning sun poured through the many leaded panes of glass.

Honoria Wyngate loves sunlight to see by and warm her old bones, the queen thought, in a sudden rush of affection for the old woman. And, no doubt, she needed light to do her fine work of sewing strands of hair.

Feeling like a Peeping Tom, Elizabeth nonetheless stepped up to the bow of window and glanced in. Baskets of hair sat beside a long workbench directly under the window, all lit by splashes of sun. Raven-dark hair; nut-brown, blond, russet tresses, and the same red-gold hue as the effigy's wig.

"She'll have answers for us," Elizabeth said as Jenks, Ned, and Gil joined her. "Or her granddaughter will."

The queen stood on tiptoe and looked beyond to a ladder-backed chair near the empty, cold hearth. Her own shadow fell across the sunny space. Then she saw the old lady, sitting on the floor with her head on the seat of the chair. But the tilt of her neck was strange, and those thin, old limbs were sprawled in sleep at an awkward angle.

"Jenks, open or break down that door!"

He obeyed, but before he could draw his sword to lead the way in, Elizabeth pushed past him.

Chapter
THE TENTH

*Venus claims dominion over the herb meadowsweet or
mead sweet. Therefore, it is good to stay bleedings and
for other women's problems.*

NICHOLAS CULPEPER
The English Physician

T HE EVER-SWIFT JENKS REACHED THE WRINKLED,
hoary-headed Honoria Wyngate with Elizabeth, and
Ned came close behind.

"Is she dead?" the queen whispered.

"Mayhap she just stumbled or got a dizzy spell and knocked
herself out!" Jenks said, resheathing his sword with a loud
scrape.

"Or she's just asleep and didn't hear us," Ned offered.

Elizabeth touched the wig-maker's arm as if to rouse her. It
was stiff and cold. "See," the queen said, her voice still hushed, "a
puddle of blood on the chair seat where she must have struck her
head. But let's make certain she's gone."

When she did not budge to touch her again, Ned felt for a
neck pulse, then shook his head.

"If a long life is any kind of good life, she had that," Elizabeth said, as if pronouncing a benediction. "She looks so frail. No doubt she could have slipped and fallen, but in this instance, I cannot help but be suspicious."

After all, she thought, this would not be the first time lately that someone she needed to question had been snatched from her grasp. No one had seen the effigy placed in the coach on Knightrider Street; both Lucinda, the lace girl, and her paramour had disappeared; and a corpse had materialized in the royal privy fountain of a crowded palace with no one to question but a greedy bargeman lurking outside who saw but shadowy form with no face. And now this.

She stepped back and turned away to survey the room. It was immaculately kept, but for one thing. The ashes from the cold hearth were trailed and smeared far into the room, even across a Turkish carpet the old woman surely must have valued. The queen walked closer to the hearth.

She knew her people watched her, waiting for a command to leave this sad scene. She straightened and stepped back. "Guards," she called to her four men who had followed as far as the door, "two of you draw swords and search this house for an intruder or signs of one." They instantly obeyed, clattering through the single interior doorway to the sprawl of small rooms.

"Despite her age and frailty, you're thinking foul play, Your Majesty?" Ned asked, coming to stand beside her at the hearth.

"I'm fearing it. Look at this."

She bent closer to study the ashes that marred the clean-swept floor and bright-colored carpet. This soot told a tale as clearly as one of Gil's charcoal drawings.

"Gil," she said to the boy who had begun to sketch Honoria Wyngate, "draw the pattern of these ashes on the hearth first, then the body."

"I see what you mean, Your Grace," Ned agreed.

"I believe someone set this room aright, but either in haste or carelessness forgot to clean this evidence left underfoot. Something has been dragged through the remnants of charcoal residue. And see here," she said, pointing to the smears on the old woman's skirts and slippers.

They all jumped when a guard asked from the door, "Shall we search this room, too, Your Majesty?"

"No, just the others," she said without looking at him.

"We did and no one's hiding here'bouts and nothing seems amiss," he reported.

"Two of you stay at the back door and the others search outside for fresh foot- or hoofprints. For anything!"

The men clomped out again, but Elizabeth kept staring at the fine, filmy trail of ash that was thick on the edge of the cold hearth but dissipated near the chair. "See," she said, pointing, then blocking their approach with both arms when Ned and Jenks came too close and nearly tipped Gil into the ashes. "The proof of her struggle, feeble though it may have been, is written on the hearth and on the bottom of her skirts. *She* is what was dragged or lifted to the position she is now in."

"Maybe her granddaughter helped her to the chair when she felt faint, and ran for help," Jenks surmised.

"And never came back?" Ned challenged. "More like it was their family argument that put the old thing here like this. Perhaps the girl wanted to take over the trade sooner than Dame Wyngate thought she should. Or the girl had a lover of whom the old dame did not approve," he added, pointing to the prints. "It looks like a man's and a woman's steps here."

"It does indeed, and not Dame Wyngate's," Elizabeth theorized. She turned back to remove a linen slipper from the woman's right foot. "See?" she said as she held the ash-smeared slipper over the print of a woman's shoe. "Honoria Wyngate's foot is smaller, and there is no heel on this slipper as the other woman wore. We must find her granddaughter to see if this could be hers."

"Then you credit my theory the girl—a girl, at least—could be guilty?" Ned said, his eyes lighting.

"I suppose that could be one reason she's evidently not come back and the body has already gone into what the doctors call rigor mortis, which takes several hours. But what if foul play has struck the girl too? Mayhap she has been abducted from here."

"To what purpose?" Ned asked.

Elizabeth shrugged as she placed the slipper back on the woman's foot should the local sheriff or justice investigate this. "The possibilities do boggle the mind," she admitted.

"The man was big, I warrant," Ned surmised, dangling his own foot over that longer print.

"It may be the very sole that Robin and Henry Sidney obscured in their fall off the ladder in the privy garden," the queen mused. "Jenks, when we are ready to go, I want you to run ahead to inquire in the village whether the granddaughter's been seen. And get a description of her in case she's guilty and a fugitive. But we will not report this murder until we are ready to leave, so that Gil has time to complete his drawings. Meanwhile, Ned and I will minutely inspect this place for any correspondence or receipts she may have naming someone who bought a red wig."

꧁   ꧁   ꧁

Dear Dr. Clerewell,

I must, of necessity, ask that you to treat this as privy correspondence. You saw the results the other day of our being discovered together talking overlong.

I thank you for your help and for not claiming a fee in the matter of Gil's learning to speak so he can, as you say, "tell his tales." Meanwhile, I am pleased to keep your secret while putting on trial the V.M.E.

But as to the business with the Queen's Evil: by tradition she enters the Abbey through the main west door just before ten of the clock. She will progress the entire nave to the high altar where the poor victims await her. The ceremony is very well guarded and goes by rote, so there is no hope for success there.

However, after it, as she recesses, it is possible to approach her. Have your friend kneel in the aisle, close in front of the queen to stop her. You will then both have a quick moment's access to her, especially if she is caught off guard. I must needs remain hidden so none of her retinue spot me, though I will get you into place and be there watching—and praying—for victorious results.

I shall meet you both at Westminster Palace river stairs.

Mistress Sarah Wilton

Meg was proud of this letter, for she seldom wrote out that many words at once. She wished she could show it to Ned, who had taught her to read and write. She even wished she could show it to Her Majesty, to prove how far she'd come since Her Grace took in that bedraggled, befuddled kitchen herb girl four years ago.

Sadly, she'd never dare show it to either of them. But to buck herself up for what momentous deed lay ahead, Meg made a copy of the missive. Drying the ink carefully, she rolled it up like a little scroll and stuffed it down her darned stocking with the note from Dr. Clerewell.

But as she started down the stairs, she began to fret. Ben might not read well, but he could pick out people's signatures. So she went back, took both notes, and hid them instead in an herbal drawer downstairs behind the alabaster box of Venus Moon.

 ❧   ❧   ❧

L OOK, YOUR GRACE," NED CRIED, FLOURISHING THE small piece of paper he'd found stuck on a nail in a raft of others on the mantel. "Maybe Dame Wyngate meant to burn this but didn't get to it. It was under these other receipts."

Annoyed he took so long to tell her what it said, Elizabeth snatched it from him. " 'For a fine red wig with a slight sheen of blond, two pounds, four shillings,' " she read aloud. " 'To be in upswept fashion in current court style, suited for light coronet.' That's it, Ned, for all the deuced good it does us when she's dead, because there is no name of the buyer here. Do those other receipts have names?"

"Most do," he muttered as he scrabbled through them. "Just a few without, and I don't see any pattern. Some have dates, some don't."

"This one doesn't. Then we must immediately locate her granddaughter, and she will know who bought the wig."

She heaved a huge sigh. "Keep looking here," she ordered him, "and bring Gil out with you when you're done."

Elizabeth motioned for her two guards to remain at the door and stepped out into the sun. The little world of a woman's works and long life had suddenly seemed to close around her with foreboding. The stench of death was not yet in the room, but she felt it was, like some foul disease clinging to her skin or hair, or insidiously seeping into her lungs. What could be the link between the demise of an anonymous young woman bled to death by leeches in London and an old woman who hit her head to draw blood in her home in Chelsea?

She spun and rushed back into the house. "I didn't want to move her body, but lift her head off the chair," she ordered the startled Ned.

He looked as if he'd argue, then obeyed, pulling the body up a bit by the shoulders and awkwardly lifting the head from the sticky pool of blood. It had pulsed from a small, neat, shallow stab wound in her temple, at the very site physicians bled patients for disorders of the head and mind.

"A lancet wound," Elizabeth said. "She's been bled too! First a poxed effigy that looks like me, then a young woman leeched in the pattern of the pox, then an older one, lancet-bled. Definitely done by a doctor!" she cried. "I knew it—one of those Papist physicians who holds a grudge against his queen!"

"Or some layperson or quacksalver who's worked cures in the past when she or he shouldn't have," Ned mumbled.

The queen strode back outside. Sucking in a breath of fresh air, she walked the stretch of lawn toward the brook. Beyond it, frost-blasted, tall grass waved in a fallow field mostly gone to weeds. She stared at the remnants of wildflowers and herbs, trying to calm herself. But instead, back leaped that tormenting memory of that long dead day she'd seen the poxed mother and her children begging near the herbal fields of Chelsea, though at the other end of the village. And then it hit her.

This field had obviously been full of meadowsweet and woodruff this summer, the two herbs with which the linen body of the effigy had been stuffed. Those herbs could grow elsewhere, but things were starting to point to someone who had a certain familiarity with Chelsea. Mayhap the old woman did not include the name of the buyer of that red wig because she knew him and where to find him, just on the other side of the village, ensconced in the home of his deceased friend and mentor Sir Thomas More.

"Ned, Gil, guards, to me!" she cried.

Two of her men emerged from the bank of the stream on a dead run, as if they'd already been on their way. The others gathered around her too. "When we get back, I'm issuing a formal warrant for the arrest and questioning of Dr. Peter Pascal," she announced. "But right now, we are going calling on him at his house on the other side of the village."

"But it's likely he's gone to London, Your Majesty," Ned reminded her. "You said before he was to spend the day with Dr. Caius, vetting victims of scrofula for the ceremony tomorrow."

"I know that, but I don't want to see him until I have him under arrest—until, as Cecil would say, we have our case prepared to argue before the bar. I'd rather see his house when he is not there. I will tell his family or servants I was out on the river and decided to stop."

"Which he won't believe," Ned muttered.

"Neither you nor he will gainsay me. I don't believe him, either, anymore, so it is checkmate."

"And the queen is a far more powerful chess piece than one of the pawns," Ned put in quickly.

"If he is not home, I will leave two guards behind to watch for his coming should we miss finding him in the city," she said and turned to walk away.

"Your Majesty," her guard Clifford called to her, "we were just coming up from the stream to tell you there's fresh hoofprints in the mud. Maybe Jenks should check local stables for a horse with muddy shoes. And maybe its rider dropped this."

As she spun back, Clifford extended to her on a thick chain a muddy, gold-encased timepiece the size of a fist. "Got some fancy scrollwork on it, right there," he added, pointing his big finger at the open cover.

Ned stuck his nose close before Elizabeth could see it clearly in the sun, but she elbowed him and he stepped back.

"Didn't wash it off, 'cause the mud makes it easier to read," Clifford explained. "If'n I could read."

"The timepiece has not even run down yet," she noted, "so it was not dropped long ago."

"Bull's-eye," Ned whispered to her. "The kind of mechanical timepiece a well-to-do physician would carry to count pulse beats."

"With his engraved initials back-to-back in a special design," she observed, her voice rising in excitement. "A fancy *P*—no, two of them entwined! My instincts are exactly right!"

"At least it looks," Ned said, "that Peter Pascal's our man."

              ✒   ✒   ✒

T HIS SUDDEN, UNANNOUNCED VISIT TO HIS SANCTU-ary, as you put it, will no doubt tip him off," Ned warned as they approached the large, frame and timber house overlooking the Thames. "His family or servants will surely tell him straightaway we've been here, especially if you have his portable timepiece from near the site of a murder."

"First of all, no one is going to mention a murder or that timepiece," she said, raising her voice. "Is that understood?"

Murmurs of acquiescence and nods all around. Elizabeth felt the timepiece resting heavily in the pouch hanging from her belt. "Clifford," she ordered, "knock on the door, but Ned Topside will announce me, and no one mentions that Jenks has gone to snoop around their stables."

A male servant of middling years, lantern-jawed with graying hair, opened the door for them. His mouth fell open at the size of the armed retinue, though their swords were sheathed. His gaze darted to Elizabeth, standing in the center of her men, but no recognition lit his face.

"James Witherspoon, house steward, at your bidding, milady," he said with a half bow.

" 'Tis your own queen who stands before you, sirrah," Ned announced with a sweeping gesture, "Elizabeth of England."

At that, the man nearly fell backward. He looked so stunned they could have walked right in.

"My good man," she said, stepping forward, "we were passing by on the Thames, and I said I had a good notion to see the home which Dr. Pascal now owns, the former abode of Sir Thomas More, of whom the doctor thinks so highly. May we not come in?"

Whatever the man's orders to guard the place, he stepped back and bowed low. Elizabeth entered and, with Ned, Gil, and two guards in tow, began to take a tour while the others waited outside.

"I have always been curious about Sir Thomas More," she told the man as she glanced around the first room, one with such dark, old-fashioned walnut wainscoting that it seemed to keep sunshine at bay outside. Assuming this man would also venerate Sir Thomas, Elizabeth tried to sound impressed with the place. And, though she gracefully accepted the glass of Rhenish she was offered by another servant from a silver tray, she did not drink it.

" 'Tis the very room," the steward told her, soon warming to his task, "where Sir Thomas sat with his family for a Hans Holbein painting. The doctor tried to recover it, but the crown keeps what it has, pardon my saying so, Your Majesty," he added hastily. "Holbein was sent by the king, your father, before His Majesty turned on—before the times shifted."

Elizabeth could tell this James Witherspoon, house steward, was used to giving these explanations slanted toward those who favored the Catholic Mores over the terrible Tudors. Yet she held her tongue.

Numerous, only slightly different sketches from the one of More that Elizabeth had seen in the Tower decorated the walls here.

"My master has a fine hand for faces," the man told her.

"Ah, a doctor who can draw."

"Many do, I hear, Your Majesty," he countered.

Elizabeth gave Gil a sharp look to stop his signaling that he thought the sketches were *flat* and *eyes too close*.

In each room they entered, more servants peeked from doorways or down staircases to catch a glimpse of their queen, but if she looked at them, they scurried away like mice.

"And the doctor's family?" she asked.

"Sadly, he is a widower with no heirs," the steward said, shaking his head. Elizabeth set her wine goblet on a heavy chest she passed in the hall to go upstairs. All the furniture was of her parents' or grandparents' eras, probably possessions of Sir Thomas. She suddenly fancied it had never been moved nor the arrases or hangings taken out-of-doors and beaten. She had the continual urge to sneeze.

The staircase treads squeaked in protest as the large party climbed them. At the top hung a life-sized, three-quarter oil portrait of Sir Thomas, garbed in black, somberly holding a copy of his book *Utopia*.

"Did your master do that one too?" she inquired.

"Oh, no, Your Majesty. Hung there for years, that has. Belonged to his widow—Sir Thomas's, that is."

She realized that Pascal's clinging to the past indicated he was hardly the forward-looking physician Dr. John Caius seemed to be, but what she saw here proved little else. Whatever dire deeds the two doctors might have planned, Elizabeth sensed that this servant knew naught of them. So as not to tip her hand that she was overly suspicious, she did not ask to see the cellars. However, that reminded her that she must have the College of Physicians' cellars on Knightrider Street thoroughly searched. They were the only part of their building she had not seen.

The rooms upstairs were all linked by doors, yet most also

had access to the narrow hall. The floors creaked when they trod them, as if ghosts walked here.

"The chamber that is closed at the very end of the hall," she observed, "would overlook the river, I believe, and catch both morning and evening light."

" 'Twas Sir Thomas's library, but now Dr. Pascal's and quite sealed off," he said, pointing to the large lock on the door.

Hair prickled on the nape of her neck. "Ah, but I would love a look inside. Imagine, men, a glimpse into not only the library where Sir Thomas wrote his great masterpiece, but where the brilliant preserver of his memory works to further the art of medicine. Cannot it be entered through one of these other chambers?"

"Your Majesty, I beg of you!" the poor man cried and looked as if he'd dare to throw himself in her path as she entered the chamber next to the locked one. Both Clifford and Ned stepped between him and the queen.

She found the adjoining door in this room, evidently Pascal's bedchamber, closed too. The steward's reaction—which could be simply his rightful instinct to protect his master's privacy—piqued her curiosity even more. She opened the back door to the study, shivering when it creaked in protest.

"I hear that oft at night from my chamber in the attic," the steward admitted, strangely making no further protest. Could he be curious to see in too? "The doctor works all hours," he explained, "but he said I'm not to oil the hinges. And the staff is never to touch or move anything but in the kitchen or our rooms above."

Elizabeth peered around the door she'd opened. As with Sir Thomas More's cell in the Tower, the shutters were closed, but no candles burned here. Instead, sword-edge-width bands of sunlight sliced into the shadows, revealing the contents of the room.

A spartan desk, one piled with books that smelled of mold and lay an inch deep in dust. Writing pots of ink long gone dry. Quills with their nibs cracked and feathers eaten by moths. Bookshelves laced with spiderwebs hovered on each wall but the one with the altar and prie-dieu draped in faded folds of black velvet like a mourning pall. On that altar, unlit banks of votive candles, a gold crucifix, its gleam dulled by dust. And spread across, like an altar cloth, an animal pelt of some sort, as if there had been a sacrifice, though not—this time—a human one.

She almost jumped out of her skin when Ned said, "Shall I open a casement, Your Majesty?"

She shook her head as she reached out to touch the rough fur of—a shirt. A hair shirt, such as ascetics, martyrs, and, she'd heard, the fanatical, Spanish-born Queen Catherine of Aragon used to wear. But this one, no doubt, once rubbed raw the back of Pascal's second St. Thomas. People had whispered that More did not even take it off upon the scaffold.

"Oh, he's left it home tod—" the steward blurted before he evidently realized his mistake.

"So Pascal wears this or another hair shirt as other tortured souls who wish to augment their penance of sin?" she asked, turning away from the altar. "And what sin would a well-respected physician wish to do penance for?" she demanded, more of herself than the poor servant. She had to flee this chapel chamber; once again she felt the walls closing in.

As she was ready to pass back through the partly closed door, she glimpsed something hanging behind it. Though it disgusted her to think Pascal was finding ways to bleed even himself, she seized the thing by its rawhide handle and took it with her. The thongs, tied with pieces of sharp bone on the ends, snagged at her skirts as she walked, and she hid the whip called a scourge beneath her cloak as she exited the house. She was not certain if the

servants knew it was there or if she had taken it, but poor James
Witherspoon looked as stunned as she felt.

"You may tell your master, when he returns," she said to the
man, now blinking in the bright sun as he followed her outside,
"that I found his private Chelsea cathedral dedicated to Saint
Thomas More most enlightening."

As she headed for the barge at the water stairs, trailed by her
men, Jenks joined them, out of breath.

"Did you find a horse with muddy hoofs?" she asked, still
striding toward the barge.

"Not that I saw, and the stableboy claims Pascal's too fat to
ride anymore."

"Ha!" she said, but she felt deflated. Why didn't all the pieces
of the Pascal puzzle fit? "He may be bald as a marble ball, but
that does not mean he still couldn't visit the wig-maker," she insisted.

"But before I approached them, I did overhear the two
grooms mention the wig-maker's granddaughter, running their
mouths with village gossip," Jenks told her. "Guess the girl fell
and broke her arm Friday. Since Pascal wasn't here, she hired a
barge to London to get it set and never came back. A pretty
wench, that's what they were saying."

Elizabeth felt sick to her soul. "Broke her arm . . . couldn't
find Pascal and went to London for help," she whispered. "To
find him or any physician? Ned," she ordered, gripping her
hands so tightly together her fingers went numb, "go back to the
tavern and get a more complete description of that girl. I'll wager
a throne I can tell you what she looked like down to a strawberry
birthmark on her throat."

Chapter
THE ELEVENTH

*The pimpernel is of the power to mitigate pain,
to cure inflammations and hot swellings and to help
the King's Evil.*

JOHN GERARD
The Herball

WELCOME BACK TO COURT, DEAR COUSIN, AND
my Lords Lennox and Darnley," Elizabeth declared
with a set smile on her face and a slight inclination of
her head. A few hours after returning from Chelsea, Elizabeth
Tudor sat on a raised dais in her presentation chamber, under the
scarlet and gold canopy of state emblazoned at its top with *E.R.*
Though she tried to sound pleasant and pleased, her voice could
have etched steel.

The queen's cousin Margaret curtsied, as her husband,
Matthew Stewart, and their son, the seventeen-year-old Henry,
bowed. As ever, the woman somehow overshadowed both her
handsome heir and her brawny husband. But, Elizabeth vowed
silently, she shall never again overshadow her queen.

A few well-chosen advisers stood below the throne, and the

ladies-in-waiting surrounded her, but by usual standards the vast
room was greatly devoid of courtiers. It wouldn't do to make this
anything broaching a state occasion, Her Majesty had told Cecil.
He was presently conferring with his man who had examined
both Katherine Grey and her husband before they'd been sent
into exile. Obviously, that news had not spread yet, or Margaret
Stewart would not dare to look so smug.

"We are grateful to be with you again, beloved cousin,"
Margaret replied with a broad smile that flashed her large teeth.
She had some sort of metal filigree box in her hands, mayhap a
gift, Elizabeth noted.

"It has been far too long," the queen declared, "though you
seem to thrive distant from our presence. Clever doctors, I take
it, have kept you and your entire family hale and hearty."

If that barb pierced the Stewarts' bubble of a triumphal return, no one showed it. The attractive Margaret, curse her, had
always been popular at court. If she soon had the usual contingent clinging to her skirts, so much the better. That way the
Stewarts would not so easily spot the spies assigned to each of
them the moment they'd stepped off their barges.

"How I have missed Whitehall and London," Margaret went
on with a dramatic sigh that would have done Ned Topside
proud. "Though of course," she added, almost preening, "I was
reared at Greenwich with your sister and know all of her—now
your—palaces intimately, Your Grace."

This half-Scottish daughter of King Henry VIII's sister had
been treated almost as a sister to Mary Tudor, while Elizabeth
used to be oft sent away for suspected disloyalty. Even now the
forty-seven-year-old Margaret craned her neck to look about as
if she owned Whitehall and everything in it.

Elizabeth dug her fingernails into her clenched palms. When
Mary Tudor was queen, Margaret had been assigned precedence

over the Princess Elizabeth. Even now, with her fate in the current queen's hands, Margaret dared to stare down her prominent nose at Elizabeth as if she would shriek a laugh, point, and shout again, "Protestant usurper! Daughter of the great whore Boleyn! Walk behind your sister and me! Your father has made a fine marriage match for me, but he can't even stomach you in his sight."

"And my young Lord Darnley," Elizabeth said as she rose and descended but one step to tower over the Stewarts, "how does your lute playing these days? Did your parents mayhap send you to France to find a better tutor than we English can provide?"

The rustling of satin gowns, all sounds, stopped. Everyone knew full well that Margaret and Matthew Stewart had defiantly dispatched their heir to the French court for a daring and dangerous reason last year. He was to entice the newly widowed Mary, Queen of Scots and France, to fall in love with him, for his royal Tudor blood made him a political marriage prize. Damn the Stewarts, connivers all.

"Indeed, Your Grace," the lad replied, straight-faced, "I learned a good deal while in France and would play for you, if you wish."

"When you do I shall closely watch your fingering to see what I can learn anew from you and your parents' endeavors and desires," Elizabeth replied as her gaze snagged her cousin's again.

"And that reminds me," Margaret said, lifting the filigree box, "that our son brought back for you from the queen herself a special gift. Sadly, kept away from you as we were, we could not present it to Your Grace until now."

Elizabeth came down another step. "From our kin Mary, you say? What is it then?" she asked warily, keeping a good distance as if some viper would coil from the depths of the small box.

"The latest rage in French cosmetics, Your Majesty," Margaret explained, "cochineal and alabaster facial powder. 'Tis such a lovely shade of rose I was tempted to try it myself, but Queen Mary told our dear son it was for you alone."

Elizabeth loved pretty, new things, but for all she knew, the shimmering stuff she saw within the box could be some dreaded poison. If only Meg Milligrew were here, she'd recognize the substance for what it truly was.

"It looks lovely," Elizabeth declared, "but I would be pleased to share it with you, cousin. I will see that some is sent you and have someone report back to me on how it looks on your face."

From the box Margaret extended, stiff-armed toward the queen, emanated an enticing aroma. Indeed, a floral or herbal fragrance must be included with the powdered shells and alabaster. Yet, considering the source, the queen scented a trap.

She reached out to click the box lid closed, nearly in Margaret's face, but the scent of powder had already permeated the air. Elizabeth jammed her finger under her nose to keep from sneezing, but several others, including Mary Sidney, exploded in racking *ca-choos*.

"I have no doubt, Cousin Margaret," the queen said, sounding stuffed-up now, "that you will report by hook or crook to Queen Mary concerning what I have said and done in the reception of this gift—and in *all* things."

For one moment, Margaret's face froze and her eyes stayed wide, as if she might sneeze herself but was determined not to. As if painted, her counterfeit smile did not shift nor did the brazen woman blink.

Elizabeth swept from the room while everyone dipped or bowed. The family wars, both domestic and foreign, would continue, the queen thought. But at least now the most intimate battles would be under her watch and on her playing fields.

❧   ❧   ❧

AFTER A SPECIAL EARLY EVENING PRAYER SERVICE AT Whitehall, beseeching power for the queen's healing touch on the morrow, Elizabeth rose from the royal pew. Gray shadows crawled in even here amidst lanterns and candles; the autumn wind howled outside. Harry Carey, standing in the doorway at the back of the chapel, gestured to her.

"Pascal's been brought in," he mouthed before she reached him. Since her cousin Margaret was among her women trailing behind, Elizabeth lifted a quick finger to her lips.

"Where?"

"At the Royal Physicians' Hall, examining candidates for the curing ceremony."

"I mean not where was he taken but where is he *now*?" she whispered as they began to walk together.

When her women caught up with her, even blunt, bold Harry evidently recalled this was covert business. He darted his eyes twice in the opposite direction from the royal apartments.

"Ladies," Elizabeth said, turning to face them with a smile, "my dear cousin Harry has a surprise for me, and I will join you later."

"A fine new hawk, no doubt," Margaret Stewart put in as if given leave to speak, "from the queen's Master of the Hawks. Always you are so generous to us, your blood kin," she added with a flash of smile, though her voice was edged with sarcasm.

Elizabeth bit back a sharp retort. Motioning two guards— Jenks and Clifford—to follow, she preceded Harry in the direction he had indicated, then turned to Jenks as she walked. "Hie yourself to my privy library and fetch that bag with the timepiece and scourge we found in Chelsea and bring them to me posthaste in . . . In?" she prompted Harry.

"Ah, so no one would catch wind of it, I stowed Pascal in the gatehouse chamber above the Sermon Court," he said as they walked the corridor overlooking the tiltyard.

"Good, for I shall preach him quite a sermon and, I swear, he will confess—to something. Make haste, Jenks," she urged as he dropped back. She heard him break into a run going in the opposite direction.

"But I was thinking," Harry told her, "if you have Pascal arrested, you'll be short a physician for the curing ceremony in the morn. And if you yet want me to take a few men and search the cellar of the Royal Physicians' College Hall while that ceremony's going on, I won't be about to protect you there."

"Harry, I will be fine. I believe it is God's will I continue the healing ceremony. It is in a public, holy place which will be packed with my full contingent of Yeomen Guards and Gentlemen Pensioners, not to mention my closest courtiers."

"Namely, Lord Robert Dudley, who watches you—well, like a hawk."

She said naught to that as they climbed the lantern-lit stairs to the gatehouse. "As for being short a physician," she told him, "I shall tell Dr. Huicke, despite his age and bad knees, I need him there tomorrow. God knows, I ignore my household physicians too much lately anyway. They've been vexed to no end that I have twice summoned Dr. Burcote."

Despite her assurances to Harry, the queen was quite anxious about the service for the Curing of the Queen's Evil tomorrow. She was no coward, but she wanted out of London where a poxed effigy or leeched body could appear in her privy, protected property. She yearned for open spaces where villains could not materialize from nor melt into crowds.

From Hampton Court she could see more clearly and plan her next moves. It was but a short barge ride from London, so she could easily dispatch her Privy Plot Council members to do what they must, arrest who was guilty. Cecil had deduced from his interrogator's questioning of Katherine Grey and her husband that, even if they were being used by outside hostile forces, they were hardly instigators. Then who was?

Harry opened the door for the queen, and she entered. Peter Pascal's great bulk blotted out the last of the outside light from where he stood at the window. The chamber contained several armchairs set back against the walls and three tapestries of a hunt scene. Lanterns hung from the old wall sconces. The queen indicated that Harry's two men should step outside, but she kept him and Clifford with her. Pascal made a bow so low he almost toppled onto his face.

"I visited Chelsea this day," she began, moving into the middle of the room while the men seemed to crowd the corners.

"I heard such, Your Majesty," he admitted after a brief, awkward pause. "My steward sent word you were just passing by and examined my house, including my privy chapel. And that you dubbed my home a cathedral to my mentor—"

"Is it not?" she demanded, her voice rising. "I swear you are practicing idolatry at the least! Do you not adore Sir Thomas More as if he were some saint to you? And would you not do anything to avenge his loss, even on the one who had naught to do with his demise?"

"Naught to do . . ." he choked out before he seized control of himself. His voice had momentarily gone so high-pitched he almost squeaked. "Your Majesty, the men who died because they would not sign your father's Act of Supremacy making him—now you—head of the English church, your birth which caused—"

"Enough!" she shouted, smacking her fist into her palm instead of his face. "Let the past be past! Let us pursue this another way, then. To what lengths would you go to discredit, annoy, or try to terrify me? You and your crony, Dr. Caius, who used to serve at court, think you know all my medical secrets, do you not? The queen fears the pox, you tell each other, and she detests being leeched. We shall show her! We will work closely with those who would usurp her place, starting with the Scottish Earl of Lennox, mayhap poor, pliable Katherine Grey. Let us encourage her to bear heirs to supplant this queen."

He stared aghast at that tirade, then seemed to recover himself. "I—well, yes, both of us did urge the Lieutenant of the Tower to allow Katherine to meet and have talks with her husband—"

"Talks? 'S blood and bones, if my learned doctors believe only talks would result from two defiant, passionate young rebels being left alone together, I have no hope of medical progress in my realm. So do not ask me again for corpses to dissect, though you would love to dissect me!"

"Your Grace, I beg you," he said, clasping his fat fingers together so they went stark white, "have pity and mercy, for I am guiltless of your other accusations of trying to harm your person. Physicians take an oath to do no harm, to rescue, to preserve."

Finally, the man looked and sounded terrified. Good, she thought, for it was high time to turn the screws again. But where was Jenks? As if her desire had summoned him, a knock sounded on the door. He entered, out of breath, with the sack she had called for.

"Ah," the queen said, taking it and drawing out the still mud-encrusted timepiece, which she dangled by its short chain. "Look what has turned up. Do you know where you lost it?"

He stepped forward but did not reach for it. "I evidently lost it where you found it, Your Majesty, but since it was lost indeed, I know not where."

"Do not mince words with me!"

"I swear by all that's holy, the last time I had it was at the physicians' hall the day after your visit. That would be Saturday, September the twenty-sixth. I thought I laid it down on the table in our council chamber. I have searched high and low for it, as it was a gift from . . ."

"From?" she prompted.

"A dear friend."

"Let me guess. Sir Thomas More?"

He squared his trembling shoulders. "God's truth."

"Peter Pascal, Physician of the Royal College of London," she droned as if she would pronounce some dire verdict, "did you treat a Chelsea girl, one Anne Wyngate, for a broken right arm Friday last?"

"Anne Wyngate? The old wig-maker's granddaughter? I did not, and haven't seen her for days," he declared, his voice steady now. "Why, I spent that day—that very day you visited the Royal College of Physicians—with you, Your Majesty."

"A scant two hours I can vouch for. And for all I know, Anne could have sought your help the next day in London or Chelsea."

"But what has any of that to do with my lost timepiece? And something else I recall now," he added, his words becoming so rushed they slurred. "It was lost somewhere at the College. On the day you sent William Cecil to peruse our books—that very Saturday morning you just mentioned—I told him I had lost my timepiece, that I was looking for it. I am certain I did, so ask him!"

Evidently emboldened by his defiance, Pascal reached for his timepiece, but she snatched it away and dropped it back in the bag. "Your timepiece is sullied, and your testimony may be, too, doctor. But let us examine one thing more together."

She drew out the leather, plaited scourge that she had seized from his study and shook it once at him. The little pieces of bone at the end of the thongs clicked together. He gaped at it as if it were a sheath of serpents.

"And your house steward inadvertently mentioned," she went on, "that you wear a hair shirt like that relic of Sir Thomas on the altar in your privy shrine to him." She fixed him with her narrowed gaze. "Will you deny using that and this, too, so I must have my men bare your back to testify against you? For what misdeeds or secret sins does a learned, wealthy physician punish and flagellate himself, Dr. Pascal?"

"I—I . . ." He staggered back into the wall, then righted himself. "For not being worthy of him—Sir Thomas. I live my entire life morally, helping others to be more worthy. But I swear I am innocent of harming the Wyngate girl—or you."

Their eyes met and held. She had given John Caius another chance, and her proof was yet tenuous against Dr. Pascal too. Nor could she afford to gut her Royal College of Physicians by sacking its leaders, not yet, not before the ceremony tomorrow. And not when she was determined to advance the estate of medical arts in her realm.

But it was this man's pitiful admission from the depths of his soul that had softened her rage at him. Each mortal, she well knew, however brilliant, blessed, or powerful, carried dark faults and failures within. It was a bloody, brutal struggle to try to cure the plagues of one's past.

"Swear not to me, nor by your Sir Thomas," she said, her voice quiet now. "If Lord Cecil says you speak the truth about telling him you lost your timepiece by early Saturday, I will see you at the ceremony tomorrow morning, where you will do your duty under the watchful eye of those I can trust. I do not wish to let your patients nor my people down."

"I—yes, of course, Your Majesty," he said, blinking back

tears with a sniff. "Dr. Caius and I will do our duty. We will be certain everything goes well at—at the Queen's Evil ceremony."

"I tell you flat out," Elizabeth said, enunciating every word, "and you may pass this on to Dr. Caius. As to duty, you shall both be removed from yours and have your licenses revoked should anything go even slightly askew tomorrow or hereafter. And while I am away at Hampton Court, you will have men with you to observe your every move, moves which must be your striving for the good of my people's health.

"Harry," she said, turning away from the wide-eyed doctor, "hold Dr. Pascal here until I speak with Lord Secretary Cecil, then have one of your men escort him either to prison or the physicians' hall. Your other man will find Dr. Caius and remain with him."

In a change of heart, she handed Pascal the sack with the timepiece, but threw the scourge at his feet. With Jenks and Clifford in tow, she headed for her privy quarters.

"A moment, Your Grace," Jenks said as he followed her into her apartments for a Privy Plot meeting. No one else was in the presence chamber yet. Jenks went down on one knee though he looked up at her.

"Your Gracious Majesty," he began, his face so in earnest, "I've protected you for years and would give my life for you."

"I know that, my man. Say on."

"I do not like the tactic of allowing those we suspect to keep close to your person, guards or not."

"I have had Katherine Grey and her lord sent to separate rural exile, and word of that will be a warning. Everyone else is under watch, whether they know it or not, even my Lord Dudley. But," she added, wringing her long fingers, "I yet hope those behind this effigy plot are so desperate that they will make another rash move and so be snared."

"But they are getting more desperate in their deeds," he argued. "First just that poxed dummy, but now corpses."

"I do the work of our blessed Lord's healing touch tomorrow," she assured him, wishing she could likewise comfort herself as she bent to touch his shoulder. "All will be well, for He has put me on the throne of this realm and, no doubt, means to keep me here a good while."

"Hmph," Kat said, making them both jump as she came into the room from the queen's bedchamber. "Wish I hadn't heard your brother and sister say the same in their youth, then both ruling but a few scant years apiece."

"But neither was healthy as I am!" Elizabeth shouted, throwing up her hands. "Is no one on God's green earth, not even my intimates, on my side?" She stomped into her bedchamber and slammed the door.

≈   ≈   ≈

TRUMPETS ANNOUNCED THE QUEEN'S ARRIVAL AS SHE walked the long aisle of the Abbey's nave toward the altar. Gowned in black and gold, wearing the traditional embroidered apron for the ceremony, she pulled a long velvet train her ladies held for her. Courtiers, including the Stewarts, awaited her arrival. Pikemen lined the way to hold back those in the pews or standing in the crowded church; her Gentlemen Pensioners followed, interspersed with ladies-in-waiting, also all bedecked in ebony hue. Before the altar awaited the black-garbed physicians, those of the college and the queen's household, fourteen in total number. Only the afflicted, waiting their turns off to the side, were clothed in white.

The scrofula, or Queen's Evil disease, was similar to the small pox in that it could cause facial disfigurement and blindness, but unlike the pox, it was not often fatal. Instead of sunken pits on the skin, neck tumors were its dreaded signature and legacy. But for salvation by the royal touch, which the English and French had long sworn by, the disease was treatable but not curable.

Pitying the waiting victims, Elizabeth darted surreptitious looks at those she would be touching: forty-some folk, as many men as women and several children. Her gazed snagged Dr. Caius's then Pascal's. Both looked wary, watchful. Mayhap, she thought, she had put—if not the fear of God—the fear of queen into them.

Turning carefully while her women draped her train behind her, Elizabeth Tudor sat on the throne and steadied herself for the ritual that would precede the touching.

                                                  ☙   ☙   ☙

WOULDN'T TOUCH THIS WEIRD RUBBISH WITH A pikeman's staff," Harry Carey whispered to his companion as he lifted their lantern toward the glass jars on the shelves in the cellar of the Royal College of Physicians. "Looks like a damned butcher's shop. Wait till she hears about this."

"But it could all be part of their trade," Jason Nye, one of Cecil's scriveners, muttered. Two of Cecil's other secretaries were keeping the doctors' servants busy upstairs with questions. They'd gone to the front door while Harry and Nye, like foul footpads, had sneaked in the back.

The two men stood, Harry in disgust, Nye in awe, of things floating in what appeared to be—smelled to be—vinegar. An eyeball, an ear, a hand, a woman's breast, and things unnameable.

"They could have gotten those through accidents or necessary amputations," Nye said, as if defending the doctors. "Or on a hunt. But for the hand and breast, they could be animal parts."

"Could be," Harry agreed, mesmerized as he squinted at the

organs. He had seen such when deer were gutted but not pickled and put on display. "How about these then?"

They moved on to shelves of bones—obviously human—a rib cage, even a grinning skull which Harry was tempted to turn to the wall.

"When the sextons bury new folk in city graveyards, you know the older bones are put in charnel houses or sometimes tossed aside, least of the poorer sort," Nye said.

"Still, this kind of thing will give her reason to pursue them further, though I think she was wondering if we'd find corpses or at least effigies here. Look, you're the scrivener, so why don't you go through that stack of papers quick while I rummage about a bit more." Harry pointed to a pile of paper impaled on a thick pin, the kind the doctors employed for bleedings if they didn't want to use a lancet.

"I'll need our light then," Nye informed him and moved away with it.

Harry didn't like the idea of poking into the shadows down here, but they were both armed. There was absolutely nothing to fear, he tried to buck himself up.

❧   ❧   ❧

ELIZABETH FOUGHT BACK THE PANIC SHE OFTEN FELT when she faced those who were so grievously afflicted that it made others stare. She tried to look only into the eyes of each scrofula victim as various doctors ushered them forward. Most of the ill women seemed awestruck and the men resigned; tears tracked down several cheeks. The children shuffled forward trustingly, and the queen squeezed each of their shoulders to stay them. One poor man, evidently a patient of Dr. Pascal, got a coughing jag and flecked her apron and hands with his saliva before Pascal pulled him away.

With each touch, her chaplains took turns reciting, "He shall lay hands upon the sick, and they shall recover." Another intoned the Lord's Prayer as the sufferers continued to come two at a time to kneel before her. The queen placed her hands on the head of each and made the sign of the cross on their foreheads. The latter was a part of the ritual that rattled both the Protestants and Puritans, but, in this instance, she didn't wish to tamper with tradition.

Each time, she repeated, "I touch thee and God heals thee," then hung a newly minted gold angel coin on a ribbon around the patient's neck. The coins bore the image of the archangel Michael, and she knew a fierce underground trade in them abounded. People believed that, if they could not be touched for the Queen's Evil by their monarch, perhaps owning an angel coin, called a touch piece, could heal them.

❧   ❧   ❧

CAN'T BEAR TO TOUCH, LET ALONE SMELL SOME OF these healing herbs down here either, like they're moldy or rotten," Harry told Nye as the man skimmed through the papers stuck on the spike. "I'd be a night soil man afore I'd be a doctor."

"Mm," Nye said, bent over one parchment for a long while. "They do smell horrid, so you'd best tell Her Grace that. Physicians are supposed to buy herbs fresh from the apothecaries."

"The Royal College is on a crusade to shut them down if they don't toe the line, so maybe this tripe is evidence against them," Harry muttered.

"That's what a lot of these other papers are about," Nye said. "Lists of apothecary shops they intend to raid or examine somehow, some with charges already against them."

"No correspondence with Katherine Grey or the Stewarts?"

"Ah, no, just a fascinating letter from a London doctor from Norwich, about a water droplet vapor theory of spreading disease. It really makes sense that plagues and pestilence are not just God's judgment, since the good die as fast as the evil. At least, I always thought so. You know, my lord," Nye went on, "had my family money or position, I'd have wanted to be a physician, but here I am, Lord Cecil's scrivener—and covert informant."

"Damn it, if there's nothing in that pile worth a fig, stop dawdling. At least we found no sign of effigies no matter how well Pascal can paint or Caius can mix plasters. And no skeleton or corpse; that's what the queen was fearing, I warrant. Come on, man. Let's go!"

∽   ∽   ∽

IT WAS TIME FOR THE QUEEN TO DEPART, BUT ELIZABETH hated to leave the afflicted. She wished she could do more, speak with at least one individually, encourage another. It was tempting to break the pattern of the ritual, to tell each sufferer she grieved for them, would pray for them. But that might sound as if she doubted their cure. On cue, with a final hard look at Drs. Caius and Pascal, she rose, then waited for her ladies to lift her train.

Faces of people she knew and those she didn't blurred by as she made her way down the long aisle in stately fashion, looking straight ahead. Cecil had half vouched for Pascal's truthfulness about losing his timepiece, as her secretary of state recalled the man told him that he lost something at least. 'S blood and bones, so many strands of this web must be unwound.

First, she must confer with Harry and Cecil's man about their search of the cellar of the Royal College of Physicians. Cecil was also trying to discover whether Caius and Pascal, when they were supposedly called to Oxford and Cambridge instead of tending to poor Kat, could have visited Margaret Douglas and her son at Sheen.

Suddenly, just ahead of her, a disturbance ... a reed-thin girl with a sad countenance kneeling in the aisle.

"Please, Your Gracious Majesty," her tremulous voice carried to Elizabeth as guards hastened to step between the women. "If you please, Your Majesty ..."

"Stay your hands!" Elizabeth called to her guards as they converged to move the girl back into her place. "Does she need the queen's touch or to ask a boon?"

Behind the young woman, on the edge of the aisle, half sat, half leaned a handsome man with piercing gray eyes and a slightly swollen face on one side, though not in the neck where scrofula showed itself. Mayhap he was the woman's husband or brother, and a toothache had puffed half his face like that. He knelt now as did others, even in their pews when they saw the queen deigned to stop.

"Another angel?" the queen asked. "Is there another coin?"

"The number was counted exactly," someone answered, a voice like Dr. Caius's, from the retinue behind her.

Elizabeth placed her hands on the girl's trembling, thin shoulders. She had her hands thrust into her sleeves, and her mouse-brown hair spilled partly over her face. Her complexion looked perfectly smooth and pale, yet her eyes seemed overly bright, feverish, unlike the other sufferers. Though she wore a sort of wrap around her neck, the queen could discern no tumorous swellings there.

"Is it the scrofula?" she asked the girl.

"More than ..." she got out before she nodded or hung her head.

"Be bold in the face of the hard times," Elizabeth told her. "The queen touches thee but may God heal thee."

She lifted her hands to the sufferer's head. As if her companion could sense the girl would falter or swoon, he reached for her, evidently to steady her shoulders or help lift her chin. No, he pressed a sachet of some sort to her nose to keep her from fainting. But the thin thing exploded into a series of violent, racking sneezes.

The queen stepped back. "See to her comfort and care," she told the girl's companion, who nodded and pulled her back into their pew, covering her nose and mouth with a large handkerchief. Exhausted now, the girl seemed to swoon in his arms. "My lady," Elizabeth said, turning back to Mary Sidney, "see that she gets some coins if not an angel."

"You are the angel of us all," the man with the girl said in a deep, fine voice. That very moment the queen glanced across the rapt crowd and saw Meg Milligrew in the shadows of a gray stone pillar, her clasped hands pressed to her mouth, watching. For the first time in two years, their gazes held. As the former herb girl lifted her hand in a weak wave, Elizabeth thought Meg looked guilty—caught at something.

While Mary Sidney spoke to the man with the girl, the queen turned away with a brief nod at Meg, then walked from the Abbey into clear light and fresh air.

Chapter
THE TWELFTH

*My opinion is grounded upon reason too, not upon
fancy nor hearsay. . . . All modern physicians know not
what belongs to a sympathetical cure, no more than a
cuckoo knows what belongs to flats and sharps in music.*

NICHOLAS CULPEPPER
The English Physician

"YOUR GRACE, I WISH YOU WOULD HAVE TAKEN AND
tried that powder from your cousin Margaret," Mary
Sidney protested. "But then I wish you'd wear my mermaid pin again," she added under her breath, with a little pout.

"Don't let Margaret Stewart take you in too, Mary, with her
cleverness and charm." The queen answered only Mary's first
concern, for she saw the mermaid pin as a reminder of a dreadful night. "She may be my kin, but she is not my friend."

"Oh, I would not, Your Grace," she insisted. "I just meant the
powder was such a soft color, and it smelled fabulous, if a bit
strong. I think the scent was lavender and meadowsweet, but I
wormed out of Margaret that it had madonna lily root crushed in
it too. I've oft said, the bright red face powder we English use on
our cheeks is so stark against our white-as-milk complexions."

"Mary," Robin Dudley said sternly, "our queen needs naught to enhance her charms, especially not something sent from the Queen of Scots."

"Thank you, Robin," Elizabeth said and smiled his way. She felt so free and alive out here on the Thames, with the crenellated walls and chimney clusters of Hampton Court coming into view above the bright autumn trees. But the way Robin kept eyeing her, top to toes, made her blush in the cool breeze.

The royal barge, easily discernible by size as well as by its banners and crimson bunting, shot smoothly upstream with twenty men-at-oars bending their backs together. For once, the queen felt sorry for their labors, as her back ached. Yet whether commons or courtiers, ashore or adrift, folk they passed cheered and hurrahed to lift the royal spirits.

Perhaps after all, she would not have to dismiss the realm's chief physicians, thereby dealing the English medical arts a severe blow. Her cousin Harry and Cecil's man Nye had found nothing amiss in the cellar of the physicians' hall, though they had found plenty that was distasteful. But should she turn up more proof that her physicians were in league with the Stewarts, who were no doubt in deep with Mary, Queen of Scots, she'd mete out justice to them all.

"I'd swear that was Ben Wilton just shot past us in a rowboat," Ned Topside interrupted her thoughts.

Elizabeth threw off the blankets of crimson velvet from her legs and stood, arching her back. "In that distant craft?" she asked, pointing.

"The same."

"Not with Meg again? This far from London?"

"Not Meg, this time, unless she was hunkered down in the bottom of the boat. She's been known to hide herself."

"Meaning what?" Elizabeth demanded as she sank back onto

her seat and Ned folded his legs to sit again on a plump cushion at her feet. "I saw her plain as could be in the Abbey at the healing service two days ago," she went on, when he did not forthrightly answer. Though Elizabeth had wanted to set out for Hampton Court that very day, forty-eight hours of cold, pounding rain had much delayed them. "Ned," she pursued, "you look like the cat which swallowed the canary. Tell me flat what you mean by Meg hides herself."

"When you are in public, she likes to watch you from a little distance," he began, then seemed to wilt under her narrow-eyed gaze. "All right," he blurted, "I've learned that she was standing in an alley on Knightrider Street the day the effigy appeared in your coach. I even questioned her about it."

"On your own, without telling me?" she demanded, smacking her hands on her skirts.

"Nothing really came of it you don't already know, Your Grace, and for months—years—we weren't to speak of her."

"Mayhap not, but I have sent my courtiers and servants to buy from her nigh on since she left, though without telling her who sent them. Just as, dear Ned, should I dismiss you for keeping things from me, I would send Jenks and my other guards to hear you reciting doggerel in some tavern."

Ned jerked even more alert. "If you must know, Your Majesty," he blurted, "without telling her why, I did take a cutting of Meg's hair to compare to the effigy's wig."

"I caught you at that, and you still did not explain your actions. Your findings?"

"Its hue came close, I must admit. You see, you were so set on doctors being the ones skilled with plasters, wax, and false faces—"

"Doctors *and actors,*" she said, hitting his shoulder with her fist.

"Yes, well, the point is, apothecaries are skilled with those things too. I went off on a wild-goose chase, panicked it could be Meg. But now I—it just can't be," he added, rather lamely, she thought. "She could never have pulled all that off. And then, as Cecil always says, *sui bono,* what's the motive? I cannot fathom she'd want revenge, as she adores you—still."

"Unless she thought that by rattling my inherent confidence with threats of disease I would take her back. She used to dose me with herbs. Meg is at heart a healer. But even if she managed to buy or filch some effigy, she's not a murderess. Still," she mused aloud with a little shudder in the river breeze, "there is that ambitious husband who managed to be an eyewitness to some supposed doctor climbing my privy walls. When you met with Meg, how did you judge her emotional temperament?" Elizabeth asked, motioning Robin away when he looked as if he would interrupt.

"She misses you, Your Grace," Ned said. "She is clearly frustrated by being sent away from your service for something she believes Sarah Wilton—her former self—got her into. The marriage with that lout, I mean."

Elizabeth gripped the arms of her chair. "Yes, nothing worse than that, I'm sure. She'd lied to me, and I thought she must repair her marriage, but mayhap it is broken beyond repair."

"Oh, it always looks so beautiful in its autumn garb!" Kat Ashley cried. Elizabeth swung around to see her dear Kat pointing at vast, pink-bricked Hampton Court Palace set in its parkland and orchards. "So romantic," Kat enthused about her favorite place.

"By that, I hope you mean," Elizabeth called to her ladies, clustered a short distance from her own canopied seat, "that the view is exquisitely fair and you do not refer to the fact my father brought five of his six brides here to honeymoon."

Though she had meant it as a jest, everyone quieted. It was

common knowledge that the queen's mother's initials, once entwined with King Henry's, had been chiseled off when she was
beheaded to be hastily replaced by Queen Jane Seymour's. Still,
Elizabeth loved the place and felt close to both her parents here.

The infamous Cardinal Wolsey, who had presented the
building and grounds to the king as a gift that was really a bribe,
had chosen this site because the air was so salubrious. The cardinal had been obsessed with good health, so Elizabeth was doubly
glad to be here. God forgive her, she wanted to distance herself
from those poor souls afflicted with the scarring of the Queen's
Evil and get miles away from poxed effigies and dead women's
bodies. She wanted to shake off the cloying scent of the Scots
queen's gift of bloody-hued powder offered by the wily Margaret
Stewart, the odor of intrigue all around her.

She shook her head to clear it of too many disturbing images,
like the face of that poor girl who had kneeled in the aisle at the
Abbey. Mary Sidney had inquired where she had lived and found
it was in some dreadful place called Gutter Lane. Yet when she
and Harry had tried to take an angel there, the landlady claimed
she'd never heard of the girl or the man with her. Then Elizabeth
recalled again Meg's face as she stood behind the ill girl and her
doctor, fearful, hopeful.

"Ned," she said looking down him, "when this barge returns
to London to fetch more of my things, bring Meg Milligrew to
me on it. Just Meg, not Ben Wilton. Say only the queen has need
of some of her favorite strewing herbs, personally delivered. And
do not set yourself up as Meg's interrogator on your own."

"Of course, Your Majesty, I wouldn't."

"Ha," she said only, as she turned her eyes toward her safe
haven of Hampton Court.

                               ✧   ✧   ✧

THE FIRST TWO DAYS IN THE COUNTRYSIDE, ELIZABETH tended to state business but also led her courtiers on constitutional walks and pulse-pounding rides through the surrounding forest. On her way back to her royal apartments, she passed through Base Court, then under the Queen Anne Gateway, named for her mother, and into Clock Court. With everyone close around her, she looked up at the ornate astronomical clock above the arch.

"*Tempus fugit,* my queen," Robin whispered, but she ignored the fact he dared to add, "and for a beautiful young woman, adored by one particular man, who has loved her always, *carpe diem.*"

Elizabeth was thinking that she must indeed seize each day, hold to each moment she was queen. She must protect her realm from all plots that would do her person and her people harm. Staring at the intricate copper dials she read the hour, the sign of the zodiac, the month and day, and the number of days since the beginning of the year. Even the moon's phases and the time of high tide at London Bridge were clearly marked. It was a brilliantly conceived, ornate machine, a far cry from Peter Pascal's physicians' timepiece, and yet it could not give her the answers she must discover and link.

"I have much to do," she said only and walked briskly upstairs with everyone scurrying behind her. But she paused at the top of the stairs to catch her breath. She had perhaps overdone her exercise lately, for her back hurt even more. If truth be told, she ached all over. Her heart pounded, and she was perspiring overmuch.

"Mayhap I should lie down for just a moment before my next meeting," she told Kat quietly as she reached her privy chambers and went in. She walked directly to the windows and threw the casements open to look out over the fading evening sky that sil-

houetted the twisted chimneys, mazes of rooftops, and the proud
statues of heraldic animals called the queen's beasts. As if she
dozed standing, disjointed images danced through her tormented
mind: queen's beasts, queen's evil, queen's cure, queen's kingdom.

෴   ෴   ෴

"TIME?" ELIZABETH SAID, SITTING UP IN HER BED,
where someone had pulled a coverlet over her. Darkness
had descended. Only a few candle flames flickered. "What time
is it?" she demanded.

Kat came close with Mary Sidney. Dr. Huicke, with two
other household physicians, appeared over their shoulders.

"It's near morning," Kat said brusquely, pushing Elizabeth's
shoulders back so she lay down again. "You were running a slight
fever from all your exertion yesterday, so we thought it best not
to disrobe you, and just let you sleep, though Dr. Huicke plans to
bleed the fever out of you."

"No bleeding," the queen commanded. "I am fine and—'S
bones, Kat, you let me miss my meeting with Cecil and the others last night!"

"My Lord Cecil thought this best too," Mary put in. "Please,
just lie back, Your Grace."

"Stuff and nonsense! I have much to do!" she protested and
sat up again until the rush of dizziness hit her. "Give me something to drink. If I have a little fever, I need to replace the liquid
I'm sweating out, don't I, doctor? I'm parched. Well, do not just
stand there. Someone fetch me ale or beer!"

Mary instantly offered white wine, which the queen drank
straight down. The aftertaste revealed some sort of medicine was
in it. She realized her hair was loose and matted to her forehead;
her gown felt clammy. Oh, hell, she'd caught a chill on the river

or hunting. Perhaps she had best sleep this off. How had it come on so fast?

"I need to make a diagnosis, Your Majesty," old Dr. Huicke muttered, daring to swipe at her wet throat then smell her sweat as if she'd given him leave to do so. "I fear something more than fever."

"Just let me sleep!" Elizabeth shouted, but her own voice sounded as if it came from far outside her. "I'm just fine!"

❦   ❦   ❦

I'M SCARED TO DEATH," MEG ADMITTED TO NED AS THEY alighted from the royal barge on the landing at Hampton Court. She was also thrilled to death, merely to be in Ned's company. She carried the smaller sack of her crushed strewing herbs, and Ned, bless him, hefted the one that was nearly as big as a woolsack. "I prayed for this, Ned," she bubbled on, "dreamed of it—that she'd summon me for strewing herbs or for anything!"

"Don't get your hopes up too high," he warned as they walked up toward the sprawling palace together.

But Meg could have danced across the moat and not even used the bridge. "Even when her Tudor temper blows," she told him, "she does seem to get over it. But it's taken her so long to want to see me, mayhap to ask me to serve her again."

"Hell's gates," Ned muttered, "she still cares for Robin Dudley, too, but she's never quite let him back in her heart, so stop this silly prating!"

"But he's a man, and you know the queen with men . . ." Meg went on, then let her words trail off. The moment they entered the palace proper, she could scent something amiss. Messengers ran to and fro while courtiers stood in clumps whispering. No one smiled or laughed. Ned, too, picked up on it.

"I'll bet bad news has come about the Scots queen," he confided, keeping his voice low. "Up in Edinburgh, she is, just biding her time to cause trouble. Why, if she weds again before the queen and has an heir— Look, there's Jenks."

Meg was dismayed when Jenks's face did not light to see her. He barely slowed his feet as he went by. "The queen's sore ill," he muttered, keeping his voice low as if Her Majesty would overhear and cuff him.

"Of what?" Ned called after him, but Jenks didn't turn back.

"Come on," Ned said. "I've always been able to cheer her when she's low, even with one of her headaches, and I wager she'll be glad to have your strewing herbs too. What's in them, did you say?" he asked, bouncing the aromatic bag he carried for her.

"Mostly meadowsweet and woodruff," she said, then added calmly, however hard her heart was pounding, "and I've something else to tell her of, though it's back in London. You know how she always fusses about her complexion. I've something good to hide scars or blemishes, should she ever need it."

      🙠   🙠   🙠

FACES. SOLEMN, SAD FACES LEANED OVER HER, CAME and went. Kat's, Mary's, Cecil's. Beloved Robin's. And someone else, a doctor, more than one, prying in her throat and probing with needles to draw blood before she cursed them away. Which doctor was that? Surely Cecil would not let Pascal or Caius near her.

They spoke darkly of diagnosis. No matter. She wouldn't let them bleed her, screamed when they tried to use a lancet. "And no leeches," she was sure she told them. "No leeches and don't you dare tie me down or I'll have your heads!"

But those familiar faces merged with dreadful demons. The faces of beasts, queen's beasts. And a loud ticking, ticking of a gigantic clock, her mother's clock or that evil doctor's, dropped in the mud when he tried to kill that old woman.

"Lovey. Lovey, you have a rash of little spots. You must let the doctors treat you. It could be the pox."

"Get away from me! Just let me sleep!"

Kat is an old woman. Kat is ill and doesn't know what she says. Call that foreign doctor. The doctors of the realm cannot be trusted. Don't let Kat die.

"Do not let Kat die," she ordered them.

Or was someone trying to kill her, Elizabeth, the queen?

Sounds and senses slowed, dragged. Dizziness sat on her chest and poked in her head. She seemed to be spinning, even when she clung to Kat, even when she thought she must be lying still and exhausted on her bed.

"That's all right now, lovey," a voice said, a nice voice. "Just drink this for Dr. Huicke then."

Something cool spilled down her throat, clear down between her breasts. Was she naked and floating in a fountain? Was she dead? No, she was so hot, and her head hurt.

"It doesn't look good," a man's voice said. "Those pustules clearly indicate the pox. We'd best send for Lord Cecil."

Elizabeth screamed and sat straight up, hitting at all of them, fighting, flinging halfhearted curses and fists. "No, no! Get away from me! I don't have the pox, never have the pox. No doctors. No doctors!"

She fell back gasping. She couldn't breathe. Everywhere she looked—in the box of French powder, in the fountain and the coach, was a scarlet river deeper than the Thames. In her veins, behind her eyes, behind the plot to hurt her, she saw only blood-red fear and evil.

HOURS, DAYS LATER, WILLIAM CECIL SAT OUTSIDE THE doors to the queen's chambers, as if he were another of her guards. He could not bear to sit inside any longer, listening to the terrified and terrifying ravings of the most brilliant woman he had ever known. He shook his head, angry with himself that he had thought of her in the past tense. But clearly showing the pox on her hands and face, she had been delirious for five days. She was barely clinging to life with a disease that killed one-fourth of those it assailed. He was scared to death that he and England were going to lose her.

Other members of her advisory council kept coming up to him with ideas and questions. Who would rule if Elizabeth died? She had no heir and had named no one. Surely, not that Papist, French and Scots Queen Mary. And Cecil didn't trust the queen's hovering Stewart kin any farther than he could throw her Grey kin, though the latter had been sent away to permanent house arrest. Though Dr. Peter Pascal from the Royal College of Physicians had arrived and was demanding to see the queen to diagnose and treat her, Cecil had ordered him not to be admitted unless Her Majesty expressly asked for him. And then Cecil intended to go in with the man, who hung about like some bloated harbinger of doom.

Cecil sniffed hard and wiped his nose as his eyes skimmed the others, crying, whispering. Every now and then the exhausted Mary Sidney would pop out of the sickroom to give her brother and everyone the latest word on how the queen was faring. Dear old Kat Ashley had refused to leave Elizabeth's side.

Her stalwart cousin Harry paced the corridor until Cecil almost screamed at him to stop his footfalls back and forth, softer, louder, as maddening as dripping water. The Stewart contingent of Margaret and Matthew sat on chairs, probably imagining themselves on the soon-to-be-vacated throne of England. Earlier, he'd noted they were whispering with Dr. Pascal. Gil Sharpe was crouched like a whipped pup by the queen's door, scribbling circles on a paper with black chalk.

And then Cecil lifted his gaze to note Ned Topside with Meg Milligrew huddled in a distant corner with two plump sacks at their feet. Seeing the herb girl here after her long exile brought back memories of earlier days when the motley band of what Elizabeth had always called her Privy Plot Council had struggled to save her so she could claim her throne.

Cecil rose from his seat and motioned Gil to follow. The boy leaped straight up with his hands still on the paper. He'd never yet, Cecil thought, lost the amazing agility of a thief who climbed on roofs and in and out windows. With Gil on his heels, Cecil made his way through the crowd toward Ned and Meg.

"Ned, mistress, with me," he said quietly and led them and the glum Gil down the corridor, away from the clumps of courtiers.

"How fares our queen, my lord?" Ned asked.

"God's truth, man," Cecil said as he slumped into a window seat and they dropped their sacks to stand before him, "events are not encouraging. It is the pox for certain."

"Can I not go to her?" Meg cried.

Cecil frowned and shook his head. "Her Grace summons up the strength to curse or throw off her household doctors' hands and, in the end, they are afraid to restrain or tie her down."

"Frail as she looks, she's strong," Ned insisted, his usually robust voice gone shaky. He put a hand on Gil's shoulder as if to steady himself or the lad. "She'll pull through."

"God grant it," Cecil said wearily. "And what is Mistress Milligrew doing here, and what is in the sacks?"

"Her Grace sent Ned for me and strewing herbs," Meg declared defiantly.

"Where is your husband then?" Cecil inquired.

"I haven't seen him for two days. I told Bett to tell him where I was when he came back, but as he hasn't showed up looking for me . . ." Her voice faded to nothing but a sigh.

"You do know that Ben Wilton was lurking a fortnight ago near the privy garden walls of Whitehall?" Cecil asked. "He claims he spotted a man who appeared to be a doctor climbing a ladder there."

"The night a woman's corpse was left in the privy fountain," Ned blurted before Cecil could stop him.

"A corpse? I—no," she said, looking shocked but angry too. "I didn't know. Of course, that's a public barge-landing there, and Ben, being once a barger, has friends around the place, no doubt."

One thing about the girl, Cecil thought, was that she was easy to read—at least she used to be. Yet how smoothly she had just slipped in an alibi for her husband. Cecil had never been as convinced as the queen that Meg could not recall her past—in a Papist family that had once served Queen Mary Tudor and had sworn to keep Elizabeth from her throne. Hell's gates, he scolded himself, this was no time to be going off the deep end mistrusting everyone in sight.

"I swear," Meg said, propping her hands on her waist, "Ben told me naught of that, though I don't know why. He's always asking me things about the queen and boasting anytime he's near her."

"I thought *you* could tell *me*," Cecil said, "and perhaps the queen thought you could tell her. Think on it. But it may all be moot," he added, shaking his head again, "if the household physicians can't calm her down in there and treat her—"

"My Lord Cecil!" Harry Carey called and windmilled his arm from a ways down the hall.

Cecil bolted to his feet, pushing between Meg and Ned while

Gil jumped lithely aside. "Has Her Majesty come to the crisis?" Cecil cried.

"No, she's talking again, but making terrible sense. She insists she's of sane mind and, should she die, wants to name Robert Dudley as Protector of the Kingdom."

       🙚   🙚   🙚

ELIZABETH HAD TO GASP FOR EACH WORD, EACH breath. "I will not have my tricky female cousins on my throne—none of them," she managed. She gripped Cecil's wrist. His skin felt icy. Her skin was on fire, as she always felt when Robin Dudley looked her way.

Robin had stood by her when they were facing death in the Tower. He had sent her flowers, loaned her money. He could not help it that his wife took a tumble down the stairs. And as sick as Elizabeth felt, she knew Cecil would bring back Katherine Grey to be queen if she died, because of her Protestant leanings. But she could not die. No one was getting her throne, not the Stewarts, not the Greys. Not that Scottish queen, whatever her name was. And not her Catholic sister, Mary Tudor. Or had Mary died and become an effigy, staring at her?

"Robin—Robert Dudley—I name as Lord Protector of England until a suitable regent—or monarch—can be found—if I—do not survive," she rasped out, speaking directly to the distraught-looking Cecil, though her entire council crowded around her bed. "Swear you will do it—swear," she demanded in a rasping wheeze.

Looking sick unto death themselves, each man, beginning with Cecil, nodded or murmured assent. She seized a thought then, before it flew away. Few could stomach Robin any more than Cecil could, but she knew they would have to work with him if it came to that. If not for their dead queen's sake, then for the kingdom's.

Exhausted to her very bones, swimming in the sweat of the fountain, she fell back on her pillows and was instantly asleep. But she heard voices floating, wrapping themselves around her after most of her council filed from the room.

Kat spoke. "She claimed she was sound of mind just before she said that, Lord Cecil, but she must have still been delirious."

Cecil's voice. "The damage is done. I'm taking things into my own hands before that traitor's son sits the throne. Protector, indeed. He'll try to become king. We'll have another war, like when the Greys and Dudleys tried to seize the Tudor throne from Queen Mary."

Kat. "We must tie her down and treat her. Her doctors have tried feverfew and figs to make her sweat out the poisons. Bleedings, which she fought, marigold in white wine, avens root, and much saffron, lupin, and snakeweed. And, of course, precious ground unicorn horn that helped me so, and then Dr. Huicke sent for the physicians from the Royal College in London and—"

"You must hold them off. I am fetching someone else."

"Not Dr. Caius? Pascal already waits without these doors!"

"Kat, I am going to find your own savior, if I can get there and back in time."

Again Elizabeth sank into the depths of velvet darkness. People kept fussing over her, wiping her face with a cool cloth. Was she dying? If so, maybe her own mother's hands were on her, sweet and soothing.

You shall not be afraid of the terror by night, nor the arrow that flies by day, nor of the pestilence that walks in darkness. Psalms, Elizabeth thought. Was a minister here reading Psalms, or were they in her own head? They should recite the one that would keep her safe from doctors who would harm her: *I have enemies against me. I will repay them. An evil disease, they say, clings ... clings ... to me.*

"I don't have the pox, cannot have the pox," she tried to tell the minister, to tell her mother, to tell her father too, if he would listen for once. "I don't have a rash and see no pox on my skin. See?" she insisted and groaned to find the strength to lift one hand before her own eyes.

But there, clear as can be even in this dim light, were the pustules in the pattern that had been on that mother and her children in Chelsea so long ago, and on that effigy, the effigy that had been made for a queen's funeral.

Elizabeth the Queen screamed and screamed.

❧   ❧   ❧

M Y LORD CECIL," MEG CALLED AND DROPPED HER BAG of strewing herbs to chase him down the corridor. Lord Hunsdon was hard on his heels too, but Cecil did not break stride, even when a woman's faint scream sounded, echoing behind them.

Meg wished that had been Catherine Howard's ghost screaming again, for she walked these halls at night, but she knew it was the queen.

"Come with me, mistress," Cecil ordered, not turning back, but flicking a wrist at her. "No reason for you to stay longer. I'll leave you in London. And Gil Sharpe, to me!" he called, and Meg saw the queen's young artist materialize from somewhere. "It does you no good, lad, to be moping around here. Best you be with your parents now and come back when Her Grace is—is much recovered."

"I don't know about Gil, but I want to be here," Meg protested. "I'll give her my herbs, at least. And I know a doctor who could help in London, a fine, learned one from Norwich, one who has worked with pox patients, the man she saw with that sick girl in the Abbey's aisle."

"Not now, mistress. Hold your tongue like Gil does and walk as fast."

But a shout behind them halted their haphazard parade down the hall. They stopped and turned to see Lord Robert Dudley hurrying after them. The man had a cluster of courtiers with him, including Matthew and Margaret Stewart. And Dr. Peter Pascal was clinging like a burr.

"My Lord Cecil, you cannot leave now," Dudley insisted. "The queen—and I, as possible, future Lord Protector—might have need of you. Where are you going?"

"On important business of the realm," Cecil clipped out and didn't bow, though Meg dropped the queen's former favorite a quick curtsy, and Gil bent in a half bow. "Now, if you'll excuse me, Lord Robert," Cecil said and left the man sputtering at being summarily dismissed.

"Where is the man Her Grace said is keeping an eye on Dudley?" Meg overheard Cecil whisper to Baron Hunsdon, who walked at his shoulder, while she and Gil came behind. She pricked her ears up even more.

" 'Tis me, my lord," the queen's cousin said, "along with an informer who reports to me and is serving as his new footman. So we are leaving Dudley behind, basically unwatched."

"Thank God Her Grace is surrounded by watchers right now," Cecil said. "Kat's turned guard dog, and even Mary Sidney would die before she'd let anyone—including her own brother— harm the queen. I believe Her Grace will be safe here, as safe as someone stricken with smallpox can be."

"Tell *me* where we're going then?" Lord Hunsdon said.

"I believe you know where to find that German Dr. Burcote from fetching him before."

"Aye, if he's still in town, or in England, for that matter."

"If he's not, we're doomed."

Chapter

THE THIRTEENTH

*Diverse physicians do boil with the root of alkanet and
wine, sweet butter until such time as it becomes red,
which they call red butter. It be good to drive forth the
measles and small pox, if it be drunk in the beginning
with hot beer.*

≈ JOHN GERARD
The Herball

GRAY SHADOWS CLOTTED IN DOORWAYS AS MEG AND
Gil trudged up the Strand from the Whitehall landing
where the royal barge had put in. En route Meg had
overheard that Cecil and Lord Hunsdon planned to ride
posthaste to fetch a German doctor, then return to Hampton
Court. It was not at all the way Meg had planned things, hoped
for things. Though Cecil had put Meg off when she'd tried to
mention Dr. Clerewell, she was determined to contact the physician and beg him to hie himself and some Venus Moon Emollient
back on another barge with her.

Meg and Gil passed a few people who whispered fur-
tively, scurrying through the dim, windy evening. The parish

night watchman trudged toward them with his lantern yet unlit.

"The queen dire ill at Hampton Court!" he called in his loud, singsong voice. Meg grabbed Gil's arm so hard he winced. "The queen dire ill of fever at Hampton Court!" He went on, passing them with a solemn nod, as if to verify his dreadful words. "Time o' night to stay within. The queen dire ill . . ." his voice trailed off as he disappeared around a corner.

Gil's wide, watery gaze met Meg's. So Londoners did know and were waiting, like everyone at the palace, to learn the queen's fate. At least the watchman had not blurted out that Her Majesty had the small pox, for that could cause even more panic.

When Gil shuffled along even slower, Meg gave him a poke in the ribs. Ordinarily, if she had been gone nigh on six days with the apothecary shop untended, she'd drag her feet too, afraid Ben would beat her and accuse her of dreadful things. But when he heard she might soon be back in the queen's good graces—if Her Majesty lived—Ben would surely even run her errand to fetch Dr. Clerewell so she wouldn't have to send Gil or Nick.

Poor Gil seemed as sunk-in-the-depths over the queen's illness as she was. He'd hardly responded when she'd signaled to him on board the barge to ask how his cure for muteness was faring.

Medicine made my throat sore, he'd finally answered her.

"Have you tried to talk more than usual?" she'd asked. "Have you really *wanted* to talk more?"

He'd shaken his shaggy head.

"Gil, that's part of any cure or healing, wanting it. But," she'd muttered, "I still say valley lily is what's needed and not the doctor's rosemary cure."

Gil had only shrugged and plunged back into his dark mood. Now her insides plummeted farther as she saw that the shop was black as pitch. She wondered if Ben had just gone out again or had he left her for good—it would be for her good, all right. She'd expected him to follow her to Hampton Court, demanding his due if the queen took her back. She fumbled for her key tied in the corner of her cloak and unlocked the door.

But Bett and Nick clambered down the dim stairs to greet them. "We been staying here, since folks knew you were gone," Nick said. "Didn't want these herbs to get thieved."

"We were going to bed," Bett went on. "The queen—she's not—not . . ." she stammered as she hugged Gil.

"Still hanging on, but the truth is she has the small pox."

"Lord have mercy," Nick said, starting to cross himself before he jerked his hand down. Bett began to cry while Gil just hung his head.

"Secretary Cecil's gone to fetch some special doctor to take back by barge posthaste," Meg explained. "But I want to have Dr. Clerewell go to the palace with me to offer his expertise. If he will, considering that he said the doctors haven't yet approved his Venus Moon . . . Oh, curse it," she muttered. "I wasn't supposed to tell who made the emollient. Bett, Nick," she went on, clasping their hands hard, "you've got to swear you won't tell anyone I let that slip—or that Her Grace has the pox either. She refuses to let any doctor make the diagnosis or treat her for it, stubborn to the end. . . ." Her words trailed off, and an awkward silence ensued, as if they were grieving her loss already.

"You want me to go fetch Clerewell then?" Nick offered. "I can slip 'round the night watchmen, see if the doctor will agree to try to help Her Grace. If only Ben were back, you could have him row the doctor to the palace."

"Row me and the doctor," Meg added. "You haven't seen Ben, then, either of you?"

"No," Bett admitted, reaching out to squeeze Meg's shoulder. "But then he always did stay out nights more and more of late."

"As much as I don't want him here, I hope no ill's befallen him," Meg said, walking behind the work counter to feel in the waning twilight shadows for the herb drawer she wanted. She'd get the Venus Moon out next, but she wanted to give Gil some chopped valley lily to chew. She owed Bett, Nick, even the boy so much for being here with her through the bad times as they once were through the good. And if it was the last thing she did, she was somehow going to get the good times back again.

"I'll return soon's I can," Nick promised. He darted upstairs and came down with his coat on and a lantern lit for them. He kissed Bett and ruffled Gil's hair, then hurried out the still-open door.

Meg seized a handful of dried lily valley stalks and thrust them in Gil's hands. "This is my own herbal cure for your muteness. Even if you continue to take Dr. Clerewell's rosemary tonic, chew this when you can. And practice trying to talk or you'll stay as rusty as . . ."

Her words trailed off as four men, three of them clearly armed with drawn swords, filled her front door to block out the last remnants of daylight. In the single, dim lantern glow inside, she could see their silhouettes but not their features. For one moment she thought Ben was back with some of his cronies, for several of them were large men with beefy shoulders. But the one in front, legs splayed, who must be their leader, was gaunt as a rail.

"What do you want at this hour?" she demanded.

"A look around your shop, Mistress Sarah Wilton, alias Meg Milligrew," the gaunt man said ominously. He extended to her a piece of parchment with a blob of wax on it. "Fetch more lights for this den of darkness!" he ordered his men.

"Now, see here! You can't—" Meg protested as they produced and lit lanterns.

"This, mistress," he interrupted, "is a warrant duly signed and sealed by the London Royal College of Physicians and is being served to you in person by Dr. John Caius, president of said college. Read it yourself if you can. Our license from the queen gives us *ex officio* authority to search the property of apothecaries and make arrests against those of you acting illegally."

"But I have a license too and permission papers, which—"

"We deem you have been cooperating with and selling illicit drugs for an unlicensed Dr. Marcus Clerewell, providing him with herbs *et cetera*—and, I might add, for just now prescribing something of your own accord I overheard, when you 'physicians' cooks' are never to prescribe. *Ergo,* you, mistress, are under arrest. Search this shop, men, sparing no space where anything might be hidden."

ॐ   ॐ   ॐ

IT WAS AFTER MIDNIGHT WHEN CECIL AND HARRY, WITH Dr. Burcote in tow, glimpsed the lights of Hampton Court from the royal barge.

"The vay you describe Her Majesty, my lord," the little German said, "I may already be too late."

Cecil and Lord Hunsdon had rousted the man from an early bed, forcing him to dress quickly and gather up his things. He'd been muttering to himself in two languages ever since. But those last words sat so hard on Cecil's heart he could not answer.

"*Ach*, if I am too late, I vill be blamed for not saving her life or her beauty," Burcote groused, sliding down the bench and shifting his gear with him. "Vould they hang me for a scapegoat?"

"I'll hang you from this canopy," Harry threatened, "if you don't keep a tight hold on that bag of tricks you've got there. Here, let me carry it off the barge and to the palace for safe-keeping."

He snatched the large hemp sack the doctor had been guarding, but let him keep his worn leather satchel. "What's in here, anyway?" Harry demanded. "Why can't you doctors do a better job curing or healing pox?"

"See?" Burcote challenged as the queen's oarsmen bent their backs to edge out of the main current toward the landing. "See? Blame for those ve fail, but no praise for those ve save. And vat's in there? Something that may save her, that is all. Alkanet leaves, flowers, and roots. Because they dye the hands a bloody color, ve know they fight the diseases of red rash."

"Hell's gates," Cecil put in, "she's far past the rash stage."

"*Ja,* so the best French alkanet is her only hope!"

"French?" Cecil and Harry remonstrated together as the barge bumped the landing.

"The best is from France, like this, though, if I had time, I vould fetch some from Margate."

"If she's conscious when you use it," Cecil said, "don't tell her it's French. But we're going to just tie her down to treat her. I swear I never saw a more willful woman in sickness or in health."

"What else is in here?" Harry pursued, bouncing the sack as they stood to get off. "What's the big, soft thing I feel?"

"A crimson cloth, of course," Burcote told them as if they were dunderheads. "*Ja,* to vrap her in to draw out all the red pox and poisons."

Cecil and Harry had just helped the doctor out onto the landing when they heard running feet. It was Jenks, looking harried and out of breath.

"She's not taken a turn for the worse?" Cecil demanded.

"Dr. Huicke says she's reached the crisis. Dr. Pascal is demanding that her ladies let him in to treat her or the queen's death will be on their heads."

Pushing past Jenks, Cecil and Harry each took one of Burcote's elbows and half hustled, half carried him up the gravel path toward the palace.

"Dr. Caius hasn't showed up too, has he?" Cecil threw over his shoulder as Jenks jogged behind them. "Or have we heard from the man we assigned to stick with him?"

"Haven't so much as heard from either," Jenks said. "But Lord Robert says he'll let Dr. Pascal in soon if the queen doesn't rally, despite all her women's and her own protests. But wait. What I wanted to tell you is that you'll never get this man in through the courtiers and doctors. I came down the back privy steps, and that's the way we should go in—if it's—" Jenks's voice caught. "If it's not too late."

Forced to remain in the apothecary shop, Gil and Bett stood by the stairs, as upset as Meg. She leaned with shaking legs against her work counter while her bins, jars, drawers, and shelves were searched in such a roughshod manner it amounted to a ransacking. Curse their black souls, they'd been tearing her precious property apart for hours. She still held the warrant in her hands but had not opened it. It must invoke the queen's name, and Meg could not bear that.

"And what is this?" Dr. Caius demanded, extending before her the alabaster box of what remained of Venus Moon Emollient. It was the moment she had dreaded.

"I—I am not at liberty to say right now—until I receive permission," she said, knowing how lame that sounded. She could only hope that Nick brought Marcus Clerewell, he would see her plight, and explain everything. After all, he'd said he'd applied for a license to sell it. If only she had not sworn to him she would keep secret the source of this miraculous emollient.

"These papers stashed in the same drawer may explain, doctor!" one of Caius's ruffians told him. Sick at heart, Meg saw him extend to the doctor the letters she and Marcus Clerewell had exchanged over her helping to bring his scrofula patient before Her Majesty in the Abbey.

"Those are privy correspondence," Meg insisted.

"Naught is privy here," Caius said, smoothing the letters out side by side to read them on the counter.

"Well, well," he said, taking his time to peruse them fully and rubbing his skeletal hands together as if he were washing them. "*Spero meliora.* I believe we may have stumbled on more than just illicit practices by yet another wayward apothecary."

"A person not in the formal list of scrofula victims is permitted to sue for the queen's healing touch!" Meg insisted.

Carefully refolding both letters, Caius muttered something to his men, who shoved Bett, Gil, and Meg upstairs and began to search things there. Meg noticed the window overlooking the street had been left ajar, probably since Nick and Bett first spotted them. How she wished she could just fly out it, back to the palace to be near the queen. Once, Elizabeth Tudor would have rescued her from any harm.

Meg gazed at Gil, whom the men had pushed into a corner as they sliced her mattress apart with knives, throwing straw and wool batting everywhere. They fanned the pages of her four precious books and threw them down, only to step on them as they banged through her few pewter plates and cups. They tossed her box of tiny treasures, ribbons and pins, trifles the queen had given her, and Ned Topside's cherished handkerchief on the floor and crunched through them.

As they ripped clothing from the large, humpbacked chest at the foot of the bed, she protested, "My husband—those are his goods too."

"We've already questioned him," Dr. Caius said.

That jolted her. "Have you been holding Ben? He's missing."

"You're the apothecary here, he told us. But I see our net must widen," Caius said, not answering her question. "We'll also take this shop woman and the lad with us for further inquiry, men," he added with a nod toward Bett. "And that Cotter aide Mistress Wilton sent out a while ago to fetch Marcus Clerewell."

Nick. They had Nick and had evidently stopped him right outside the shop hours ago. Then Dr. Clerewell knew nothing about helping the queen. And no one could bail her out of this new nightmare but Clerewell. They must already have him too and had gotten out of him something about her helping test his Venus Moon. But if he was still free from them . . .

The moment Caius looked back toward his men, Meg turned to Gil and signaled to him. *Try to find and bring Dr. Clerewell. If you can't find him, tell Ned or Jenks of this. Can you get out the window?*

Gil did not even take the time to signal in return. He bolted lightly to the window, squirmed through it to stand momentarily on the sill with his torso outside, and reached high for something Meg couldn't see. Then, silently, long legs and all, he disappeared upward. Her captors didn't even notice Gil was missing for a good while, and their hue and cry on the street snagged them only night air.

༃   ༃   ༃

I T's been the longest night," Kat greeted the four men as Jenks, Cecil, and Harry brought Dr. Burcote and his goods through the privy entrance into the queen's bedchamber.

"You must sleep," Cecil told Kat. "Too many nights you and Lady Mary have stayed with her like this."

"*Ach,*" Dr. Burcote said the moment he saw the queen, "I said you should have fetched me sooner, Lord Cecil. Quick. Quick now. Help me vrap her in this cloth," he ordered. He took his bag from Harry and flipped the crimson sheet open. "Then ve lay her before the hearth and build up the fire to make her sweat it all out into this red color. How long has she been insensible like this?"

"Off and on," Mary said as they uncovered the sweat-drenched queen, clad only in her shift. But for her head, they wrapped her mummylike in the crimson cloth. The four men lifted her carefully onto cushions on the hearth. As if they were palace wood fetchers, Cecil and Harry hastened to build up the flames. Soon the chamber was hotter than the hinges of Hades, Cecil thought, as they all perspired with the queen.

Evidently the increased heat or jostling made her stir. She slitted her eyes open; they fixed on Burcote, kneeling at her side.

"They think I have the pox," she said, weakly but distinctly.

"*Ja,* Your Majesty. God's truth, you have the pox and bad. But now you know your enemy, you vill fight to defeat it."

"My enemy," she said. "I've been thinking—dreaming that it's those doctors."

Burcote shot a puzzled look at Cecil, who only shook his head. The queen seemed to nod, but before she drifted off, Burcote raised to her cracked lips a goblet of alkanet in hot beer. She drank it greedily, though some spilled.

Cecil sent Kat to bring in Robert Dudley so he could see the queen was being treated and halt his clamoring outside to be let in. "You sneaked that man in," Robert remonstrated, pointing at Burcote, when he saw the situation. "And without my express permission."

"Hold your tongue," Cecil told him curtly. "Her Majesty is not dead, and it will take that for you to be giving orders or permission for anything. You can see she is a bit more peaceful, and surely you want that."

"Of course, I do," he muttered, raking his hand through his hair as he bent over her. "But I'm staying."

"Staying outside," Dr. Burcote put in, coming to stand at Cecil's side. "Ve call you soon as ve know anything."

Dudley went beet red, or else the heat of the chamber was getting to him too. "I'm staying," he whispered. "I'll be *by* the door, but on *this* side of it, after I tell everyone out there that all that can humanly be done is being done—but not by whom." He glared at Cecil, then Burcote. He walked away to open the door only wide enough to slip out, then left them.

"Shall I lock him out?" Kat asked, despite how Mary kept wringing her hands.

"No, Kat. He'll serve to hold the hounds at bay, and he—he loves her too."

Even when Dudley returned and didn't keep well back, Cecil and the doctor let him hover. This was no time to argue; they still might have to work together to keep the realm going if Elizabeth was lost.

They all sat or knelt on the floor by the hearth, clustered around the queen's prone, thin form until their knees locked or their backs ached and they had to move or stand.

Cecil had just started to doze off, leaning on the mantel, when his head jerked and he bolted awake. Burcote was comforting Mary Sidney, who kept shaking her head and crying. Panicked, Cecil bent to be certain the queen was still breathing. She was. Then he noted that Burcote was pushing Mary's sleeve up her arm and pointing out something on her wrist. She recoiled in horror and clung to the closed draperies, sobbing silently into their deep folds. Robert noticed, too, got up, and rushed to comfort her.

AT FIRST LIGHT, CHURCH BELLS BEGAN TO RING ALL over London. Meg panicked that the queen was dead, but then remembered it was the sabbath day. And she recalled where she was: in a filthy, straw-strewn cell at Bridewell Prison.

They had put her by herself, though she'd insisted she not be separated from Bett. She'd heard strange screams and cries all night. Bridewell had inmates publicly flogged and even hanged, but surely not in the middle of the night.

Aching all over, she lay flat on her back, staring at the vaulted stone ceiling as it went from black to gray when muted morning light made its way in. Bridewell had once been a palace but now was a sprawl of separate entities: a workhouse for vagrants, a hospital, and this dank first-floor prison. Desperate for a sniff of fresh air, she rose and looked out her slit of slatted window.

She could see the great Thames glittering below where the smaller Fleet River poured into it. Pressing her cheek to the cold, damp stone window frame, she could barely glimpse the famous Bridewell landmark on the Thames. A wooden bridge, built in Venetian style, arched over the Fleet between Bridewell and old Blackfriars Monastery lands. The queen's father had ordered this palace built but soon abandoned it when the summer stench from the garbage-ridden Fleet became so rank. Even now, in fairly brisk weather, the smell made Meg want to puke.

She jumped away from the window as a key grated in the lock. The same crude, beefy woman who had locked her in here last night entered and thrust a dented pewter mug full of gruel at Meg.

"Eat quick 'cause you got a 'terr'gation coming."

She banged back out. Meg could not stomach the cold, congealed stuff. How far away the fancy fineries she'd used to eat at court, some from the queen's own table.

Soon she followed the woman down the hall and up a curving flight of stone stairs into a chamber with a deep window overlooking the Thames and a single table and chair. Dr. John Caius sat at it; behind Meg was a secretary, standing at a small, rickety lectern, with his pen evidently poised to take down all she said.

"Who is Dr. Marcus Clerewell to you, Sarah Wilton, alias Meg Milligrew?" Caius asked without ado.

"A customer of herbs," she replied crisply. She recalled Her Majesty telling her once that Lord Cecil had counseled her, before she was queen, never to embellish an answer, only to give the interrogator the minimum of what was asked. Meg was quite pleased her voice was strong. Caius's head snapped up at her simple reply, which gave her the idea. Not only would she not cower before him, but she would use the tone and diction Ned Topside had taught her, court talk for when she used to emulate the queen herself.

"Then why did you send your man Cotter to fetch him at night, last night?" he plunged on.

"I had just returned from Hampton Court where I learned the queen, whom I used to serve, was very ill. Since I knew Dr. Clerewell had dealt with pox patients, I thought—"

"Been to court after being expelled from there, have you, and trying to get close to the queen again, *sub rosa?*"

Meg wanted to blurt out that the queen had sent for her, but she still wasn't certain why and didn't trust this vile man not to read something dreadful into it. Besides, she didn't know what *sub rosa* meant. So, fighting for calm, she returned to his earlier question.

"Dr. Clerewell had told me he was adept at treating pox patients. He had bought herbs from me for such purpose. I had hopes he would be able to volunteer his services to Her Maj—"

Caius's bony fist banged the table. "*Maxima Regina* has edu-cated, royal doctors, has the Royal College of Physicians, includ-ing me, at her beck and call and you—*you* presume to decide who will treat her? I'm sure you would have liked to treat her too, and for a handsome reward! Don't put on your I-once-worked-for-the-queen airs with me, Mistress Apothecary. Don't you try to lecture me!"

"I was merely answering your question, doctor," she retorted in such ringing tones his dark eyes bulged.

"The papers, sirrah. Come on, come on!" Caius ordered the man behind her. His lackey leaped forward with two letters, which she recognized as hers and Clerewell's. She knew now she should never have saved them, but she had been so proud. How she had reveled in the fact Clerewell admired her for once work-ing with the queen.

"I shall now quote that Norwich, unlicensed doctor—"

"He never told me he did not have a license. He is a brilliant man who understands his patients' sufferings because of his own."

"Do not interrupt me, mistress!" he shouted, holding one let-ter up before his eyes to catch more window light. "I am quoting here directly," Caius went on with a sniff. "This Dr. Clerewell writes that you and he 'have forged a partnership for particular causes.' Through 'your former days in service to our queen and your skill with herbal healings,' he claims he 'may accomplish his aim.' And what might that aim be, mistress? Your husband, when questioned, admitted that Dr. Clerewell paid you hand-somely—*very* handsomely—*id est,* for mere herbs."

"No doubt you should have Dr. Clerewell speak for himself, as you have evidently let my husband do so, doctor."

"Has Clerewell sworn you to silence in some secret pact?"

"He asked me to be discreet about some things, and I would honor that."

"Aha," he said, leaning back in his chair and looking entirely pleased for some reason she could not fathom. "Then to your reply to him," he said, switching letters. "You insist on 'privy correspondence' and say you are 'pleased to keep his secret while putting on trial the V.M.E.' What secret, precisely, mistress? And those three letters are your code for . . ."

"Again, you must ask him."

"You refuse to answer. Write that down, man. And note, too, that the letter continues in like vein as the accused advises Dr. Clerewell on how to 'have a quick moment's access to her'—*id est,* to Her Majesty—hoping 'she is caught off guard.' And then the most damning words: 'I shall be there watching—and praying for—victorious results.' "

"What are you implying?" Meg demanded, gripping her hands so tightly before her that her fingers went numb. "The doctor asked me how he could get a scrofula patient touched by the queen when you did not include her in your set list."

"Ah—accusing me again. You are bitter and subversive against the grant of power to the Royal College of Physicians to control London's apothecaries, are you not? But I repeat, woman, what exactly does your code V.M.E. mean? You might as well admit it, for I have ferreted out your secrets."

"My secrets? Many an apothecary has hinted to a customer what old healing herbs may work for a cure as I did to Gil Sharpe. And many have sold something they did not have permission for. But I did not sell that ointment in the alabaster box! I will pay a fine then, but—"

"A fine?" he bellowed, his voice mocking. "Mistress Sarah Wilton, alias Meg Milligrew, there are no fines for treason, but only torments, trial, and death. Though the queen's license gives the Royal College permission to jail apothecaries who subvert our power and grants us leave to incarcerate you in any prison but the Tower, you have been brought to Bridewell."

Meg shook her head to clear it. Had he said treason? But that meant against the queen. Either he was mad or she was. She tried to follow all he had said. Bridewell was a political prison. Then he must have said treason indeed.

"I cannot fathom what you mean," she insisted, sounding deflated and frightened. "All of your words and accusations are as obscure as your fancy Latin phrases."

"All right then. *Inter nos,* mistress, let me clarify. I believe you and this missing Dr. Clerewell are in league to harm the queen. You arranged for Her Majesty to be frightened, perhaps even warned, by presenting her with a poxed effigy outside our physicians' hall, hoping to cast blame on us. You had Dr. Clerewell place a leeched body in her privy fountain..." His dreadful words rolled on while she just stared agape at him.

"Then in the sacred ceremony at Westminster," he went on, "which was under the Royal Physicians' watch and care, you planned to—"

"To what?" she cried, grasping where his accusations might be going. "You are insane!"

"Am I? All my evidence and your confessions lead me to believe that you and your cohort Clerewell meant to assassinate the queen in the Abbey, then make a quick escape through the ensuing chaos and the crowd."

"No!" she gasped, staggering back. "No—I—"

"Yes, and I shall formally accuse you of such treason. But then, I surmise you changed your mind, perhaps because there were so many of us doctors standing by. So you connived to go to Hampton Court, hoping to get near her there. But that brings me back to this letter which incriminates you with your 'praying for victorious results,' as you put it. And your code of V.M.E.? I warrant that stands for the 'Victorious Murder of Elizabeth,' does it not?"

Meg wanted to deny it, but she was as mute as Gil. The walls wavered. She fought to keep her balance, for she must not appear guilty. Yet the ceiling spun, and the floor leaped up to meet her.

Chapter

THE FOURTEENTH

*Take cucumbers, camphor, blanched almonds and the
juice of four lemons . . . This not only helps fiery faces,
but also takes away spots, sunburn, and all other
deformities of the face.*

The Herball

T HE MOMENT THE GUARDS THREW NICK COTTER
out of Bridewell Prison, he headed toward home. He'd
been questioned hard by Dr. Caius about Meg's doings,
mostly things he didn't know and couldn't believe. But Nick had
finally admitted that Meg had tried a fancy face cream on Bett, so
Bett wouldn't be tortured for answers, as the doctor threatened.
The man had barely mentioned how Meg had told Gil to chew
lily valley root, which Nick figured was all she'd really done ille-
gal. The questions about treason had to be rubbish.

But the ones about Meg's feelings toward the queen scared
him. Did Sarah Wilton, alias Meg Milligrew, want revenge? Did
he ever hear her talk about dosing the queen if she took sick?
And then so many lamebrained questions about things like was
Meg good at wax and plaster.

"Of course she's good at wax pills and healing plasters!" Nick had finally thundered at Dr. Caius. "I even helped stir up a big bowl of plaster not long ago, lots of it!"

Now, striding toward home and Bett, Nick nearly jumped out of his skin when a tall figure suddenly appeared at his side. But it was Gil, like he'd just stepped out of the wind.

The lad inclined his head, and they hied themselves into an alley.

Been home, seen Bett, Gil signaled to him. *She was let go too. Had to go in from roof. Someone watching the street, maybe for me.*

"Well, they let me out proper, so I'm going home," Nick said.

Gil shook his head. *Bett says you go find Dr. Clerewell, and I go tell Cecil, Ned, or Jenks.*

That short speech took Gil a long time, as Nick had never learned the signals for people's names. Gil had to mimic Clerewell's big hat, Cecil's beard and his importance, Ned's giving a grand speech, and Jenks's using a sword until Nick picked up on exactly who he meant.

"No more word on the queen's health?" Nick asked.

Gil shook his head and hit his heart with his fist. *That* was clear enough, at least. Nick clasped the boy's shoulder, then set out for the Cheapside doctor's shop where he and Gil had gone for help once before.

❧   ❧   ❧

MEG RETURNED TO CONSCIOUSNESS, FLAT ON THE stone floor of the interrogation room. No one else was there.

She tenderly fingered the bump on her forehead and moved her limbs. Bruised, shaky, she did not try to sit up. If they thought she was still unconscious, maybe it would give her a little reprieve from the terrible things Dr. Caius had been saying. She still heard his voice echoing deep inside her.

No, that *was* his voice. Maybe in the hall. She closed her eyes and concentrated on what he was saying. He was obviously conferring with someone, but that person's voice did not seem to carry. Or was Caius dictating to his secretary again?

". . . enough evidence to have her summarily hanged . . ."

Whatever did *summarily* mean? Meg wondered. But she sat bolt upright at the import of his other words.

"With the queen at least indisposed and the court in upheaval, they won't even know until it's over. *Maxima Regina* ordered us to hasten to our business, so this will show her . . . Make a dramatic example of an apothecary, but for a high crime, not mere misdemeanor. How I have longed to get even with the queen for dismissing me—*me*—from royal service as she did, yet I need her goodwill. And disposing of a would-be assassin who played on the queen's worst fears which she learned as an intimate at court before being dismissed . . ."

The words rolled over Meg, but she could grab so few of them. Concentrate—she must concentrate. She rose groggily to her feet and pressed her ear to the door. But the sound was not filtering in there. She moved again into the center of the room, then realized his voice was coming along the floor, from under the heavy wooden door.

She lay back down, this time on her belly, pressing her ear to the ground just the way Jenks had taught her to listen for the beat of distant horses' hooves.

". . . to keep her in the queen's prison, I had thought I'd have to use the abandonment of her daughter against her, charging murder . . ."

Daughter? Whose daughter? The queen had no daughter.

". . . but the child is not dead, just given away and . . ."

Curse it. She'd missed something. *Whose* daughter?

". . . but won't have to now with the two letters she and Blackwell—ah, I mean Clerewell—exchanged. Nasty business when a child gets involved anyway, especially a poxed six-year-old who's best left where she is out on the heath."

His voice came closer, clearer. "I'd best go look in on her again, but I think I have plenty here to get her on the execution list. Imagine that—the queen, if she lives, will lose her former herb girl, who yet adores her. After *Maxima Regina*," he went on, his voice dripping sarcasm, "dismissed me from a post that should have been mine yet, after she refuses to give me the corpses we need . . . Ha," he shouted an exultant laugh, "now I shall give *her* a corpse, one she knows well this time."

Daughter. Six years old. Poxed. Out on the heath?

Caius returned to find his prisoner standing by the window, breathing hard.

"I heard what you said," she accused. Her head was throbbing, spinning.

"You hit your head and must have been delusional so—"

"No! Did you mean *I* have a six-year-old daughter? You see, there are years—things I can't recall."

"Now that's convenient. I rather think—"

"Where is she?" Meg screamed.

"—you are very dangerous," he got out before Meg launched herself at him, fingers curved like claws. He was so surprised he went off balance, slamming into the wall, tipping to hands and knees on the floor while Meg tried to scramble for the open door.

But his secretary and a guard filled it to stop her flight.

෨ ෨ ෨

E LIZABETH'S STRENGTH CAME BACK SLOWLY, SOME-times in waves, but then ebbed. They still kept the room dim. Mostly just Dr. Burcote and some of her ladies were in attendance, especially Anne Carey, Harry's wife. Elizabeth had been told Kat was exhausted and Mary needed her sleep. God bless them for tending her for . . .

"How long was I—not myself?" she asked Dr. Burcote as he bent near to time her wrist pulse.

"Today is Saturday, October the seventeenth, Your Majesty."

She tried to recall when she first fell ill. On the fifth. Twelve days ago! Twelve days her kingdom had gone on without her. A dozen days she had not pursued whoever had tried to frighten her and—mayhap—to kill her with the pox. She had so much to do.

"Send for Lord Cecil," she ordered Burcote, snatching her wrist back. "But do not go far. And do not let my royal court doctors nor those from the Royal Physicians College bully you," she added as he nodded and obeyed.

She felt better already. God had spared her life. And Dr. Burcote had assured her she had relatively few and shallow pox marks. Her mind was working. She was giving orders, making plans.

Cecil joined her immediately, or had she drifted off to sleep again?

"I believe we have our beloved queen back with us," he told her as he took the hand she offered. Tears shimmered in his eyes.

"My lord, I know you and Dr. Burcote tell me true. How many marks on my face? They won't give me a mirror. Count them."

He leaned closer. "Two high on your forehead, Your Grace, two along your chin, a few scattered on your cheeks, but Burcote says you are healing. . . ."

"I have them on my arms and legs, but I am praying they will heal shallow, all of them."

"Praise God your life was spared. Your beauty always came from your strong spirit and marvelous mind, as well as from your face and form."

"Spoken like a fond suitor, as well as a wily lawyer and my principal secretary, my dear Cecil. But—the God of my salvation forgive me—I cannot bear to be marked and scarred."

"We had your old herb girl here for a while waiting to see you before I took her back to London. She mentioned something special to cover pox marks, something about a doctor . . . I cannot recall, but I can fetch her for you again."

"But first, I want to find the person who did this to me. Cecil, I swear, my being smitten with the pox was part of a hateful plot. The effigy of a poxed queen, the leeched body of the wig-maker's granddaughter in the fountain—now this. I have been thinking there were certain incidents which might have caused this."

He looked amazed. "Such as?" he asked gently as if she were delirious again.

"Margaret Stewart's special gift of bloody-hued powder from Mary, Queen of Scots, of course! It made everyone sneeze. God only—and Mary and Margaret—knows what was in it."

How dare he smile. "Do not coddle me, my lord!" she told him.

"I am simply overjoyed that your brilliant powers of deduction are back already, Your Majesty. As ever, you are astute, for through the man watching Matthew Stewart, I have intercepted and had copied—the original has been sent on—a letter Margaret wrote to Queen Mary in Edinburgh."

"It says the powder was poisoned, or carried pox or—"

"No, but it clearly suggests that, should the Scots queen wish to wed Lord Darnley, so that their heir might bind the Tudors and the Stewarts, and should you—sadly—die of the pox . . ."

"The treasonous bitch—both of them!" Elizabeth exploded, smacking her fists onto her mattress to bounce the bed.

Dr. Burcote poked his head through the other side of the tapestried hangings. "Please, Your Majesty, Lord Secretary, she must not become so excited that—"

"I'm fine, doctor," she said with a dismissive gesture. "Cecil, be certain that neither the Stewarts nor their son leave these grounds. And send for Meg Milligrew again. Meanwhile, I still want Caius and Pascal watched day and night. Well, what is it?" she demanded when Cecil shook his head.

"Pascal was here for days, insisting he treat you," he explained. "But he disappeared in a fit when he heard we'd brought in Dr. Burcote, and in the confusion of your crisis, we lost him. Nor have we heard from our man with him. The same with Caius, only he never appeared here, nor did the man watching him report to us."

"It's them, perhaps in league with the Stewarts and the Scots queen," Elizabeth vowed. Yet she knew full well that, besides Pascal's patient's coughing to fleck her with spittle, the young girl who had kneeled in the aisle had done so too.

Anger and energy coursed through her. She slid her feet to the side of the bed while Dr. Burcote appeared again, holding up his hands as if to stop her.

"Cecil, send for Kat and Mary Sidney," Elizabeth ordered. "I long to see and thank them—and I will need their help to get dressed. What is it now, damn the two of you. Stop shooting each other glances as if you are my mute artist and I some silly fool!"

"Your Grace," Cecil said, grasping her hands, both of them, though she had not indicated he might do so, "Mary Sidney is ill of the pox too."

"Mary? Beautiful Mary? And caught it from me—or from whoever did this to me?"

She tried to stay strong, but could only seize her hands back, cover her face, and sob in great gasps. She shuddered again as if the fever were on her, the marks all over her.

"Fetch Kat Ashley," she heard Cecil tell someone.

Burcote kept repeating, "Calm down now, *ja,* keep calm or those marks vill get all fiery again. . . . "

" 'S blood and bones! How can I calm down," Elizabeth

yelled, "when no one will tell me anything? And when I have both revenge and justice for myself, poor Mary, and two dead wig-makers to tend to now!"

෴   ෴   ෴

NICK KNEW HE'D BEEN DRUGGED, BUT HE COULDN'T shake off the heavy weights that held him down. He remembered now—Dr. Clerewell had not been tending the other doctor's shop in Cheapside, so he'd gone asking for him along Gutter Lane where he'd said he lived.

Nick tried to sit up but his limbs were made of stone. And those terrible sounds, the moans and shrieks. Closing his eyes tight shut, he tried to remember more.

"A Dr. Clerewell, you say?" an old crone had asked on the fourth floor of a crooked, narrow building on Gutter Lane, where someone had sent him.

"Aye, the same," Nick had assured her, wishing he had so much as a groat in his purse to loosen her tongue, but the Bridewell guards had cleaned him out. "Large feathered hat, has—or used to have—scars on his face, that's him," Nick had told her.

"Oh, thought tha's who ye meant. Lives in Chelsea, 'e does, only rents a room 'ere so's 'e can say 'e's a fancy London doctor."

"Clear out in Chelsea?" Nick had asked. And here he couldn't hire a boat to go find him there. He'd have to run home to Bett, tell her what he'd learned, get some money, and head out again. He'd been about to turn away when the old crone had spoken again.

"A man downstairs knows just where 'e lives, so you can ask 'im direct."

Nick had gladly followed her back downstairs—and he'd seemed to be going down, down ever since. He could remember asking the man about where Clerewell could be found. The man had pointed out into the street, and Nick had turned to look before the whole world had gone black.

"No, no not the leeches again!" a woman screamed so close that Nick jerked upright, craning his neck to see. Not the Gutter Lane crone's voice this time, but someone young. Someone terrified.

Shock after shock rolled through Nick Cotter as he looked groggily around. The scene was the way he'd always thought of hell, but this was hell with artwork. On the stone walls were crude drawings of what must be corpses: people cut open, parts of bodies, all drawn in black and white.

He heard before he saw it then. Two men dragged a gaunt, limp body from a cage. Must be a corpse, leeched white as it looked, a young woman in a shroudlike shift. Nick squinted as the men pulled the corpse into a distant room. And then he saw something that shook him even more.

Looking every bit as mean as a Bridewell guard, Ben Wilton sat across the stone-ceilinged room before a dark door, holding a coiled whip. Between Ben and himself, Nick was looking at rows and rows of caged human beings. Ill. Scarred, maimed, half-dead. He knew better than to yell to Ben for help, because he was seeing this through his own set of bars. But worst in all this horror, he saw Gil too trapped in one of the cages, wild-eyed, his mouth open in a silent scream.

❧   ❧   ❧

B ETT SHARPE, I MEAN COTTER, IS HERE, YOUR GRACE," Kat Ashley said as Elizabeth tried on several hats with veils. She was not hiding in bed or her rooms one day longer, but neither was she going to have people staring at her healing pox marks. Even if she must go about like some veiled beekeeper or tavern doxy, she had things to do.

"She's come with Meg Milligrew, you mean?" the queen

asked, fluffing out the veil she preferred because, though it looked opaque, she could still see through it quite well. "I told Cecil to send for her straightaway, and that was yesterday."

"Not Meg," Kat said. "Bett alone and so distraught I gave Jenks permission to bring her up the back way."

"It's something about Gil," Elizabeth muttered, jamming the hat on and jumping to her feet. "I pray naught has happened to my Gil."

Elizabeth walked slowly but steadily to her privy sitting room as Jenks brought Bett in. The only other time she'd been out of her bedchamber in a fortnight was to visit and comfort Mary Sidney. She had worn the mermaid pin, held Mary's hand—for once one had survived the pox, for some reason it did not strike again—and had vowed when she saw how much more heavily Mary was stricken with the pox that someone would pay.

"I am glad to see you," Elizabeth said before Bett even curtsied. Bless the woman for not gaping at her or trying to peer behind the veil. "Is Gil well? And Nick, too, of course?"

"Don't know, as both have gone missing, Your Majesty, Nick since he got out of Bridewell, I take it. Gil could have gone too, but he 'scaped."

"Bridewell?" Elizabeth repeated. "The hospital or the workhouse?"

"Oh, no, Your Majesty, the prison. Took there by Dr. Caius. I was too, but they let me go after some questions, things about plaster and effigies and corpses. And Meg's feelings for you, which is only being hurt and missing you. I was praying Gil'd come here, but I hear not," she rushed on, wringing her hands. "I told him to go to you and"—here she lowered her voice though only Kat stood nearby—"your Privy Plot Council what solves crimes and helps those in need and that's all of us, 'cluding poor Meg."

"Meg Milligrew isn't missing too?"

"Oh, no, Your Majesty, I know right where she is. Still in Bridewell—the prison—but I fear they're going to keep her there or worse for doing some sort of treason 'gainst you, which she never would."

"What?" Elizabeth screeched so loud her veil belled out. "Kat, fetch the others of the council. Now Bett, start over again, slowly, leaving nothing out. I've been a bit unwell and weak lately, but I'm better now."

⁂

M EG HAD LOST TRACK OF TIME. SHE KNEW SHE WAS doomed, and she almost didn't care anymore. She'd lost the life she loved as herb girl to the queen—with the dream of being court herbalist someday. Her parents' apothecary shop, which had been her only love since she'd left royal service, was in shambles.

Something dreadful must have happened to Gil. She could feel it in her bones. Ben and Dr. Clerewell had evidently abandoned her, but Gil never would. And that blackguard husband of hers must have deserted their daughter, when she got the pox, shuffling her off to someone out in the heath, wherever that was. Or could that craven bastard have given her away? More like, knowing Ben, he'd sold her for a servant or some such fate.

If there was one thing Meg would like to live for it was to see her girl, poxed or not. And, of course, to see the queen again, for word had come, even in this hellhole, that Elizabeth had survived the pox.

Meg turned sideways on the pallet of rough straw that had served for her bed these last nine days and pulled her knees almost up to her chin. It was warmer that way in this cold, stinking place. She'd never live through the winter here, but she wouldn't have to try. Somehow, Dr. John Caius had gotten her on a list of people to be hanged first thing on the morrow. So today she was just going to lie here and dream of taking her girl—whatever her name was—to court to meet or see the queen. Kat would be there nodding and smiling as if she were the little one's grandmother. Jenks would give the child a ride on his horse, and Ned—dear, pompous Ned—would make them both laugh with his funniest speeches and wry faces.

The key jangled in the lock, and the door grated open. "Get up," the guard named Clary ordered. "You're being took out today instead."

"I—not today. You mean—Dr. Caius arranged it?" To her accusation of treason he had added charges of deadly assault on his person. Did that mean he could bump up someone's execution?

"Far's I know. Get up, I said. Men downstairs to take you."

Meg knew it was the time of day when those who were to be flogged or hanged were rousted out. When she tried to hold back, Clary seized her arm, bent it up behind her back, and marched her out and down the main stairwell. Below, in what was once a great hall, a few prisoners stood in line, hands bound behind them, nooses already about their necks, the way the condemned were always marched to the scaffold.

"No," Meg screamed. "No! Not today! I haven't seen a judge! Dr. Caius is not a judge! The queen's own artist—Gil Sharpe—he's coming here with a message from court!"

She kicked at Clary, but two guards came up the stairs to help subdue her. As if she were a sack of hops, they carted her roughly downstairs to join the others.

THE FIFTEENTH

*There have been many ridiculous tales brought up of
the mandrake plant, whether of old wives tales, or some
runnagate surgeons and physick-mongers I know not,
but by someone that sought to make themselves famous
and skillful above others. . . .*

JOHN GERARD
The Herball

THE GUARDS CARRYING MEG DOWN THE STEPS SHOVED
her at two others. One looked so like Jenks, Meg almost
threw herself into his arms.

It *was* Jenks.

"It's all right, Meg," he whispered and flashed some sort of
rolled document before her.

"Not—from Dr. Caius?" she cried.

"From the queen. You're to come with us for questioning."

"But I've been questioned—by Dr. Caius."

She nearly panicked again. Last time the queen had questioned her everything had gone wrong, so wrong. And that was just over borrowing a gown and forging the royal signature.

But Ned was here too, her Ned. He cupped her shoulders in his hands to make her look at him. She sagged against his touch so that he was nearly holding her up.

"Meg, we know you've been through hell," he said so quietly she almost couldn't hear him above the caterwauling of other prisoners. "Bett told us the queen's royal physicians have closed your shop and have been asking questions about your trying to harm Her Majesty. I thought at first you might be suspect, but we don't believe a word of it."

"We? Her Grace, you mean."

"She said you would never harm her and thought Dr. Caius has set you up for it to be another dead body."

"Another dead body? You mean, like that girl in the fountain? Who was she, anyway?"

"It's a long story," Ned said. "We've all been led a merry—"

"Not so merry," Jenks interrupted. "We'd best be going—"

"—a merry chase right toward a trap," Ned went on, ignoring Jenks's advice just as he always had. "You'll come with us without one more peep, won't you now, sweetheart?"

Meg nodded and blinked back tears so she could keep watching Ned. If the devils in this dreadful place grabbed her and hanged her right now, at least she'd go comforted that the queen's Ned and Jenks had come for her. And Ned had called her sweetheart.

ఞ   ఞ   ఞ

THOUGH MEG HAD SPILLED EVERYTHING TO NED AND Jenks—who told her she'd just have to explain it over again to the queen anyway—she couldn't stop crying in relief.

"You're safe now," Jenks had tried to assure her more than once, patting her on the back. "She'll never believe you meant to hurt her. I heard her say more'n once, Meg's a healer."

"She did?" Meg said, dabbing at her eyes. Ned was nodding at that last comment too. She sat up a bit, blessing the way the barge kept rocking her into Ned, back and forth, back and forth as rosy-hued Hampton Court came into view. Despite the gray, chill day, it had never looked so lovely.

Meg had already washed the stench of Bridewell off at Lord Hunsdon's house at Blackfriars, though neither Lord nor Lady Hunsdon was there. And, another blessing. Waiting for her after one of Lady Hunsdon's servants helped her bathe was a gown of the queen's to put on. Granted, it was a plain dark blue one Meg recognized as one of Her Majesty's old riding habits, but a royal gown nonetheless. And to think she'd once been in trouble for wearing the queen's attire without permission. She also wore what looked to be a pair of the queen's scuffed riding boots and a cape and hood to ward off the river wind.

"I feel like the whole earth is still rocking," Meg admitted when they helped her out on the landing.

"*As if* the earth *were* still rocking," Ned quietly corrected her grammar, just as he used to, but she didn't mind a bit now.

"I said you should eat something," Jenks scolded, "and not just drink all that wine back at Lord Hunsdon's."

"I was thirsty. But it's going to take me days to get that place—and Dr. John Caius—out of my gut, not to mention the pasty slop they serve in there. I swear, I'd rather eat apothecary plaster!"

She saw Ned and Jenks exchange surreptitious glances. Her steps faltered. This surely wasn't some elaborate ruse to entice her to let down her guard and then accuse her again? She'd finally figured out that Dr. Caius had been trying to make her admit she'd fashioned an effigy of the queen from apothecary plaster and wax and stuffed it with herbs.

"Not that way," Jenks said, steering her around the Base

Court instead of into it. "Her Grace doesn't want anyone to know you're back, at least not till 'much later. She has plans for you."

⁊   ⁊   ⁊

'SBLOOD," THE QUEEN CURSED WHEN SHE SAW MEG, "how dare John Caius and his cronies put *my* apothecary in *my* prison! I shall tell the man I've sent courtiers and commons to buy herbs from your shop, and he shall pay for that and more. I see you've suffered greatly, Meg Milligrew. But for your lack of pox marks, you look nearly as bad as I do, so that will serve quite well."

After her curtsy, Meg was so overwhelmed she stood as mute as Gil would have. Those purchases from Lady Cecil's servants and from well-heeled minor courtiers—the queen had sent them?

"I—I long only to serve you, Your Majesty," she managed to choke out. "And ever did."

Her eager eyes drank in her queen at close range. Elizabeth wore a veil attached to a brimmed hat, and Meg feared she must be dreadfully scarred, but none of that mattered. Pinned on the queen's gown over her heart was a pretty mermaid pin Meg had never seen. Mayhap a gift from Robin Dudley, for that's where the queen used to flaunt her most precious pins. Meg could not stem the flood of tears that began to spill down her cheeks. The queen produced a scented handkerchief from up her sleeve and held it out.

"We shall cry for our losses later," Elizabeth told her, taking her hand, "for we have much to do. I have not even time for you to fetch me some pox doctor Cecil said you mentioned," the queen went on as she pulled Meg over to sit her at her right hand—usually Cecil's seat—at a long table.

"Your Grace," Meg blurted, "that miraculous emollient has been confiscated by Dr. Caius when he and his men searched—indeed, looted—my shop. And I fear he may hold prisoner the man who made the emollient too."

"Then we shall find him, find both of them," Elizabeth declared, gesturing to the others who came into the room to sit. "Mistress Meg," Lord Cecil said solemnly in greeting as he took the chair next to her. Kat hugged her from behind. Jenks and Ned sat on either side of Lord Hunsdon, both grinning. Gooseflesh gilded Meg's skin. She was back among Her Grace's covert Privy Plot Council.

"You must tell us all you know, Meg, all that has passed, especially concerning your struggles with Dr. Caius," Elizabeth instructed her. "You see, more are missing than that doctor friend of yours and his medicine, namely Gil Sharpe and Nick Cotter."

Meg nodded. "My husband too." She almost blurted out the few things she knew about her stolen daughter, but she wanted to tell of that more privily, then beg the queen for help.

"What is the name of the doctor we must seek, the one who stands also accused by Caius?" the queen inquired.

"Dr. Marcus Clerewell, Your Grace. Of Norwich, practicing on Cheapside but living in Gutter Lane, so Nick said."

"Bett told me the same," the queen admitted, making Meg recall that Her Majesty often knew more than she let on. Her hidden eyes seemed to burn into each of them in turn through her veil. "My friends, I am beginning to discern a pattern in this web, and I intend to find and squash the deadly spiders spinning it."

AFTER THE MEETING, THE QUEEN ROSE SWIFTLY, NODded to her Privy Plot Council, and fled to her bedchamber.

Despite the happy reunion just now and the plans she had laid out, she feared she was going to lose control and command of things again. Her stomach roiled as horrid possibilities racked her. When she heard Kat's footsteps behind her, she went into her privy closet and closed the door.

Their meeting had covered much ground, yet she had not shared her conclusions with her friends. Though she had held her own flesh and blood at bay so far, her kin lusted for her throne. She had gainsayed and offended the two leaders of her Royal College of Physicians. And she had balked at permitting human bodies for their dissection. How widespread was the hatred of her? How many of those she suspected could be linked in this hellish plot?

Ripping off her hat and veil, she bent over to be sick in her washbowl. The retching stopped but her thoughts would not.

Her enemies had maimed and murdered to attempt to kill her courage and resolve. Someone, somehow, had almost assassinated her with the pox. Though they had not yet seized her throne, they had usurped God's very control of disease and death. So wasn't dissecting the dead bodies of persons they abducted and killed—even Nick or her dear Gil—only the next logical, horrible step?

⁓   ⁓   ⁓

THROUGH HER VEIL, ELIZABETH TUDOR FROWNED AT the blank stone facade of Bridewell Prison as they passed by. As bidden, the oarsmen of a plain, working barge put in at the Blackfriars landing just across the Fleet. She could not wait to get her hands on the mastermind—or perhaps minds—behind the pox plot. And, however tired and off balance she still felt, she would never do that recovering and cowering in a rural palace.

Her entourage included four men she considered her bodyguards, each armed to the teeth: Jenks, Ned, her yeoman Clifford, and her cousin Harry. Harry had more men here at Blackfriars they could use. So that no one watching would realize she was a lady of import and influence, she had brought only one female companion, Harry's wife, Anne. The Carey home at Blackfriars would be their covert base of investigation in London.

Cecil and Kat had been left at Hampton Court. Cecil would see to the nation's business while Kat buffered everyone from Meg Milligrew. For the first time in two years, Meg was portraying the queen of England, albeit from behind a veil, claiming she needed more bed rest for the time being. The queen had vowed to help Meg Milligrew discover where Ben Wilton had sent her poor child. Meanwhile, the barge had just dropped Bett and another guard off at the public landing near Whitehall so that she could return to the ransacked apothecary shop in case Gil, Nick, or even Ben returned.

Dr. Burcote, richly rewarded with a fine leather satchel and much coin, had remained behind to tend Mary Sidney. Elizabeth did not want him where the Royal College physicians could sanction him. She was tempted to simply have them arrested, but she'd promised herself she would not set back the English medical arts by gutting the leadership of her London College—unless it came to that.

"Now," Elizabeth said, even as they stood on the windy barge-landing, "do not fret for me, for I will be fine here with the Hunsdon household men for extra guards. Each of you must hire a barge at the public landing, be about your given tasks, and report back to me here as soon as possible."

Murmured assents and nods. Good, the queen thought, for she was leaving no stone unturned, even backtracking to the earlier clues.

"Anne, I pray you," she told her friend, "do a better job of cross-questioning the workers in the Royal Wardrobe than poor Kat did. Go now. We have immediate and important work to do!"

꩜   ꩜   ꩜

THE QUEEN PACED THE DINING CHAMBER OF THE Hunsdons' house at Blackfriars, listening avidly to each report. She had ordered them all to sit but her, a breech of protocol, but she wanted them to realize only their tasks of discovery mattered now.

"So, Anne, the new guard was also able to describe the man who came to lease my gown," Elizabeth asked excitedly.

"He's not so new, Your Grace, but one who alternated with the guard who fled with the lace girl," Anne explained. "But yes, he glimpsed the man with the very gown that turned up on that poxed effigy in your coach. 'Twas a sketchy description, but something to go on, I reckon. The man who leased the gown had a grand, feathered hat. Oh, and as Kat had ascertained afore, he spoke very well, mayhap with some foreign phrases."

"Dr. Caius, with his incessant Latin," Harry put in smugly.

"I think not," Elizabeth corrected. "That hat makes him sound like that Dr. Clerewell Bett and Meg told us of. If so, hat or not, I wager he's the man with the girl who knelt in the aisle at the Abbey.

"Ned and Jenks?" she prompted. "Your findings?"

"Nick was seen trying to track down Dr. Clerewell," Ned reported, "just as Bett said. We talked to an old woman at the place the doctor let for a time on Gutter Lane, a vile flea-trap. Under my clever cross-questioning, she admitted Nick was there, but says she told him she had no idea where Dr. Clerewell had gone, nor did she know where Nick went after he left her place."

"It must be that same old woman who put me off," Anne declared indignantly. "You know, when I tried to take some coins to that sick girl after the Queen's Evil ceremony. An old beldam said Clerewell had never lived there!"

"I can see why you believed her, but Ned, reader of parts and people, did you?" the queen demanded, hands on her waist.

"She was beady-eyed," Ned said, "and nervous, as if she hadn't learned her part well."

"Let's cut to the quick," Elizabeth insisted. "The crone was lying. This entire plot is stitched together with lies, and we cannot afford to believe anyone."

"We can go after her with more force," Ned said, "and—"

"Move on for now," Elizabeth ordered. "She could, no doubt, be put to the rack and not be able to tell us where to find the mastermind. Cousin Harry, I dare say you have something to contribute. Did you find any records of Dr. Caius's interrogation of Ben Wilton at Bridewell?"

"If Dr. Caius interrogated Ben Wilton at Bridewell, Your Grace, it wasn't recorded—no records of Clerewell, either, and you think the royal doctors would have hounded him as they did Meg."

"Then either Caius questioned Ben and Clerewell elsewhere," the queen concluded, "or they are in league with him. The rest of your report, then, Harry. Tell us of your new search of the cellar beneath the Royal College Hall after you left Bridewell."

"This, Your Grace," he said, extending a piece of paper to her, "could be a key clue. My Latin's a bit rusty, but Cecil's man Nye translated the body of it last time I was there. I didn't think it of import till Meg told us about Dr. Clerewell. And, now that he could be tied to the taking of your gown that turned up on that dummy . . . "

Elizabeth snatched the piece of paper and walked away to get window light. She held out the hem of her veil to see it more clearly.

"What is it, Your Grace, my Lord Hunsdon?" Ned finally asked.

"A petition, entirely in Latin, to the Royal College of Physicians," Elizabeth said, beginning to pace again. "From said Marcus Clerewell, late of Norwich, now practicing his craft in Cheapside. A request for the recognition of something he calls the water droplet vapor theory of spreading disease. And he lists here several Italian doctors who promote the theory."

"Italians," Ned echoed with a sniff. "Catholics, in short. Do the names include that Italian doctor who wants to cut up bodies, the one who is Dr. Caius's friend?"

"You mean Andreas Versalius," the queen interjected. She put one hand on the tall back of a chair to steady herself. "No, his name is not here, and the word you want is *dissect*."

"All right, dissect," Ned muttered. "Then what about that Italian doctor's name who fashioned the so-called life mask or bust of Katherine Grey?"

"Yes, Stefano Natus is noted here," she told them, slapping the paper down on the table for them to see. 'S bones, she wished Cecil were here to help sort all this out. "See the notation in a second hand—also in Latin—there? That florid, robust writing? It reads that Marcus Clerewell is not licensed in Norwich but is a runnagate—a mountebank."

"A fake doctor?" Jenks asked, turning toward her wherever she paced in the room. "A quacksalver? Then why wouldn't the royal doctors have him arrested straightaway when they found this out?"

"Unless he's in a different prison," Harry said.

"Or unless it was somehow to their benefit to blackmail Clerewell," she added. "Or if he's in thick with them."

"What?" several people chorused.

Her veil bounced as she nodded, and she kept fingering the mermaid pin as if it were a talisman of good luck. "As you see," she explained, "there is also scribbling on the page in a third hand, the tight, spare writing. That says Marcus Clerewell may actually be one Mercury Blackwell, who was banished from Norwich for selling fake cures for pox scars."

"But who wrote what?" Anne asked.

"I don't know," Elizabeth admitted. "But I could hazard a guess that the crisp, tight hand is like Caius and the robust, broader strokes like Pascal. We'll need more proof."

"So what's this water droplet theory?" Harry asked.

"As Dr. Burcote explained the theory," Elizabeth said, each word spoken deliberately as she reasoned everything through again, "it is the spread of certain vile diseases or contagions by an ill person's sneezing or coughing tiny droplets which are then inhaled into another's pores, mouth, or lungs. No one knows what causes the pox or bubonic plague either, so this could be valid."

"What's our next step?" Harry inquired.

"Harry, you must return yet again to the Royal College of Physicians to find samples of both Pascal's and Caius's written hands—in Latin—and do not confuse which is which. I believe that whoever merely noted that Clerewell is a runnagate may not be in on this plot, but the doctor who pursued Clerewell and learned he had faked cures and had worked with the pox—that doctor could have bribed or blackmailed him to help in this plot, even trying to set Meg up somehow."

"I'll bet it's Caius," Jenks muttered. "He's the one in charge. But then, it could still be both doctors, working together."

"It could indeed," the queen admitted as her stomach knotted again. "Harry, as soon as you find those handwriting samples, come to Cheapside. The rest of us are going shopping there for a runnagate doctor."

HOUGH IT WAS LATE AFTERNOON, LONDONERS STILL scurried from shop to shop on crowded Cheapside. Food mongers, trying to sell the last of their day's wares, shouted above the din, hawking pigs' trotters, oysters, and fried fish. The veiled queen and Lady Anne stood back under the overhang of Goldsmith's Row. Ordinarily, Elizabeth would have loved to be incognito to wander from shop to shop, to mingle with her people unseen and purchase pretty things, but today she had ugly business to see to.

Jenks and Ned soon returned from their task of inquiring where a Dr. Pribble practiced. "Bett's right," Ned said, out of breath. "It's that one on the corner, and he's in. We saw a man just enter with a bloody nose, like maybe from a fight."

"Ned, Jenks, and Anne, come with me," the queen commanded. "The rest of you wait here, but do not clump together nor call attention to yourselves. And keep an eye out for Lord Hunsdon, as he should join us soon." They left Clifford in charge of the four other armed guards, all doing their best to hide their weapons and blend into the crowd.

At the doctor's front door, Elizabeth and Anne stood back as Ned and Jenks argued over who they should say they were. Annoyed but hesitant to scold them in public, Elizabeth glanced through the narrow bull's-eye glass window next to the door. When she had looked in the wig-maker's window, she'd seen her body. Now, despite the distortion of the glass, she startled to see another old woman, but very much alive, facing away, leaning intently, one hand to her head as if it hurt.

"I thought you said a wounded man went inside," she interrupted Ned and Jenks.

"True," Ned said, stepping back to look through the window

too. "Oh, that's the old beldam who answered the door to let him in. Heard her tell the injured man she had to run back upstairs to clean, but guess she didn't."

Elizabeth swore under her breath and shoved Jenks aside to rap on the door herself. "It doesn't matter what we say to get in to see the doctor," she told them. "What matters is what we can get out of him."

T HOUGH NICK WAS NEARLY DYING OF THIRST, HE'D QUIT drinking the flat beer the keepers of this hellhole provided. It must be drugged. So he'd been dribbling it on his filthy body instead. His head was clearing some, though he'd almost rather be unconscious or dead, considering things he'd seen in here.

Whole jars of leeches put on screaming, tied-down people. Slowly they quieted, died, and were carted off to another chamber, where who knows what went on. He'd seen some steaming, creamy stuff, like maybe molten wax or plaster, smeared on people's faces, then peeled off. Tumors, like the ones from scrofula, had been cut off people's necks and packed in jars.

"A gift fit for a queen," he'd heard Ben Wilton say of the tumors. Ben was the main guard here, though he usually just sat around with a whip or whacked noisy people with a club. The fact he knew Nick and Gil cut them no slack, so Nick thought they weren't getting out alive.

Fit for a queen, Nick thought. Deuce it, surely the queen wasn't coming here.

When Gil was conscious and not having something thrust down his throat, the boy tried to signal across the cages to Nick until Ben reached in with a club and knocked him down. Nick wanted to rip his bars apart, but he still played like he was drugged. He knew that gutter cur'd just as soon club him too, and then he'd be leech food. He was pretty certain poor Gil had signaled, *I been eating Meg's cure. Makes my burning throat better.* But he knew he couldn't have read his boy right when he thought he added, *men in next room, chopping corpses.*

❧   ❧   ❧

"I SAY WE SHOULD HAUL DR. PRIBBLE TO THE TOWER AND tear the truth out of him," Ned groused as they dejectedly left the doctor's shop and moved away through the swirl of pedestrians. The doctor had insisted he'd never met Nick or Gil, nor did he know where to locate Dr. Marcus Clerewell if he wasn't in his chambers on Gutter Lane. He had admitted, though, that Dr. Caius had recently come looking for Clerewell too.

"And probably found him and either eliminated him or joined ranks with him," Elizabeth said with a weary sigh. Old Pribble had been such a bumbler that she believed him. Besides, she had another plan, pure woman's instinct, or maybe that of a cornered animal when it scents its hunters are too clever.

"Anyway, that's what I'd do," Ned muttered, trying to see through her veil. "I'd use the thumbscrews or the rack to make anyone involved tell all they knew."

"Oh, yes, I'll just decree they all be hauled into Bridewell or the Tower," Elizabeth said, her exhaustion and frustration edged with sarcasm. "Including the old crone from Gutter Lane, my Stewart cousins, Katherine Grey, and her little son. 'S blood and bones, *I* am the one on the rack, so you'll not tell me what to do. Ned, go back to Dr. Pribble's and bribe that old woman to come talk to me. I swear we saw her eavesdropping."

The queen was getting more dismayed that Harry had not come yet, but she didn't want to upset Anne by saying so. It wasn't long before Ned returned with the old woman in tow. While the others stood scattered at a distance, Elizabeth and Lady Anne huddled with the woman at Goldsmith's Row. She was grinning to have received an entire crown and bent a crooked curtsy to Elizabeth and then Anne.

"I warrant you know I'm the one who asked the questions inside," Elizabeth said. "Your name?"

"Millicent Mabry, milady," the white-haired woman answered readily, almost feistily, gripping her coin tighter. "Dr. Pribble's elder sister, I am, the one should have been the physician in the family had I been born a man."

"Is that why you listen at his door when he thinks—and you make a point of saying—you are going upstairs to clean?" Elizabeth prompted. "I assure you I will not tell him. I understand your yearning to be the one in command when your brother is instead."

"Oh, aye, milady. Well, since you caught me at my game, I'll tell you straight I heard what you asked him afore, about that half-handsome Dr. Clerewell and the mute boy."

"And his father," the queen prompted.

"Oh, aye, saw him too. More dim-witted than the boy, though the boy's mute. You won't believe this, but the lad's an artist for the queen!"

"Indeed? Say on."

"He made Dr. Clerewell angry not wanting his cure, biting off his tongue stick, and arguing with his hands, like he does. Peeked in as well as listened that day, I did. Such an int'resting malady, muteness."

"Have you seen other doctors here," Elizabeth went on, "important ones, perhaps to see Dr. Pribble or even Dr. Clerewell?"

"A tall, gaunt one, several weeks ago, came to see my brother but wanted Dr. Clerewell. Chief physician, the visitor was of *Maxima Regina's Collegium,* that's the way he put it."

"Yes, I heard Dr. Caius came calling. I will see more crowns are yours if you tell me true what else passed between them."

"Don't know for a certain. My brother sent me for hot ale for the two of them, and that Dr. Caius wouldn't even stay to drink it when I brought it down. On his way out the door, but heading for Dr. Clerewell's place, I warrant, since my brother shouted out to him which way was Gutter Lane.

"Now," Millicent Mabry went on, "if that fancy Dr. Caius would have asked *me*—like you're doing, milady—where else to look for Dr. Clerewell, I could have told him. Overheard him say once to a patient scarred near as bad as he was—till he got his face mostly cured, that is—that he'd take her to his doctor friend in Chelsea, to a sort of hospital to cure her."

"To Chelsea?" Elizabeth cried. "Chelsea, *not* Cheapside?"

"Why," she said, drawing herself up to her full, short height, "guess I know Chelsea from Cheapside, milady. I'm no fool."

"Indeed you are not. And this doctor friend of Clerewell's in Chelsea was named Dr. Pascal, was it not?"

"If he said that, didn't hear it. But I know Dr. Clerewell was interested in curing scars on faces, like on his own. Is that why you're searching for him, then? I mean, with your veil and all . . ."

"Partly, yes," Elizabeth said, pressing three more crowns from her hanging purse into the old woman's hands. "I tell you, Millicent Mabry, if there were women doctors, your sharp mind and keen observational skills would have made you a fine one. I warrant your queen would have made you the first female fellow in that vaunted *Collegium* of Royal Physicians," she added as she turned away. Her entourage materialized around and behind her as she headed at a breakneck stride toward the Thames.

"What did she say and where to now?" Ned asked.

Elizabeth stopped to face them. "Anne, you must go back with one of your guards and wait for your lord to come to Cheapside and then follow us to Chelsea—Peter Pascal's house.

It will be dusk soon, so there is no time to return to Blackfriars for the barge or extra guards."

"But—you mean you're going to Chelsea now, Your Grace?" Anne asked, her face and voice alarmed. "Without even one lady with you?"

"Dear Anne, I have been in worse scrapes before. I have men I trust, and none know who I am. Besides, the last time I went calling on Peter Pascal, I did so openly and that was a mistake. I have been surprised for the last time in this, and now it is their turn."

Chapter

THE SIXTEENTH

Those of our time do use the flowers of Borage . . .
for the comfort of the heart and to drive away sorrows.
Borage is called in shops Borago. The ancients thought
it always brought courage.

JOHN GERARD
The Herball

T HE CREAK OF BARGEMEN'S OARS AND THE JERKING
thrust of prow did not lull the queen but unnerved her.
Elizabeth had once said that all roads in this effigy plot
led to little Chelsea. Now that she thought of this treasonous attempt on her life and danger to her people as the pox plot, clues
still led there. Wishing she had some herb or potion to buck herself up, she tried to stir up her courage. *"I sought the Lord and He*
heard me," she recited repeatedly, *"and delivered me from all my*
fears." But she still shook like a reed in the wind.

Though surrounded by armed men, she did not feel safe.
When dealing with unscrupulous doctors, the fear of something
invisible, some creeping blight or plague, haunted her. The little
hamlet of Chelsea was Peter Pascal's realm. Yet Dr. Caius was the
president of the Royal College, and his accusatory interrogation

of Meg and of Gil's family—as well as his being seen looking for Dr. Clerewell—made him seem the guiltier party. Unless they were all in league.

"What will we do when we arrive?" Ned's voice broke into her agonizing.

Because she could not bear to admit she was acting as much on instinct as intellect, Elizabeth told him and the other five men, "Ned, you will go into the tavern where Jenks asked questions on our other visit. You will inquire if a Dr. John Caius is known in the village. Describe him, if you must. And I warrant they will tell you that he has been a frequent visitor to Pascal's home and is there now. And then you must describe Dr. Clerewell, both of his faces. . . ."

Her voice snagged, and her fingers tightened on the hem of her veil she held down so it wouldn't flap in the river breeze. If only Dr. Clerewell, whom Meg had trusted, was someone who had truly found a cure for pox scars, if not the pox itself. As he spoke briefly in the aisle of the Abbey, the man's voice had been so compelling and caring, and yet the poor girl with him . . .

"That's it!" the queen cried, smacking her fists on her knees.

"What's it?" Jenks asked.

"In the Abbey aisle, Dr. Clerewell, alias Mercury Blackwell, passed a sachet before that ill girl's nose, not to keep her conscious or soothe her but to force her to sneeze on me. Whether he acted on his own or under Dr. Caius's aegis, his actions intentionally threatened my life!"

The rooftops and skeletal trees of Chelsea loomed at them, lit by the crimson sinking sun. "Someone give me a dagger," the queen ordered. "And keep your sword arms free."

꙰   ꙰   ꙰

PAYING THE BARGEMEN WELL—SHE HAD SEARCHED each face to be certain Ben Wilton was not among them—

the queen ordered them to wait here no matter who else tried to buy their services. "And if another London barge arrives," she told them, "inquire if it is Lord Hunsdon and his entourage, and tell them we are probably going to be at Pascal's looking for him and his cohorts."

"We could make our Chelsea headquarters in the old wig-maker's place," Ned suggested as they left the barge landing, "especially since it's getting dark."

"It's a secondary site we may have to search again," she admitted as the lights of the tavern came into view across the familiar green. "But the darkness is on our side."

They waited anxiously while Ned went into the tavern. As she paced, Elizabeth kicked through piles of autumn leaves on the fringe of the green. Finally, Ned came out and broke into a run toward them.

"Pascal's here but he's not the only doctor oft in Chelsea," he told them, out of breath.

"Clerewell or Caius?" Elizabeth demanded.

"They never heard of a Clerewell or Blackwell. But, as you surmised, they say Caius has oft visited Pascal here."

"I'll warrant he's here now, and we'll take them in one fell swoop!" she cried.

"But something else I picked up in passing," Ned said as they started toward Pascal's. "Pascal oft comes and goes not from the old water stairs by his house nor the public landing, but from Sir Thomas More's old boathouse on the far edge of his grounds. It's a place he's been enlarging and refurbishing for years with workers from the city—no local help."

The queen's head jerked up. "The boathouse was Thomas More's, and Pascal's been changing it? But he won't allow anything his beloved mentor touched to be one whit changed. Jenks, when you searched Pascal's stables, did you see such a building?"

"In the distance, but it didn't look like much. You told me to hurry, so I didn't have time to get close. I was thinking later, though, more horses might be there, 'cause I heard distant whinnying from the old place."

Her heart pounding, Elizabeth knew her next move. "Lord Hunsdon and Anne should be here soon, so I'm sending one of you men of his household—you," she said, indicating the shortest and thinnest of the lot, "to return to wait with our barge to bring Lord Hunsdon to us when they arrive. The rest of us, Ned, Jenks, Clifford, and you two from my Lord Hunsdon's household, will come with me."

"To where, Your Grace—I mean, milady?" Jenks asked as he scraped his sword out.

"Ned, take one of Lord Hunsdon's men and keep an eye on Pascal's house. With Jenks, Clifford, and Lord Hunsdon's other man," she indicated the brawnier of the two guards, "I shall take a distant look at this boathouse, then join you."

AS ELIZABETH AND HER THREE GUARDS WADED through rustling, knee-deep autumn leaves to skirt Pascal's property, her thoughts turned to Gil again. She had come to care deeply for the boy, as if he were a foster son. Gil had God's blessing with his raw, artistic talent. He had both a restless and a reckless streak in him she saw in herself, though she had learned to bridle her deepest desires. Even his muteness had served her well, for, like Cecil, Gil kept her secrets. If anything had happened to him—

"Dark as sin," Jenks whispered, pointing toward the boathouse on the bank of the Thames as dusk bled to darkness. "No one's here, at least now."

The place was a hulking pile of stones, barely one story high.

"I'd say this is a dead end and we should join the others at Pascal's," she told them. "Yet the fact he's supposedly been rejuvenating the place . . . That's just not like Pascal, unless there's some driving need or passion. Let's go a bit closer."

But the four of them froze in their tracks. On the wind came a half moan, half scream.

"Is that what you thought horses sounded like?" the queen asked Jenks.

"I guess so, but this close, it sounds like a human voice," he whispered. The sound had been so unearthly that Elizabeth began to tremble again. She was not alone, for someone's scabbard rattled.

"We're not going in, but we can try to look in," Elizabeth said. "If it's something strange, we'll go fetch the others, even the bargemen."

As they approached, the place seemed darker yet. At least from the land side, they saw no windows, no light outlining doors, just a hump of stones like a headless giant's shoulders. But then another cry, a keening sound.

"Jenks," she said, almost mouthing her words, "go fetch the others here."

"Send Clifford, milady. I don't want to leave your side."

"Go on! You know the layout, and the stables lie between us and the house!"

She actually thought he would argue more, but he plunged headlong into the night. Keeping close to the line of gnarled tree trunks, Elizabeth, Clifford, and Harry's man edged closer. They could hear the river slapping the bank now. Still in the shadow of the skeletal trees, they inched forward.

Under the tree nearest to the boathouse, a huge, heavy net dropped on them. They stood under its weight a moment, clawing, thrashing until dark forms thudded from the trees and yanked them to the ground. Men around her—more than her own—fighting, struggling, sprawled. A clang of muted metal.

"We owe that tavern tapster for more fresh blood," someone muttered and laughed.

A voice she knew? Clerewell, the man who had spoken in the Abbey? *You are the angel of us all,* he had said to his queen.

"Stop," she cried. "I command you to unhand m—"

Pressed to the ground she tried to scream, but someone stuffed veil and net into her mouth with something bitter-tasting. The blackguard held her down while she gagged and swallowed. And then she tasted nothing at all.

⁂   ⁂   ⁂

ELIZABETH AWOKE. DIZZINESS ASSAILED HER. NAUSEA. Aches. Voices. And then one she knew.

"Lady. Lady!"

Whose voice? Not Ned's or Jenks's. Mayhap Nick Cotter's. But what about her men Jenks went to fetch? Why hadn't Harry come? Harry was her cousin too, the only one who didn't covet her throne—or did he? 'S bones, it hurt to turn her head.

"Lady! Lady Elizabeth!"

Lanterns hung from wall pegs and the ceiling. She tried to move but was strapped, arms and legs, to a narrow, wooden table in a long, low chamber filled with cages.

Ah, she was caged too, like an animal. Katherine Grey's monkey had jumped on her shoulders, but hadn't there been a net in the trees? She fought to focus her thoughts. In trying to set a trap, she had obviously walked into one. These cages, smaller than hers, lower to the ground, held human beings. Poor Meg so long in prison, but worse that her own mother had been trapped in the Tower, waiting to die.

Elizabeth's vision was blurred: things were foggy, though her

veil was gone. She must have been drugged, and she struggled to
turn her head. Yes, Nick Cotter across the room had been calling
her name. But it was the person in the cage next to her that made
her gasp.

Gil. Gil on a bed of filthy straw. Gil, keeping close to the floor
but signing up at her, *Bad doctors here! Make people sick. Then kill
and cut them up!*

"Dear God, help us," she murmured. And turned to look the
other way, only to hear her cage door clang and have two gray
eyes—one with a drooping lid—stare close into hers. The half of
the face she saw at first was handsome, even striking. The other
side was a mass of welts and ridges and pits.

"Since we meet, both scarred at last, I have something to
show you, Your Majesty," the man said in his deep, pleasant voice
as if nothing were amiss. She knew instantly who he was. The
entire scene in the aisle of the Abbey flashed before her. "You see,
we doctors have decreed that everyone here must earn his or her
keep."

He moved a lantern to a hook above her. Brushing her loosed
hair from her face, he produced a small alabaster jar of white
cream and with a small knife proceeded to smooth it on her skin
exactly where she knew her pox marks were.

"Your pits aren't deep or numerous," he said, his voice soothing, though it and his gaze made her feel sick to her stomach. "I
had hoped for more so my Venus Moon Emollient could make
me rich and powerful, but too late for that now. My wealth and
power will come from my ability not to heal, but to sicken people
at my will. You'd be a prime example of that too, but the doctor
has other plans for you."

He was demented. But she must deal with him. Just let him
talk, she told herself. Gather strength and sense, find an opening.
Calm him. Stall until her people came looking for her. But she

had no doubt she would appear to have vanished into thin air. She saw not one window in this place as she glanced around, though she could feel cool air coming from somewhere, perhaps from the roof. The stench of unwashed, ill bodies was so bad in here, no breath seemed fresh.

"Perhaps," Clerewell was saying, "we'll have to see if we can infect you with the Queen's Evil and then work on your neck tumors. Now, that would be justice, would it not? Oh, by the way, never mind looking around for help. Your two companions as well as the one you sent to Pascal's are—shall we say—sleeping until we need them. And we're sending word to your bargemen that you saw your missing servants being taken away in a boat and gave chase in another. I suppose they'll jump back on your barge and chase you down the river till dawn, when here you are, all ready and willing to help us in any way."

He dropped his hand to her slender throat and tightened his grip. Across the room, Nick went wild in his cage until she heard someone stomp over and quiet him, evidently with a cudgel that slammed the metal bars.

She heard Gil rattle his too, felt him rock his cage. For some reason, Clerewell loosed his grip, and she sucked in a breath of air. Ben Wilton suddenly appeared, cudgel in hand, and swung at Gil through his bars. Ben Wilton, another piece in this puzzle. Gil quieted at once, though she hadn't heard him hit and couldn't turn her head far enough to see.

No other protests sounded from the other sick souls she'd seen here, so she assumed they must be drugged or simply beyond help. She forced herself to speak.

"If you had such a marvelous cure, why did you not come to me, petition me, Dr. Clerewell?" It took such an effort to think, to form her words. Her tongue felt swollen, and her throat hurt. She wanted to stay as mute as Gil.

"I had planned that at first," he said, straightening to survey his handiwork on her, then, without a mirror, to apply the stuff on his own scars. Thank God, it must not be acid or poison then. "But," he went on, "my plan to use Mistress Wilton to reach you took a turn, when I found one of the doctors of the Royal College was not hostile to my ideas, at least not privily so, if I could assist him."

"Dr. Caius," she said. "He came looking for you. He's made some deal with Ben Wilton to torment Sarah Wilton. He's evidently hired her husband as he has you."

"Caius?" a new voice cried. "I swear if he knew aught of my experiments or intentions he'd cast me out of the royal college and you wouldn't even have to. Caius?" the dreadful, high-pitched voice went on with a hooted laugh. "Then you are a fool, and I never took you for that, though I must say I did take you for the Protestant bitch daughter of the great whore Boleyn and of the Tudor Antichrist who ruined the true church and my mentor's . . ."

The words rolled on. Pascal. His huge shadow loomed over her before he did. When he elbowed Clerewell aside, she saw Pascal was stirring a bowl of white slop. Porridge? No, plaster!

"I do hope you've kept that effigy Dr. Clerewell and I worked so hard on," Pascal said, "though I'm now going to do a life mask of you instead of that imitation we had to use. We'll return your body to London in pieces after its dissection and beheading—in memoriam of Sir Thomas More, of course. But I shall donate this new mask for your effigy, as I'm sure the nation will want to hold a fine funeral for you before your Catholic cousin Mary's coronation."

❧　　❧　　❧

NED TOPSIDE WASN'T SURE WHETHER TO BELIEVE THE stranger at all. "What do you mean, the veiled lady has left in a boat?" he cried. "What boat?"

"The only one left at the boathouse after some men took off in another one with her servants Nick and Gil. I think those are the names the veiled lady said and gave me a crown for running to you—see?"

In the man's grimy palm lay an identical crown to the ones the queen had been bribing and paying their way with.

"She said tell you," the man gasped out, "take the barge you came in and come after her downriver. She can't lose sight of her men—man and the lad, I mean. She said I'd have to tell you because she needed the other three men with her so she'd be safe."

"Yes, all right," Ned agreed. "Keep this quiet then," he ordered the man.

"Aye, that I will," the man said as Ned and Hunsdon's man ran hard for the Chelsea public barge-landing. Thank heavens, Lord and Lady Hunsdon were just arriving.

"Where is she?" Harry demanded as Lady Anne peered anxiously over his shoulder.

"Set off downriver in pursuit of mischief, and we're to follow posthaste," Ned shouted, out of breath. "Now we can take both barges. Did you find samples of the two doctors' handwriting?"

"After my last visit, Pascal sent word all his papers were to be burned in the back alley," Lord Hunsdon called to him as both barges cast off and caught the current. "I had a deuce of a time pawing through half-charred paper. It's Pascal's writing that's spare and taut, not Caius's. The lady won't like she's been wrong in thinking Caius was the mastermind."

❧   ❧   ❧

ELIZABETH LAY TERROR-STRUCK AS THE PLASTER HARD-ened on her face. She felt the stone boathouse roof closing in on her, the cells with bars crushing her down. Two straws were stuck up her nostrils so that she could breathe, but she felt she was suffocating. Breathe slowly, she told herself, carefully.

Though they had strapped her head down now too, and two leather bands restrained her body, that traitor Ben Wilton hovered over her with a knife blade to her throat so she would lie completely quiet. Pascal was a perfectionist, it seemed, carefully smoothing the plaster over her oiled skin. Nothing, not even the pox, had been worse than this. She felt she was in her coffin already or encased in a huge stone sarcophagus under the age-old weight of Westminster Abbey.

When the plaster on her face had gone stone hard, Pascal himself returned to peel the mask off and walked away with his prize. Though she could not stop shaking, she saw her opportunity to talk to Ben.

"Dr. Caius tells me you have a daughter, one sadly poxed," she said. She sounded like a stutterer. Her teeth were chattering though she was sweating worse than with fever.

"How'd he dig that up? Pascal says he's not in on none a this," he muttered, tossing the knife—it looked like the one she'd borrowed from Jenks—from hand to hand. Now she had nothing pointed on her person but a mermaid pin.

"Where is your and Meg's child?" Elizabeth pursued. Even if he told her, she had no hope she'd live to tell Meg.

"Seein' you won't tell," Ben said with a snicker, "I'll let you in on it, Majesty. Fostered out with a fam'ly on Hampstead Heath who have a farm. Just couldn't bear to look at her."

Elizabeth thought of her own reaction to poxed people before, but no more. If she could only live, she vowed the ill and the maimed would be dear to her.

"But Meg, I mean Sarah, surely did not agree to give up the girl," Elizabeth prompted him to go on.

"Fought me about it, but I had the little wench sent away when she was out deliv'ing herbs once. 'Bout went crazy, 'n ran off, thinking she'd find her. Didn't see her for a coupla years then, and wouldn't you know, the new Queen of England shows up with Sarah in service. I thought I'd be set for life, but you had to toss her out. It's all your fault, see?"

"How long have you worked for the doctors? Was it before or after you claimed you saw someone climbing my garden wall?"

"A short while before, though Clerewell and I made sure Meg thought I was real jealous of him. She was afeared I'd knock his teeth in, 'cause I was knocking her around good when I fancied to."

Outrage and contempt racked the queen. Ben Wilton was a demon. Now, she thought, as Pascal came back into her cell, she had to try to reason with Satan himself. But words utterly failed her when she saw Pascal was carrying a large, glass-blown jar of writhing leeches.

~ ~ ~

A S TIME TICKED ON, CLEREWELL SAT ON A LOW BENCH outside her makeshift cell, for his job was now to watch her. She could hear and smell that he was drinking, for all the good it would do her if he got drunk.

She tried to keep her mind on anything else but the numerous leeches applied in the pattern of the pox to her temples, throat, and limbs. The vile knaves had lifted her skirts nearly to her hips and ripped her sleeves off to apply them, so she felt half-naked under Clerewell's increasingly drunken inspection. Each time he'd come in to take her neck pulse, she saw Peter Pascal's timepiece dangling from Clerewell's belt.

"Did he give you that fancy timepiece before or after the two of you killed the old wig-maker?" she asked.

"Actually, oh queen of royal blood," he said with a snicker, pulling off one fat leech, "I first filched it from him right under his nose at the college. I figured since I'd helped him by sneaking down an alley and planting that effigy in your coach, he owed me a little something extra," he went on with a loud hiccough. "But when I told him I'd get the leeched girl's body into your fountain, he had to give it back a second time after I lost it—the timepiece, that is."

"Lost it after you killed the old woman for Pascal."

"She didn't feel a thing," he insisted, putting a new leech in place where he'd pulled the other off. "She didn't even see it coming, though her poor lass did. Just like you—leeched into oblivion, then stripped to take a swim in your fountain."

Elizabeth gritted her teeth and tried to free her arms from the straps as Clerewell dared to slide a hand up her left leg, ruffling her petticoats even higher. "I could put some of these leeches a special place on a special virgin," he muttered.

"Stand back!" Pascal ordered, coming into Elizabeth's cell. "I was appalled to hear you had stripped that dead girl naked, Clerewell! Sir Thomas More was a religious man, and I'll tolerate no debauchery in this."

At that, the queen had to fight hysteria, desperate to turn her head away, to scream and laugh and cry. But with the strap across her forehead she could look only straight up, not over at Nick anymore nor at her Gil so close. It was just as well, she tried to console herself. If she could turn her head, she would see the leeches as well as feel them. And then, before she died, she might go as insane as her captors. Already she felt weak, so weak.

"Gil," she whispered when both men went out, and she finally heard Clerewell snoring close by, "I don't know if you can hear me, and I can't see your signals—or make them myself."

"P—p—," she heard him say. Her entire body tensed even more. It was the first vocalization she'd ever heard from Gil other than screams one time years ago. She waited for Clerewell to wake, to react. Had that been Gil? If so, maybe he was trying to spit in contempt at Clerewell.

"P—p—pin."

"What?" she barely mouthed, trying to turn her head, her eyes, but she still could not see him. "Gil, if that's you, don't let Ben Wilton see you," she whispered.

"P-pin. Fish," he hissed over and over.

Gil was talking. He saw her pin dear Mary had given her, the mermaid. He wanted her pin?

Despite the strap across her chest, she tried hard to lift one arm to unpin it. Then she knew why Gil wanted it. He had always used pins to pick locks.

She reached it and fought to undo it. Concentrate. Try. But the safety hook was so difficult in best of times. And she was so damned dizzy, swimming in that fountain, floating faceup . . .

She gasped as Gil somehow appeared in her line of sight. He was hanging from the top of his tiny cage, though still inside. Her Gil in and out of windows, stealing things, in and out of her life, stealing her heart . . .

Somehow she had the pin between her finger and thumb, but he could not reach it. Horrified at the sight of her arm laden with leeches, she moved her hand to free the pin and extend it to Gil. He worked his arm through his bars, then through hers. He seized the pin and disappeared from her sight.

A scraping. A creak. She heard Clerewell snort, then move. Across the way she heard Nick start to make a racket, shaking his cage, screaming like a man gone mad. Clerewell lumbered to his feet, staggered against her cage, then evidently made toward Nick to silence him.

Other prisoners began to stir or wake. Gil was in her cage, leaning over her. Had he picked her lock, or did Clerewell leave her door open? The boy yanked at the strap that held her head down and scratched at her forehead. He loosed her body bindings. The leeches. He was scraping off the leeches.

"Get 'way from her!" Ben Wilton shouted from across the room. "Dr. Pascal!"

Gil helped her sit up in time to see Nick snake an arm from his cage and grab Clerewell as he tried to quiet him.

"R-run. Run!" Gil croaked out as he pulled her off the table.

Dizziness spun her around; her legs buckled. She fell on her knees against the cage door. But on the floor lay the spatula with which Clerewell had spread the emollient on her face. Grabbing it, she scraped away one leech after the other from her arms. Bleeding. She was still bleeding.

Ben came with his cudgel raised, seized Gil by the throat, and slammed him back against the bars of her cell. That jolted her. She must forget all else and save herself and Gil.

Furious, Elizabeth rose to her feet behind Ben. He had a knife raised now, the one he must have taken from her earlier. He was going to stab Gil! She clanged the cell door into the back of Ben's head and saw him crumple.

Gil sucked in rasping breaths and pointed down at Ben. She saw he had fallen on her knife. A chest wound, one that quickly soaked his shirt and sleeve in his own blood.

"Take his club and knock out Clerewell too," she told Gil, grabbing the cudgel and thrusting it at the boy. "We've got to get out of here, get help for everyone. Which way out?"

Gil pointed toward the riverside—a door to a room, then evidently remembered he could talk. "K-k-keys—b-b—his b-belt," he managed, pointing at Ben, then ran to help his stepfather. Elizabeth saw that Nick had managed to pull Clerewell down, choking him so he was nearly sprawled against his low cage. Gil knocked him out cleanly and bent to pick Nick's lock.

Elizabeth took Ben's big single key from the growing puddle

of his blood and ran from cage to cage, opening doors, though Gil was just as quick with the pin. A few weak, bewildered victims crawled out; most just stared at her or backed farther in. But as Gil and Nick ran to her, Peter Pascal filled the doorway.

"Stand back," Elizabeth ordered, advancing on him. "All of us are leaving now."

"How I prayed you would never sit the throne," Pascal cried, his eyes glowing in the lantern he held and gestured with. "I even tried to enlist the aid of the Scottish Stewarts, but it seems they have their own plans and just laughed at me."

She didn't like the way he was gesturing with his lantern. "Move aside, Dr. Pascal," Elizabeth commanded, though she could barely stand. "You have done more here than sully the name of the good man who was your mentor. You have played God. Sir Thomas More would not be proud, but shamed unto death—"

"To death. To death!" he shouted to echo her words and heaved his lantern at them.

It shattered and flamed the straw on the floor between them. He threw yet another lantern from the wall and ran out, slamming the door. She heard him shoot a bolt.

Not only straw but rags and layers of bedding caught fire. It licked in one area, then seemed to spew everywhere. The room belched heat and smoke.

"Water?" Elizabeth asked.

"Not in here," Nick bellowed, then began to hack. "Nothing like that—to put it out."

"Then we must get to river water. Where is the air source above?" she demanded over the rising cries of their fellow captives.

Gil pointed upward. Black as the night beyond, a hole in the ceiling.

"If we stack some cages," the queen shouted over the mayhem, "can you climb through it, Gil, maybe unlock that door from the other side?"

With two other victims, they struggled to stack the closest empty cages, three of them. That was enough for Gil to scramble up and out. The smoke was so dense they could hardly breathe. The queen and Nick herded everyone who could walk to the corners of the room by the door and pressed them to the floor where the thick air was slightly clearer. But when Gil did not come back, Elizabeth, who had scraped off every last leech she could feel, knew she must go up too.

"I cannot let Pascal win," she told Nick as she gasped for air. "Can you get me up to the top of that first cage? And then you'd best follow me."

She half climbed and pulled herself up; he boosted her. Exhausted, drained, less agile than Gil, she twice slipped back. She had prayed that the air would be clearer here, but the smoke in the room vented upward toward the hole as if it were a chimney.

Then, above, it was not Gil's face she saw, peering through the smoke, but Ned's. Then Harry's. Hands reached for her and hauled her up.

"The door that way near the river!" she shouted, pointing. "There's a bolted door! And Nick Cotter's right behind me."

Ned and Harry scrambled down the curved roof to the ground. Shouts. Cries. Then smoke pouring out from the doorway as well as the vent behind them.

"Where's Gil?" she asked Ned.

"Gil broke his leg, Your Grace, and we found him crawling and jabbering. Once we realized you weren't on the river in a boat, we came back—then saw this smoke."

"Did you see Pascal?" When he shrugged, she shouted, "Find Peter Pascal! Search his house!"

Ned and Harry helped her edge off the humped stone roof and, with two other armed men, ran to obey. Below, others— even some Chelsea citizens now—carried or dragged the drugged Jenks, Clifford, and Harry's man, as well as the other ill and maimed, from the flaming, smoking boathouse. Anne was bent over Gil, who sprawled on the ground, his leg bent at a bad angle, but his throat working as he cried, "Ma—je—sty! Majesty!"

They all looked in the direction Gil pointed. Not far away, brightness bit into the sable sky. Pascal's house—Sir Thomas More's—flamed like a funeral pyre.

AFTERWORD

This verifies our English proverb, "Far fetched and dear
bought is best for ladies." Yet it may more be truly said
of fantastical physicians, who when they have found an
approved medicine and perfect remedy near home . . .
yet not content seek for a new farther off. . . .

                      JOHN GERARD
                      The Herball

A FORTNIGHT LATER, ONLY A FEW OF THE QUEEN'S intimates knew the real reason Her Majesty had a sudden urge to visit her father's long-derelict hunt lodge on the edge of Hampstead Heath. She felt much stronger now, she told everyone, and needed an outing. She was wearied, she said, of meetings with the London Royal College of Physicians to set new precedents and fill the vacated post Dr. Pascal's accidental death had left.

It was known far and wide that Peter Pascal had burned to death with his house steward, though the rest of his staff escaped the late-night conflagration, which was evidently sparked by a lantern igniting draperies. Elizabeth saw to it that word did not get out that Pascal's large skeleton was found, with an antique axe nearby, beheaded before the flames devoured the house. Somehow, too, Chelsea gossip said, the flames had leaped to the old boathouse and left only a charred and empty interior.

As for Dr. Caius, Elizabeth had pretended to believe he had been misguided in his zeal to punish Meg and subdue all apothecaries. In truth, she had been so relieved he knew naught of Pascal's demented doings—and she needed a brilliant man in charge of her London College who owed her his very life—that she fined Caius heavily but did not imprison him. Word had flown far and wide that the once stiff-backed Dr. Caius was suddenly working closely with the crown.

But no one except Meg knew that the queen had sent Ned Topside ahead today to find a farm in Hampstead Heath where a six-year-old poxed child resided and then to meet their entourage on the road.

"I'm so scared," Meg told the queen as they jolted along in the queen's coach. Elizabeth had come the six miles from London on horseback with many of her courtiers, but since it would never do for her herb girl to ride with her, Meg had made the journey in the coach. Besides, the queen had reckoned, it would serve well for a privy reunion hidden from prying eyes. But near Hampstead Heath, the large retinue had halted at last, and the queen had joined Meg in the coach.

"You must not be afraid," Elizabeth, fingering the mermaid pin on her bodice, tried to comfort Meg. "I daresay you—we—have both been through worse than a reunion with one's own flesh and blood. Partings are far more terrible." She thought of Mary Sidney, greatly scarred, but recovered from the pox. Her friend had insisted on leaving court for her family home at Penshurst in Kent.

"But what if my own child hates me, blames me?" Meg cried,

sniffling. "And I mean not to rip her from all she's known if they love her there, if they are her parents now."

"That is true love, my Meg," the queen told her, staring out the window so the girl would not see her own tears. "To give up that which you desire deeply for the betterment of others who are your charge and care. You know, I'm thinking of sending Gil, when his leg heals, to Italy to study his art. Look, here's Ned. Halt, driver!"

The footman opened the door and put down the steps for Ned. He dismounted and climbed in to sit across from them.

"I've seen the girl and spoken with her and the family," Ned told them. Meg clasped her hands to her mouth. As ever, Elizabeth had to jolt him from his dramatic pause.

" 'S blood, say on, man!"

"The parents have tried to explain things to her. She came to them as a small child and knows no other home. They have named her Sarah, but call her Sally."

"Ah," the queen said. "And?"

"They beg you, Your Grace—and you, as her natural mother, Meg—not to take their child. The woman never bore a child," he said, with a nervous, darted glance at the queen, "but they have loved this one as their own. 'Tis a simple farm, a good, wholesome place, Meg, on the very fringe of the heath."

He leaned across to take the hand she offered him. "So much, all at once, I know," Ned said, his voice comforting. "To be widowed, to be returned to court—now this."

"I count it all blessings," Meg said, dashing tears from her face with her free hand until Ned fished out a handkerchief and handed it to her. "Believe me," she said, crying even harder, "when I tell you both, this is one of the best days of my life."

"Tell her all you know of the girl, parents, and their farm, Ned," the queen commanded. "I shall ride horseback the rest of the way so Meg and the child can have the coach."

As ever, Robin was waiting outside to help her down, and she let him. The brisk breeze and autumn sun felt fine on her face, for amazingly, her pox marks seemed to be healing faster than before and she would employ no more veils.

She gasped to see what Ned had not yet said. On a sway-backed horse sat a stout but comely woman with a young girl seated before her—a reddish-haired girl with a poxed face.

The queen strode closer. A few courtiers clustered around, but most of her entourage awaited farther up the road. The mother's eyes grew wide as the queen smiled and nodded up at her. And then to everyone's surprise, the child squirmed from her mother's grasp and tried to slide to the ground.

Elizabeth caught her and held her close. Tears blinded her eyes, for she saw in her soul that long past day at Chelsea she had fled the poxed mother and her children. She hugged the girl tight.

"Are you my other mother come to visit?" the little wench asked.

"No, but I am her—her friend," the queen said, her voice catching in her throat.

"This doll is Sally, and she looks just like me," she declared, producing a rag figure with a smooth linen face.

"Then bring Sally, and we shall go to meet your other mother."

Ignoring Robin and Jenks, who leaped forward to help, the queen carried the girl to the open door of the coach and put her down on the top step. She caught Ned kissing Meg's hand, but he had the good sense to make a hasty exit out the other side.

The last thing the queen saw as little Sally and Meg shared a trembling embrace was the girl's dropped doll lying faceup on the floor of the coach, like a little effigy.

AUTHOR'S NOTE

READERS OFTEN ASK WHERE I GET THE IDEAS AND PLOTS FOR
this historical mystery series. They always come from actual events.
For example, the kernel of the idea for this story came from the fact
that, in 1562, a wax doll—an effigy of the queen—was found in
Lincoln Inn Fields in London. Elizabeth was so disturbed by this
that she assembled a group of advisers, including doctors, to help
her trace it and what it might mean. And since the queen nearly
died from an attack of pox that year, from the doll and the disease
came all the other research, plot ideas, and characters for *The
Queene's Cure*.

I found Elizabethan era medicine fascinating but frequently
shocking. I have only touched on some of the beliefs and cures
known to Renaissance doctors and their patients. Although
Elizabeth did not dislike doctors, she often seemed to mistrust
them. (Her modus operandi in dealing with men in general.) In
1563, the year after this story ends, her government passed a law
controlling pricing by physicians. And it was not until 1565 that
Dr. Caius and the London Royal College of Physicians were finally granted corpses to dissect. Thereafter, they held an annual
lecture on anatomy.

However, medical progress was still not swift in England.
Over two centuries later, when Edward Jenner finally found a

way to immunize against smallpox through cowpox inoculation, the Royal Society of London was the premier scientific institute of that day. In 1798 the Society refused to accept Jenner's findings, despite his twenty-two years testing the theory, so he was forced to publish the information on his own.

Smallpox is sometimes called the only disease ever wiped out by man. It was officially certified as obsolete in 1980; however, because of recent fears that smallpox could be used in biological warfare (since most of the world's populace are no longer immunized against it), the World Health Organization has been debating whether or not to keep vials of it at the U.S. Center for Disease Control in Atlanta. As a safety measure, U.S. armed forces serving in dangerous areas of the world are immunized against the pox.

As for interesting sidebars about some of the real-life characters in *The Queen's Cure* . . .

—Katherine Grey bore a second son, Thomas, in 1563. Over the years each time Katherine became ill, the queen sent one of her physicians to her. The royal physician Dr. Symonds was with her in her final illness.

—Although at this point in her reign Elizabeth could not pin treason charges on Margaret, Matthew Stewart, and their son, Lord Darnley, Darnley later figures prominently in the royal lineage of England. (*Stewart* is the Scottish/English spelling for *Stuart.*) Lord Darnley's future son will become James VI of Scotland, James I of England.

—Sir Thomas More officially became a Catholic saint in 1935. His prison cell in the Bell Tower of the Tower of London was recently opened for visitors.

—Elizabeth refused to let Mary Sidney permanently exile herself after her disfiguring smallpox. The queen often brought Mary to Hampton Court so she could see her over the years. The mermaid pin Mary Sidney gave to her friend and queen still exists.

—Elizabeth I's funeral effigy sustained water damage during World War II when fire hoses were used to put out an incendiary German bomb in Westminster Abbey. Only broken pieces of the wooden limbs remained of the body, but the head survived. Now refurbished, the effigy may be seen in the Undercroft Museum at the Abbey. The effigies of Elizabeth, Mary Tudor, and their grandparents are pictured in detail in the book *The Funeral Effeigies of Westminster Abbey,* ed. Anthony Harvey and Richard Mortimer.

In selecting contemporary quotes from medical and herbal books, I chose to include some from Nicholas Culpeper's *The English Physician*, although he lived just after Elizabeth (1616–1655). His knowledge certainly came from the Tudor era.

One of Elizabeth's court physicians, William Gilbert (1544–1603), who served her later in her reign, wrote something that I believe the queen herself could have said. It is such confidence that made her a great monarch—and in my world of fiction makes her a brilliant amateur detective:

> *There is nothing within this mortal circuit that God hath, as it were, kept to Himself, and not made subject to the industrious capacity of man to unravel.*

KAREN HARPER
December 2000